ANOMALOUS EVENTS

IN AN

AMERICAN SUBURB

Ross S. Myers

Kyknus Books

Kyknus Books

First Edition July, 2025

Cover by Miblart

The author acknowledges the use of excerpts from certain hymns and poems set out in *Hesiod, the Homeric Hymns, and Homerica*, translated by Hugh G. Evelyn-White (1914), including *To Athena*, Hymn 11, and *To Aphrodite*, Hymns 5 and 6, which have been modified for use in the novel.

ISBN 979-8-9992294-1-0 (ebook)

ISBN 979-8-9992294-2-7 (softcover)

TABLE OF CONTENTS

PART ONE

"Life is full of surprises. Why is that always surprising?"
Cathleen Schine

CHAPTER 1: THE DAY IT STARTED

Saturday morning arrived, finally. The weather was pristine, the storm having moved on. I was looking forward to my weekend hike, despite the snow that laid down overnight. First, though, were errands to check off. One was shopping. Shopping, of course, is therapeutic. American stores have insane varieties of goods and produce in stock. When I see that then, in my mind, it follows that the country isn't quite falling apart yet and society isn't collapsing.

I pulled up the checklist on my phone as I strolled into the neighborhood grocery store, recalling what I wanted. Once I got my bearings, I made a beeline straight to the dairy aisle.

Where is the butter? I thought. I quickly spotted the section which, of course, had an absurdly large selection. There's the stuff from Ireland, the stuff from Vermont, and some from "America's Dairy Farmers." But, that label didn't say exactly where it was from. *What the hell does that mean?*

For some reason, I imagined hundreds of cows lined up in an abandoned Detroit factory. *Would that be an American dairy farm?*

"Could be, you never know," I said to myself. Out loud. Looking around, I realized a tall, well-dressed woman standing near me heard this. Embarrassed, I thought, *Oh well, maybe she thinks I'm having a Bluetooth phone conversation. Maybe.*

She looked straight at me. "I know you're not having a Bluetooth phone conversation."

I felt my face blush. Did this woman just read my mind? I looked over, focusing on her. "I'm sorry, what?"

I tried not to gape at her. She was not the ordinary housewife people run into at the grocery store. She, for all the world, looked like someone who others would gladly go to the store for, or have things delivered to her. With long black hair, bright green eyes, and a brilliant smile, she was spellbinding, the kind of woman men trip over their shoes looking at. The kind that you really cannot look at and chew gum at the same time.

A huge grin appeared on her face. Her eyes drilled into me. She said, "Oh, I know. You think maybe I believe you're experiencing a mental health episode, and you're having a conversation with an imaginary friend. Perhaps you've been let out of the local facility on a weekend pass."

I took a deep breath and made an effort to respond. "Well, it is Saturday, so that would make sense. But, nah, I'm sure you know better. You can read my mind, after all. Right?"

She smiled. "You're joking, but perhaps I really can read your mind."

I was impressed with my ability to even talk back to her. By the way she squinted when she looked at me, she must have known I was drowning here. I felt my face radiating heat from feeling so flustered.

Looking at her, it occurred to me she was perhaps the most beautiful woman I've ever been near, and I was somewhat nonfunctional. It seemed as if this extraordinary woman created her own reality distortion field, in which she was continuously photo-shopped. No matter, I needed to go through the usual ritual regardless.

I managed a crooked smile and blurted out, "So you come here often?"

She beamed, looked at me sideways, and raised her eyebrow. "No, I usually have other people gladly go to the store for me, or I have things delivered."

I froze. She grinned, turned around, and briskly walked away. As she left the aisle, I heard her say, "Hope he's not chewing gum."

Monkey Mountain - 39°00'21.0" N, 94°10'54.8" W

That was my morning. When afternoon came around, I found myself still thinking about that woman. I couldn't help but believe I might have known her at some time in the past. I suppose everyone runs into people at times who look familiar, for no reason. Perhaps that was the case with her. Still, she was so remarkably beautiful, in such a unique way, that it would seem very unlikely that I could have forgotten her. Regardless, it was Saturday, the sun was out, and I very much wanted to go to Monkey Mountain. I needed to justify to myself the purchase of a new camera. I barely knew enough to bring a filter.

I loaded up my SUV and drove out into the country. It was a destination I came across on Google Maps several months ago. It did not take too long, things get rural rather quickly when traveling east. After parking in a gravel area at the southwest corner of the park, I put on a jacket, found a pair of sunglasses, put the camera strap around my neck, and grabbed the tripod. The snow covered up the trails, but I could still make them out, and I had a compass. After hiking for twenty minutes or so, I was approaching my destination, the open glade on the very top.

Monkey Mountain is a county park in a rural area. Despite its name, there are no monkeys and it certainly is no mountain. It is a hill, not especially high, but the whole park is large, several square miles. It is heavily wooded, and far away from development. No background traffic noise, and hopefully no people. I noted when I was checking it out on Google Maps that there is a distinct, open high point. I felt an urge to go there this weekend despite the snow. I certainly looked forward to the isolation and the quiet. It would be especially so because of the snow. Overnight, six inches dropped, and in the morning after the clouds cleared up it was brilliant.

Winter in Missouri creates a harsh landscape. Trees shoot up from blinding white snow, and their ebony trunks slash against the virgin landscape. The naked tops fracture the blue sky. My sudden presence scattered birds roosting in the trees. They transformed into drops of India ink that flittered from branch to branch. This infinite white, black, and blue is winter at its most extreme.

I've always felt that when one walks in the forest at the height of winter, it's a way to lose oneself, a way to detach completely from the modern world. I found it to be a great joy. So, I waded through knee-deep snow, breaking its crust as I approached the summit, far enough away that few people visit, and none would even think of in this weather. Then, something extraordinary occurred.

I don't usually wear sunglasses, except when I'm driving a car, but it was almost essential to wear them that day. The sunlight was full blast and snow blindness would have certainly been the result if I hadn't put them on. What I like about this place is that at the top the view in all directions is to the horizon. Not too many locations like that. Plus, it's an obscure and relatively unknown area, somewhat hard to get to and a difficult uphill climb.

By the time I made it to the top, ominous clouds were rolling in. I've been in high places before when storm clouds appeared. Those experiences are hard to forget. The clouds churn with power. Violent, angry, and frightening. It caused me to understand why our ancestors believed in gods. Even the gods would be shaken going through one of those experiences.

I forced my way through a rough patch of woods and kicked through the snow in what I thought was the path when I broke out into the open. Except it didn't look right to me. The surrounding trees there were just solid black. I was surprised to feel a sudden piercing pain in my wrist. Looking down, I realized I had allowed my hand to swing against a low-lying tree branch. There were hideous, huge thorns covering its entire length. One of them had penetrated an inch or so into my wrist. I recognized the tree, it was a Black Locust, a tree farmers uniformly hate. Even their tractor tires get punctured by them. While holding my wrist, I managed to trip and fall into the snow. My eyes were level with the snowfall, and it was intensely cold. This was not going well.

I raised my head, just in time to notice a shadow moving across the field from a cloud passing overhead. It darkened the whole area. Weirdly, the shadow stopped moving, and reversed course. Kneeling, holding my wrist with my other hand, I looked up. What I saw caused what I think can best be described as cognitive dissonance. It was a very large lenticular disk, silver, spinning and close overhead. I saw it and my brain told me to not believe what my eyes were seeing. I froze. Fear, shock, call it what you will, but I did not move. It stopped in midair as I focused on it. Snowflakes stirred up in the air by my boots hovered, rose, and danced. At some point, I blinked, took a deep breath, and thought of taking a photo. As I grabbed my camera to turn it on, I looked up, and it was gone. Then, I spotted it reflecting sunlight miles up in the sky. In maybe a second, it bolted from one end of the sky to disappear at the opposite end. Nothing goes that fast. It just became gone. My wrist throbbed and with that came a wave of disorientation.

CHAPTER 2: ZOE ELIADES

The house is an anachronism, a 19th-century residence in the middle of the suburbs, fortuitously placed in a hundred-acre tract that developers skipped over when building out Kansas City's residential neighborhoods. It was forgotten as the suburbs grew around it. Gated, with a long driveway, unseen from the road, leading up to the carriage entrance. The woods surrounding it are overgrown with thick brambles, making it nearly impossible to walk through.

Zoe Eliades was starting up the grand staircase when she spotted her dad at the house that day. "I ran into someone who I knew from before. He didn't recognize me. But then, we only knew each other when we were kids."

Aegeus Eliades, a tall man who appeared as young as her, looked up. "That's a long time ago."

"Essie Kemp. You remember him?"

"Wait a minute. Didn't you have a crush on him?"

"Oh yeah. He's still here in town. He's grown up, and he still has that smile. And he is very good-looking. We should check him out."

"I liked that kid. He was smart. Your mother thought highly of him. Well, we are always looking for someone."

Aegeus Eliades laughed and thought to himself. *God help him if he gets involved with my daughter.* He saw how men act when they see her. His daughter's appearance at times causes more problems than solves them, just like her mother.

He turned his attention back to the gathering in the main room. They were engaged in multiple conversations. There was laughter, loud talking, and some whispering. A number of them gave sidelong glances to Zoe as she went up the grand staircase.

When I saw him, I knew instantly who he was. My close friend, maybe my best friend, from when we were so young. He went through some rough times back then. We all knew he had a difficult family life. But, he got through that, and it likely made him resilient. Maybe that's true for me too. I've had some bad times, but I can lock all of that in. I have to. I am who I am. My family, my people, we have to be somewhat apart here. I knew I was going away, and knowing that I chose not to get too close to my friends here. Except for Essie. I was close to him, as much as kids can be to each other. I'll have to ask my mother about him. It is so odd to run into him again after so many years. And, I dreamed of him just the night before. I think perhaps the fates have something in store. I'll ask my mother. She'll know.

Chapter 3: Esmond Kemp

I've always been called Essie. Stupid, I know. Like I had a choice. So, this started out as a journal to memorialize what happened. I suppose it could be considered a diary, but I'm a grown man, so I'm calling it a journal. At least part of this is. A good part ended up being written by the author, to whom I and others have recited these events. It would be too disjointed and not make much sense otherwise. He has since developed this into something much more than my journal. I have to admit, I was very surprised by some of it.

I still live and work in a Kansas City suburb. I was in the Navy for a few years, then went to law school on the G.I. Bill. Joining the Navy seemed like a good idea. After four years at a small local college, I ended up with a history degree, and I was looking at working as a salesman for an office supply company. Nothing against that company, but I was young, and I wanted to travel and do something more exciting. I went through their various schools, and I served aboard several ships. Sea duty brings with it extraordinary experiences. Ask anyone who was in the Navy. When I was in, there were very few women and no beer on active duty ships at sea. Sometimes there were exceptions with the beer. After five years of that, law school looked really nice, as crazy as that seems. In retrospect, I'm not so sure. I think most lawyers would say the same thing after a few years in practice. Anyway, many years later, I'm in private practice. My office is in a building with a few other lawyers, some there full-time, some just part-time. We congregate like that. The offices are all on the same floor and, of course, we all know each other.

I didn't tell anyone about what happened at Monkey Mountain. The only possible conclusion someone could reach would be that I was taking drugs of some sort. My wrist got worse, then better. Aspirin, ice packs, and some leftover amoxicillin I found in my refrigerator helped. I researched whether puncture wounds from Black Locust tree thorns cause hallucinations. I didn't find anything about that, but I did find that they are slightly poisonous, depending on whether the thorns are actually Black Locust or Honey Locust. Supposedly, what those trees are called is a regional thing. We've always known them as Black Locust and learned to keep our distance. Regardless, that was my own explanation. Maybe that explains the weird time loss too. Because, it was dark by the time I made it back.

Later, I think it was Tuesday afternoon, I was walking down the hallway when I heard my name.

"Hey, Essie. What are you doing tonight?"

It was William Hurley, a lawyer in his sixties, who always had too much business and was always passing cases on to the rest of us.

"Doing nothing. Going home."

"I've got this fundraiser I'm supposed to make an appearance for this evening but can't make it. I've got night court. You should go."

"Thanks man, but I'm hungry and I want to go home."

"They have barbeque."

I made a full stop and turned around. "Okay."

———— ◄O► ————

Following my GPS to this fundraiser was straightforward, but I was very surprised at its location. The stone pillar gate, the long driveway. No one would have known there was all this open land, a creek, a small mansion, a barn, greenhouse, pond, and all of it plain hidden from traffic and neighbors.

The front door was already half open, so I walked in. I introduced myself to a gentleman in the foyer who was studying a small painting on the wall.

"Hi, I'm Essie Kemp, I live in the area. I drive by all the time. I had no idea this was here. That driveway is much longer than I expected, and the woods here, in the middle of suburbia, is pretty much primeval."

The man smiled and said, "I'm Aegeus Eliades, but call me Aggie. Nice to make your acquaintance." We shook hands.

Mr. Eliades looked at me in a strange way, smiled, and said, "You're right about this place. People are surprised to find it hidden away here. But, the good thing, no door-to-door sales, right? Well, there's lots of food. Make yourself at home and look around. How's Bill?"

"Bill Hurley? He gave me the directions for this!"

"He called me just a little while ago. Said to watch out for you. That you'd eat all the barbeque."

I laughed. "Well, no. Not if you have french fries."

Proceeding down the hallway, I stopped again and looked around. Some of the furniture was impressive. I was no expert, but I recognized a mahogany desk that looked like it came straight from King Louis XVI himself. In the hallway, there was an opened antique campaign writing box in just perfect condition, complete with polished brass corners and stocked with filled ink bottles and fountain pens. The painting Mr. Eliades was standing next to seemed like something in the French impressionist style, a woman walking down a street in Paris. I continued into what I assumed was the great room. It was filled with marvelous furniture and several beautiful paintings on the walls. They all looked like originals. No way though, this is Kansas City suburbia.

There was one unusual item on the far wall that caught my eye, a sword. I strolled over to check it out. I wondered at first if it was a museum replica. It did not seem like one. Short and thick, Bronze Age. I've always liked swords, and I recall photos of ones like this from Greek archaeological digs. Bronze is softer than iron and doesn't keep an edge very long. Whenever these swords were found in ancient Mycenaean graves, honing stones accompanied them.

I realized I was blocking the light from a nearby lamp. Viewing the sword from a different angle, the light revealed a unique, blue-green patina, with a few symbols or letters noticeable underneath. It was recently honed, since its edges were thin, brilliant gold lines, converging at its point. It was not elegant, ornate or florid, but its simplicity, in itself, its single-mindedness of purpose, lent to it a certain beauty. Still, there was no mistaking it for what it was - a deadly weapon. The blade and hilt on this one were all one solid piece of bronze. Use was made of it in the past - several gouges were honed down. I really liked it. I turned around and noticed Aegeus Eliades looking my way.

Turning to my left, I saw a long table with food and drinks on the far side. I spotted barbeque, which was the reason I agreed to show up. There were ribs, brisket, even sausage. My stomach growled. That table was my goal, so I slowly made my way there. I didn't recognize anyone. That was odd since, for some reason, I thought this was a chamber of commerce event. But, I never joined the chamber. The annual dues were just way too much.

<hr />

I sensed her presence before even looking up. I raised my head and saw her standing over me, grinning ear to ear. The most beautiful woman in the world. Well, at least in my world.

I stood up, and only then remembered I had a full plate of barbeque, fries, cole slaw, and potato salad on my lap. It went air-bound. In a panic, I reached out. Somehow, and to this day I do not know how, I caught the plate, and the food, as it landed back on the plate. Yes, I actually caught all of it in mid-flight.

Sheepishly, I turned around to look at her while balancing all of this on my hand.

Amused, she said, "Wow, I must say I am impressed. So, what's your name?"

I started to sputter and realized my mouth was completely stuffed with brisket, sauce, and bread. Most likely the sauce was dripping off my chin. Judging by her expression, it seemed she was fully aware of this temporary disability and had made a point of approaching and speaking to me just when my mouth was stuffed.

Her emerald eyes both sparkled and squinted, and she looked for all the world like she would burst to keep from laughing. Performing a pirouette and strolling towards a group gathered across the room, I heard her say, "Geesh, wouldn't even tell me his name."

Of course, she knew my name, and so did a few others there.

Aggie Eliades, out of the corner of his eye, watched this whole exchange. He raised an eyebrow, smiled to himself, and walked away, muttering, "God help him."

I vividly remember that evening. I filled up, socialized for a while, and headed for the door. I'm sure my cheeks were still a bit red from the barbeque thing. As I approached the door, I heard my name.

"Esmond. Hi, Aggie Eliades. We talked earlier."

"Well, hi. This has been a great time. The food was awesome."

"Great. Zoe told me that she ran into you."

I could feel my cheeks flushing again. Still, I learned her name! "Uh, yeah. She caught me at a bad moment."

Aggie laughed. "Well, she seems to be good at that."

"So, have you lived here long?"

"Oh, it's my family's. We've managed to hold on to it for a good many years. The location just keeps getting better as time goes on. We can hop on the freeway and make it downtown in no time. So, anyway, tell me what keeps you busy nowadays? What are your hobbies?"

I was in a good mood. It was a social occasion after all, so I answered. "Well, I read a lot. Also, oddly enough, I've started flying hobby drones during the weekends. Sometimes. You know, DJI, Hubsan, and that kind. Just so much fun!"

"Oh really, I've got one. It has a pretty good range. So, you said you read a lot. What books have you read lately?"

"Fiction when I can. Lately, I made it through a few Neal Asher and Iain Banks novels."

"Oh, Iain Banks or Iain M. Banks?"

I laughed. "Ha, so you're familiar with him. Well, definitely Iain M. Banks. There's no way I'm reading *The Wasp Factory*. I do read a great deal of science fiction."

He smiled. "They are great authors. They seem to have some insight into what it may be like up there. You fly drones, what do you think of the UFO thing? Are they drones? It still shows up in the news regularly."

At this point, it occurred to me that this gentleman was doing some exploring. But, he was the host, and seemed to be a nice guy, so I didn't mind.

I responded. "Well, there's got to be something to it. When former U.S. Presidents are talking about unknown things flying around the skies, it has to be something substantial. I'm certain all the statements by those guys were well thought out before they said them on TV."

"Do you have any theories on them?"

Well, I had theories. A lot of them. But I wasn't sure I wanted to get into a two-hour conversation on all that in the hallway with the door open, so I said, "Oh yeah. I've read quite a lot on the whole history. It's one of life's great mysteries. But you know, it would take hours."

We made eye contact. For more than a few seconds. But, it was not awkward. Nor was it threatening or intimidating. It just happened. He had silver in his eyes.

"Well, look Esmond. I'm taking up too much of your time and I know you have to get home. Let's get together sometime. I think Zoe wants to mess with you again."

Nodding my head in agreement, I said something. I can't quite remember. I think it was just, "Oh, wow."

Later on, thinking about when I was leaving that evening, there were two things I thought were weird. Right at first, when I heard my name, I'm not sure whether I actually heard it. With my ears, I mean. But I certainly heard it. Also, except for the eyes, which had silver in them, I couldn't exactly recall at all what Aegeus Eliades looked like.

Chapter 4: My Client

I don't know about you, but when I get home after dark, I always step outside and look up at the stars. People from all walks of life think about it and wonder about it. Are we alone in the Universe? Where is everyone else in this infinite cosmos? Governments, their intelligence services, universities, militaries, billionaires, and everyday people are always looking for some type of evidence of extraterrestrial, otherworldly, or nonhuman intelligent life.

It used to be, when we were young, we would all get together at someone's house, go outside and look up at the stars, and we'd talk about these mysteries all night long. Nowadays, it seems we don't. Instead, podcasts and YouTube videos have supplanted those conversations. Now, we watch and listen to famous scientists and celebrities talk and argue about these topics. They all have conflicting opinions. What does come across, though, is that they don't know any more than the rest of us. But, like everything in life, there are exceptions.

I have an interesting client who, perhaps, knows more than the rest of us. He, initially, told me he was an engineer for Honeywell. You know, the company that makes home thermostats, humidifiers, and other wholesome, everyday stuff. It turns out that the company makes other things, at least in Kansas City, that housewives don't really use.

His name is Ray Langstaff. When we first met, I asked what he did there. He stated that he made nuclear bomb triggers. That woke me up. He works at what is called the Department of Energy's Kansas City National Security Campus, which is operated by Honeywell. It manufactures nuclear bomb parts. It also conducts research and manufactures other classified material, working with Sandia and Los Alamos National Laboratories, both in New Mexico. Sandia is also operated by a subsidiary of Honeywell. He needed help with a divorce his wife filed.

Most lawyers hate doing divorces, and judges hate hearing them. I sometimes agree to represent someone in a divorce if I need the money, when too many bills are unpaid. With this client, and other people he works with at Honeywell, the government is somewhat antsy about which lawyers they retain for legal matters. There are secrets they don't want disclosed. These guys have security clearances that are far higher than what most federal employees receive. He had a Q-Level 4 security designation, whatever that means.

Ray told me the government actually had to clear whoever he wanted to hire. It turned out he could retain me since I still had a high clearance from when I served in the Navy, a top-secret, crypto, cosmic clearance. It sounds impressive, doesn't it? Not really. I was a communications officer. Every sea-going ship in the Navy has at least one communications officer, sometimes several, and they all have top-secret, crypto, cosmic clearances. So do lots of other people in every service branch. But not too many lawyers. So, I ended up representing him in his divorce.

I'm still not sure why his wife filed for divorce. I say that because Ray has a fascinating personality. People really enjoy his company. I suppose women would consider him handsome. Regardless, he certainly is not ugly in any respect. He is such an outgoing and intelligent person that it shouldn't matter anyway. It was contested, and I suppose I offered emotional support to him occasionally as things worked their way through. I believe I told him that all the travails and difficulties from his divorce would pass, and it won't have any great consequence in the grand scheme of things. Maybe that's how we ended up discussing outer space, the Drake Equation, extraterrestrial life, what happens after we pass on and, well, you get the gist of it.

I recall one time when he was at my office, and we talked about how much the government really knows about UFOs and extraterrestrials. I told him my theory about that. I suspect the government actually knows a lot, maybe an immense amount, about flying saucers, intelligent extraterrestrial life visiting the Earth, and how much of a presence they have here. But, they're not telling for a number of reasons.

There are many people, including a few Senators and Representatives, who simply do not want their reality turned upside down. Consciously or unconsciously, they are adamant in their desire to just not know. If the government is competent, which I think for the most part it is, it must have arranged for any number of studies, surveys, and evaluations to determine just how well people in general, our society, our social structures, our respect for authority, our religious beliefs, even our mental and physical health, would be affected by the disclosure of extraterrestrials and their craft flying all over everywhere. To me, it would be inconceivable that there would not be extensive, top secret, anthropological and sociological studies, and psychological profiles of a statistically significant number of individuals, all carried out to answer those questions, and to assist the government in determining how much to tell the public.

So, I believe that the government has adopted a two-track "Disclosure" strategy. It, officially, denies any extraterrestrial presence. Until recently, it denied any UFOs flying around anywhere at all. It still maintains that there's no evidence of extraterrestrial life, anywhere, anytime. That's the official line. I suppose it determined it must take this position to ensure there's no general panic, that religious leaders don't declare that extraterrestrials are demonic, and that a massive stock market sell-off doesn't occur. In short, it takes that official position so society won't collapse.

But, I believe there's a second track for disclosure. The government recognizes that a very significant part of the citizenry is aware of enough facts to have a strong, well-founded belief that the government knows a great deal more than what the official line is. For those people, the government attempts to satisfy some of their need to know by arranging for unofficial leaks, arranging for ex-government officials and ex-military personnel to reveal what they know, and making available some of the paper records and videos. All of this is done in a way that is deniable by the government. It says, or strongly implies, that the records may not be legitimate, the leaks may be bogus, and the ex-government officials and ex-military personnel may be misinformed. By releasing information this way, with a kind of knowing wink, so to speak, it avoids causing general panic, stock market sell-offs, and so on. It gets some information out to people who usually can recognize it as legitimate.

There's another angle. It's the people's "Right to Know." Really, there is such a thing. Legal papers and law review articles discuss this. UNESCO states that the Right to Know is a human right - the right of people to "participate in an informed way in decisions that affect them, while also holding governments and others accountable." The public's right to know is not explicitly written into the U.S. Constitution or any of its amendments. However, scholars argue this is a legitimate constitutional right, and it is independent of any statute, including the Freedom of Information Act.

Courts recognize that several First Amendment rights, such as the Freedom of the Press, the Freedom of Speech, and the Right to Petition the Government, and also every citizen's primary right to vote, are meaningless if information, facts, are hidden from the press, from the voters, if citizens do not have access to information about what they are supposed to vote on or petition the government about. Freedom of Speech is pretty much worthless without any knowledge or understanding. Look at "X" or Twitter. So, I think this is additional motivation for the government to arrange for all these unofficial leaks of information. Individuals in the government recognize that constitutional rights are being impaired.

I told Ray this theory. I figured he may, or may not, have some insight about whether this two-track disclosure possibility holds water. Really, I wanted a second opinion, mainly to let me know if I was just crazy. Much to my surprise, he said I was probably right and that some of the news stories on this subject can perhaps only be explained by this theory. I was relieved. It's always good to know one is not completely nuts.

But, Ray didn't stop there. He had one hell of a story, and he decided to tell me. This is it:

———◦○◦———

Ironically, it was right in front of us. An answer to that question we've all asked. Are we alone? It happened in the 1970s, when the United States launched Skylab into orbit. Like most man-made orbital objects, it required minor course adjustments. It was done every few months. Due to the vagaries of orbital mechanics, Skylab wound up in a new path it did not previously clear. No other satellites or debris were in the path. Which was why it maneuvered into that path. There was an inexplicable event. Something collided with one of the port solar panels. Indeed, the panel ended up with a perfectly round six-foot hole. The residents of the space lab at that time saw this. No ragged edges. The thing was that nothing had shown up on radar. NORAD and NASA had more than enough technical capability to track anything in Skylab's path. After this event, the NORAD duty officer & the acting commander, an Air Force general, replayed the radar display over and over. Nothing there. At this point, the ground controllers at Johnson Space Center made an emergency course change to a higher orbit, and the orbit of this undetected object was calculated to inches.

Even back then, the U.S. Air Force had hunter-killer satellites. The particular one tasked with tracking down this anomalous object possessed an excellent camera. The thing was extraordinary. It wasn't a monolith or something with antennas. It was a six-foot, pitch-black ball. Radar did not reflect off it. Even from the high-power radar station in Iceland. National Security Agency, National Reconnaissance Office, and others were brought in. At some point, someone had the bright idea to shoot a laser at it. A ground-based observatory was used. The laser used was not a weapon but was utilized for measuring the distance to the moon. So they did that.

Well, it did generate a response. An emission of some type, detectable in some spectrums, originated from this black, perfect sphere. It was not directed to some destination in outer space but to Earth's surface. The beam, which they theorized was a communication method, scanned a very wide area, not unlike a LiDAR. And this is where it gets weird. A number of national technical assets were used to determine this. It was aimed at some location in northwest Missouri.

At some point, I realized what occurred at Monkey Mountain, and the unusual interactions with people I've had lately, could well have a connection to this story Ray told me. I began to wonder whether our ordinary, humdrum life, our comforting, routine reality, could well exist alongside an extraordinary, mysterious, phenomenal reality that almost everyone is unaware of.

I asked Ray about something else. I've had strange dreams lately, some just completely inexplicable. I mentioned this to him. He noted people he talks with had unusual dreams too. Stranger and weirder than the usual ones. Apparently because of the coronavirus pandemic, people have reported unusual, even bizarre, dreams. Several newspapers and news websites published reports about this. Ray said he also had a few strange dreams. Ray was participating in a support group, apparently because of his divorce, and he said people in this group have discussed it. The next day, he sent me this email, which I think is rather insightful, and also pretty entertaining.

From: Raymond Langstaff, Honeywell National Security Campus, Kansas City
   To: Esmond Kemp, Attorney, Kemp Law Firm
   Re: Crazy dreams
   Hi Essie,
   You're not the only person with crazy dreams. After I got back to my office, I thought of this. In the support group I'm in we're supposed to keep journals, so I wrote

about how they were creating some anxiety for me. Anyway, you'll enjoy reading this journal entry:

So I have these vivid dreams when things don't go well in my waking life. They are very real. So much so that it's worrying me. Now, I wonder whether, if I die, I will live on in my dream life. I hope I do. I've had doubts though, because of what I experienced, or more exactly, did not experience the one time I had surgery. I was put under by an anesthesiologist and it was complete obliteration. No dreams. Not even a sense of time passing. I fell asleep, and it seemed I woke up immediately thereafter. It was actually several hours. This worried me to no end. No dreams. No self-awareness. Just complete blackness and no existence.

So, is this our fate when we pass on? I have no idea. Some scientists who study this sort of thing say our self-awareness is just an illusion anyway. But don't you have to be self-aware for an illusion to occur? To doubt consciousness proves its reality, right? Occasionally, I run into a well-known scientist in this field, and I'll ask him or her questions like this. For some reason, they always get mad at me.

I dated a very intelligent woman who attended Stanford, then medical school in Houston. Extraordinarily sharp. She was religious, a Presbyterian. I told her about this concern of mine. She told me not to be overly troubled about it. Just because one doesn't remember something doesn't mean it didn't occur. She noted scientists have found people do not remember the great majority of their dreams, at least eighty percent. There is just no recall of them upon awakening. I remember her telling me that, regardless, she believed all of this, all our waking existence, is a dream, an illusion, and one day it will all fade away, and we will find ourselves in a new spiritual existence of some sort. She was brilliant, and I think she was considered a genius. So, her thoughts on this carry a great deal of weight with me. She mentioned some verses in the New Testament that describe how our ordinary lives will fade away and this will come about.

So, anyway, we've got that going for us, at least if we are Presbyterian. Of course, with me having more of a 'spiritual' inclination than a denominational one, I may not qualify for that. I prefer more of a Buddhist afterlife, where we get lots of do-overs, since I screw up so much. But, I prefer it slightly modified, so that we get to do over our same life, again and again, like a video game, until we've pretty much got it down. If I had a brand new, different life each time, I'd just mess up all of those. They aren't really do-overs I suppose, more of a 'try this one, it might work out better for you' kind of thing.

Anyway, I really have no idea and I need to get some sleep.

So, you can probably tell from that, Ray Langstaff has a very interesting personality – especially for an engineer. He's definitely my favorite client. That guy has crazy stories.

Chapter 5: Ray Langstaff

I shouldn't have moved to Kansas City. No offense to people living here. I'll explain. I told my wife it was only temporary. It didn't matter. A few months after we transferred here, she filed for divorce and moved quickly to finalize it. I had difficulty going through with it. My wife, to me at least, was beautiful. I always considered myself so lucky to have met and eventually marry her. I told her that every day. Maybe she took it to heart and felt she could do better. She never took a physics course, or any science class. Maybe our marriage was doomed from the start because of that. Like so many other things, it's a mystery. I could ask her, but I doubt she would be straight with me.

After we separated, and I moved out, within a couple of weeks, some guy was living off and on at our house, while I was still paying for it. That was sleazy, and really affected me. That was when I realized I needed a lawyer. The first thing Essie told me was to find a support group, or the whole process would drive me crazy. That was good legal advice. Honeywell, thank God, has its own counseling program. For me, they had counselors with very high-security clearances. It is quite amazing, group therapists, marriage counselors, with Top Secret, even Q level clearances. They're obligated not to breach our trust. Except for the usual reasons, like, if we planned on harming someone else or doing ourselves in.

So, anyway, I am thankful to the company, and to the Department of Energy for providing that. On the other hand, I'd like to blame DOE for wrecking my life, because they wanted us to move here. I couldn't even tell her why, I couldn't tell her anything about what I really did. Security is very clear in that regard. So, the more I got involved in this extraordinary thing that is going on here, the more I just couldn't tell her. The divorce, I suppose then, is perhaps not surprising. It certainly was not uncommon. Maybe we should have just stayed in Albuquerque. That's where her family lives.

I couldn't tell her that I was on the brink of creating, maybe, the greatest invention in the history of modern physics. Nor could I tell her that one of the ways we are getting close to figuring it out is that there are extraterrestrial craft flying around the area, and we've got incredibly sensitive detectors recording every type of electromagnetic and gravitational signature they emit. It is astonishing what you can figure out by analyzing just how things generate those signatures. So, what we are doing is not so much based on a theoretical model, but trying our best to recreate something that we know already exists.

The thing is, what I was figuring out, is exactly what the scientists and engineers at Honeywell's predecessor, the old Bendix Atomic Energy Commission plant in Kansas City, along with the old Western Electric Company's operation nearby in Lee's Summit, with its clean rooms, vacuum tubes, and its gyroscopes, have been experimenting with since the 1950s. But, they didn't make any breakthroughs. Well, now we've got transistors, integrated circuits, and incredible computing power, and we can generate much more voltage in a much smaller container. So, we're almost there.

One of my only friends here is Essie Kemp. My divorce lawyer. He hates being called that. He's fairly intelligent, for a lawyer, and he's interested in the same things I am. Of course, I couldn't even retain him until they did a background check on him. Surprisingly, he had the highest a person could get in the Navy.

Things started going to pieces when I was at work, on a secure floor, and walking towards one of the computer rooms. Just as I was turning the corner to go in, I heard a drawer slam shut, and out walked our FBI security liaison, giving me a weird look. I suppose he could have been there as part of his duties, but there's no way he had the passwords to access anything.

I noticed a number of suspicious things over the next few days, particularly in my own office. Someone's been poking around, and if it was that FBI guy, I really had to think about whom to talk about it with. So, of course, it occurred to me. I had an attorney, with a Top Secret clearance.

Ironically, as everyone who has gone through one knows, going through a divorce seems to make a person a better spouse, if they ever get married again. You realize all the different ways you screwed up and commit to do better if you get a second chance. Not that it matters. I was truly alone back then, with only my work, as amazing as that is. I recognized in Essie a fellow traveler. Physicists don't usually want much to do with lawyers, but I enjoyed talking to him. That's why I blabbed about the Skylab thing. After all, the Skylab incident is one of the reasons I'm here in Kansas City. Its resolution, to find out just who its signal was directed to, was really a big deal for a while. Then Air Force Intelligence connected with DOE, and we understood that there's a group of people in the area who we're just supposed to study from a distance. Because they're aliens? No one really knows. Still, the anti-gravity program here, the Skylab transmission, the detection of anomalous objects over the region, and this mystery family, all seem connected, and it is a fascinating mystery that I really wanted to discuss with someone outside of work. The only one I really could do that with was Essie.

Chapter 6: A Short Discussion

It was the custom at the Eliades house, after these evening get-togethers, for the regulars to stay late, coalesce around the dinner table, and attempt to finish off the food, or at least the barbeque. Their conversations touched upon several topics, some serious and some not so much. Eventually, Essie's visit was brought up.

"Aggie, you talked to him. What's your read on this guy?"

"Some of you might recall him from way back. Remember that Scout troop you guys set up? He was the tall kid. That was a long time ago, and he apparently didn't recognize anybody. Zoe might have a better feel for him, but she hasn't had a real conversation with him, yet"

Zoe was in the kitchen, and stuck her head out when she heard her name. "When I was a kid, I had lots of conversations with him. Some of you did too. I hope he's the same person I knew then. He seems to have an affinity for hiking in remote areas. I think every weekend. But then, he got that from you guys, right? Back then, you guys took those kids everywhere."

Aggie laughed. "Anyway, we've got a few weeks before Phil and his group return. They'll want to set up residence somewhere nearby. So, keep an eye out for some open properties. I'm sure they'll have a few tall tales to share."

Looking over to a short bearded man sitting across the table, Aggie asked, "Louie, what's going on over at CERN?"

Louie shrugged, and replied. "Well, nothing of any consequence now. They've got those extraordinary electromagnets, you know. The Large Hadron Collider has the most powerful on the planet. CERN has eight other accelerators besides the LHC. None of them are set up for rotating magnetic fields. Until last year, there was a plan to do that with one of them, without the electromagnets themselves actually moving. I'm not sure anything would have come of it but, regardless, my group submitted a competing proposal to create and detect antimatter. Since we're funded, they went with our proposal. So we're good for at least three more years."

"Does anyone know the latest on the Chinese Institute of High Energy Physics, and their Beijing Electron Positron Collider? Dr. Chang?"

A short, seemingly nondescript, woman with a pixie haircut looked up. Smiling, she took off her large reading glasses. It was a remarkable transformation. Everyone, once again, was amazed at how singularly attractive she became, just by taking those glasses off.

"Since when did you start calling me Dr. Chang, Aggie?"

Aggie laughed. "Li, I think you picked up your third doctorate this year, so I thought better late than never."

Everyone was amused by this exchange.

Grinning, Dr. Li Chang continued. "Yeah. That group is staying with high energy particle collisions. I let it be known that the Americans gave up on rotating fields, and since they know I was working on this area at Lawrence Livermore, they figured I would know. So, we're good there too."

"Aggie, what about this group that made a breakthrough?"

"There are a few labs that are somewhat going in the right direction. We're following them. But, you're talking about the Americans here locally. Mr. Kemp, coincidentally, is a lawyer and is the attorney for the physicist, Raymond Langstaff, if you can believe it. Langstaff came up here from Sandia National Laboratories, and his wife promptly filed for divorce. Langstaff may well understand the consequences of his group's endeavors if they succeed. At some point, we might consider collecting him and laying our cards on the table. I mean, we know what will likely happen in just a few years if we don't do something. I would think anyone would do whatever it takes to avoid that. If that's understood."

Looking at Zoe, and then the rest of the group, Aggie continued. "Going back to Essie Kemp, since he's associated with Langstaff we should probably keep an eye on him anyway. If he ever remembers you guys from back then, I want to be in the same room to watch, with a bag of popcorn."

Everyone in the room laughed at that.

Chapter 7: My Winter Vacation

I knew I was dreaming. There was a gray sky that merged with a haze of naked tree branches, stretching to the horizon. Aching cold. I roll over, and it causes enough discomfort for me to wake up and visit the bathroom. I was dreaming of the Ozark Mountains, in winter. It was a very dreary image and it reflected my mood. No way I'm camping there again until it warms up. I remember the other day. It takes some time to figure this out. How did I get home? Did I imagine the flying saucer? Also, did I see a woman in the clearing? Now I have a vague image of one there. I look at myself in the mirror, and I see there are still scratches and a bruise on my temple. My wrist aches, like it is trying to remind me to pay attention to it. Black Locust trees are vicious. I hope I don't have to worry about an infection. What the hell happened that day? How did I get home?

I go downstairs and check the refrigerator. There's an abandoned bag of Delta 9 gummies, opened. I know I didn't eat those. After trying one last year, I haven't touched them since. I don't think they cause hallucinations anyway. I look at my wrist again. When I was jabbed by the thorn, almost immediately I felt incredibly cold, just before seeing the flying craft. I had something of a dissociative state of mind when that occurred. It was like an out-of-body experience.

There's an academic book describing this, written by professors from the University of Virginia. They proposed that our consciousness is more or less split in two. There's the conscious mind, and then there's the unconscious mind, which they called the subliminal mind. This subliminal mind may have its own experiences, without the conscious mind's awareness. According to them, this could be the reason for dissociative experiences, when one feels he or she is observing events from a distance. So, if this is true, perhaps everything that happened on Monkey Mountain was a subliminal experience, which means it may have been a false memory, or a hallucination. It sure seemed real, though. Yeah, going to Monkey Mountain is fun.

Anyway, I get some ice for my wrist, and go through the medicine cabinet for aspirin. Nothing handles swelling better than aspirin. Why the hell did I dream of the southern Missouri Ozark Mountains in wintertime? Okay, I have to admit to myself that I know the likely answer. I went there a couple of years ago, in wintertime. I recall that trip. I don't think it was a great experience. In fact, it was pretty traumatizing:

Spending Christmas by oneself is a gut-wrenching thing. I remember it was the first Christmas I spent alone. On Christmas morning, I got up, went downstairs to the living room, sat down, and then, then I stared at the wall for an hour. I recall getting two obligatory phone calls on Christmas Eve, from people who, I could tell, didn't know what to say. The sad thing is that back then I preferred to be left alone anyway. There were others around, there were plenty, but I could not communicate important, even intimate, thoughts to them. Many people were just too shallow, others overwhelmed with their own lives. So, I kept my nightmares, my horrors, to myself.

It used to be that when I went out, anywhere, shopping, visiting parks, anywhere in public, I would run into people, friends that I knew. More than a few and every time I went out. My friends were everywhere. We phoned and visited each other all the time. Things changed, and I would run into not even a single soul who I knew. Everywhere I traveled. My neighborhood, shopping malls, and parks, were filled with strangers who ignored me, who didn't even look at me. Like, I didn't even exist. It seemed as if there wouldn't even be a vacuum created if I was suddenly removed from life. I think the explanation, perhaps, was how I appeared. People could tell I was not someone who had a good outlook on life, and I should perhaps best be avoided. That's my theory, at least.

So, I decided to go on a road trip, to get away from all that. Down south, to the Ozarks, for some winter camping and hiking. There certainly would be solitude, and it would be a challenge. A person once told me that our ability to forget saves us from a madness some compare to hell. So, I'm sure I was hoping to find some forgetfulness there.

When I went down there, I still had a beat-up 1994 Jeep Grand Cherokee, with a straight six engine. That engine has a great reputation, it is very reliable. Not too sure about the transmission. Still, I didn't hesitate to use it. I could park it at a trailhead and not be too concerned about it being broken into, or stolen. Two thousand-dollar cars have their own charm that way.

It was December 30, early in the morning. Fifteen degrees in the Kansas City area. About the same around Eminence, Missouri. I locked everything up and took off. It only takes around four hours to get down there, if one doesn't stop too often. I noticed a line of birds, crows, hundreds of them, perched on a power line going down the two blocks or so I drove to the main road. I thought to myself, *Are they giving me a ceremonial farewell? Do they know something I don't?*

———————◀O▶———————

On the way to Eminence, I was running low on gas, and after driving a while with no place to refill I made it to a small village I think twenty-thirty miles west of there, in an area labeled on the map as the Sunklands. There was an old wooden general store with two gas pumps in front. Discretion is the better part of valour, or whatever Falstaff said, so I pulled in and parked next to one of the pumps.

It's an interesting place. The gas pumps were not modern, there was no place to insert a credit card. I looked towards the front of the store and headed over there. There was a long porch. At first, I thought the railing along the front of the porch was for visitors to hitch their horses to. Apparently not though. There were hitching posts at either end of the building. I knew they were because there were piles of horse fertilizer by them. Anyway, as I walked up the steps I noticed three elderly women sitting there on rockers. All three were looking at me.

I nodded my head. "Good day, ladies."

There was no response. They just stared back. One of them was missing an eye, the others I couldn't tell. All three had gray hair, and they were ancient.

I opened the front door and walked in. An elderly gentleman was behind the counter, resting on a stool. He was enormous, and his impressive beard flowed down to his waistline. I waved at him as I headed over to the cooler for some cola. I didn't spot any Coca-Cola or even any Pepsi, but there was Royal Crown Cola, RC. There were glass bottles in the old style, no modern cans displaying just the RC initials. Picking up two, I headed over to the counter.

"Good afternoon, I'd like thirty dollars of gas, and also this soda."

"Okay, young man. Here's the key."

Thankfully, I realized what that was for. The gas pumps had padlocks on their handles. I suppose I was on the honor system as far as how much I pumped into my Jeep. I gave him two twenties and said, "Be back in a few minutes."

Walking out, I passed the women again, who were busy sewing. All three were at work on the same piece, letting out twine and sewing. They were humming in harmony while doing that. Interesting, but slightly odd.

After pumping thirty dollars worth of gas, I walked back to return the key. They looked up at me again. I smiled and asked, "What are you sewing?"

The middle lady, in a strange, raspy voice, said, "We sew everything."

Again, I smiled and said, "Okay, well, I'd better return this key."

I walked in, headed over to the counter, handing the key back to the gentleman there. While doing that, I heard their humming change to words, words I couldn't quite make out. I remember thinking right then that things were getting a little beyond strange.

As I opened the front door to leave, the humming stopped. Walking down the steps, one of the ladies spoke in a half whisper.

"Could you help? I dropped a needle off the porch."

"Sure." I walked over. "Where is it exactly?"

She pointed down and to the right. Following her bent finger, I saw it. Pretty much where she pointed. I bent down, saw what was a knitting or crochet needle, grabbed it, and handed it to her.

"Thank you. May you have a good journey."

"Oh, thank you, Well, good day then."

I reached my jeep, opened the door, got in, started up, and headed out.

That was a most peculiar experience. That lady who pointed out where to pick up the needle, I realized she was completely blind. Yet, she pointed out where to pick it up. Perhaps she heard where it landed. I recall pulling off the road a while later to think about it. The needle was not large, and it appeared to be bone or ivory. I contemplated heading back, and making up an excuse to talk to them some more. However, I thought the better of it. It's best not to tempt fate.

I've on occasion thought of them, and wondered just who they were. I have my suspicions. Okay, I know what you're thinking. I'm implying they are the Three Fates. I'm just saying that at least it's a possibility. I recall the humming I heard, which seemed to turn into whispered chanting. That certainly created an eerie feeling for me. Regardless, it actually happened, and it was definitely out of place. In Scandinavia, they are called the Norns. In Greek mythology, they are the Moirai. The Celts knew them as the Matres. The Romans, Fata, from the same latin root word for fate. In fact, they're found in mythology all over the world.

So, this is what I think would have happened if I turned around and tracked down more information about them. I would find they are rather ordinary church ladies, who have a sewing club. They crochet colorful bed comforters for the local baptist church's annual auction, which raises money to buy new bibles, or to send some children off to summer camp. They might just enjoy interacting with passersby. That's what always happens. There's always a totally mundane explanation. Reductive materialism accounts for everything. Because, there is no magic, there is no supernatural aspect to our world. Everything that happens always has a perfectly prosaic explanation. Right?

Well, I want to think that's not entirely correct. I believe we find ourselves in a world, a universe, of infinite possibilities. Anything, possibly, could be true. The thing is, how would we know? Those three elderly ladies could be both the local church sewing club, and also Atropos, Clotho, and Lachesis, the Three Fates. As far as that goes, there could be all manner of strange, supernatural folk who are part and parcel of our everyday lives. They could be our next door neighbors. We think we know them. We may see them during our daily routines, totally unremarkable. But, really, how would we ever know? We wouldn't, until we do.

⸺◆⸺

About an hour later, I reached my destination, a trailhead at the end of a gravel road. There was a campsite maybe a hundred yards up the trail and I set up camp there. The gravel road had taken me up to the crest of a ridge, so I had a fairly good view of the surrounding area.

I started setting up my campsite, which I planned on breaking down the next morning, so I could go backpacking in search of someplace deeper in the forest. While doing so, I made up this thought exercise, which I think is interesting. Bear with me. This is it: There's a group of people who, each and every day of the week, experience several hours of unconsciousness. During the periods of unconsciousness, they hallucinate, but only rarely do they remember what they hallucinate. Their hallucinations, many times, have physical or emotional qualities and characteristics that are totally foreign to their life experiences, or sense of self. One would think that this is a most bizarre aspect of their lives, certainly the most salient. Yet they experience this, deal with it, think nothing of it, and still live ordinary lives.

So, what do you think? It is a rather large group of people. The last I checked is eight billion. Anyway, silly exercise. Still, I believe it gives some perspective as to just how weird it is we sleep a number of hours every night, and we dream while sleeping. It doesn't occur to us how mystifying this is. Also, I believe that for every dream we remember, there are many, many more that we don't. Scientists have explanations, I know. For me, it's the only aspect of my life I find to have a metaphysical or spiritual quality. And, it happens every night, every single night.

The next morning, I woke up to a light snowstorm. So now it appeared as if some mythological titan had taken a shaker and sprinkled salt all over the terrain, as far as the eye could see. I've gone camping in the cold before though, and the trick is to use layers. I brought a thick, insulated pair of pants, a heavy coat, thermal underwear, wool socks, gloves, and, perhaps most importantly, and also the silliest, a fur-lined hat with ear flaps. I packed away a ski mask to use if it got too bad. As far as food, I had this pre-packaged paste to eat, which I squeezed out and swallowed for breakfast. I also packed cans of meat, cans of wieners, miscellaneous packed MREs (meals ready to eat), and various other items. I had some cans of Sterno, along with a small folding stove to heat them with. Anyway, I started on the trail after breaking down the tent, rolling it up, and tying my sleeping bag to the backpack.

My car was back at the trailhead, locked up and pretty much empty. I was on the trail, which was what I really wanted to do. It is a physical challenge, but just as equally, it is an exercise in tolerating pain, mainly the cold and general discomfort. It's just not pleasant, and I took some pride in being able to endure it. One good thing about this time of year – no ticks, no chiggers. I hiked for several hours, eyeing my compass and map at regular intervals. I spotted random bald eagles sailing high above, patrolling the gray sky. I find them more uplifting than the enormous turkey vultures that congregate around anything that's dead.

The trail followed the ridge line, went down into a valley, and back up again. It was not exactly one of Shackleton's treks across Antarctica. Still, for me, it's not an insignificant undertaking, to hike in cold weather, to be prepared for it, to endure the wind, ice, snow, and to overcome the occasionally rough terrain.

I've had interesting experiences hiking in cold weather. Years ago, I was hiking in the foothills west of Colorado Springs, not quite sure where I was. It got dark, so I put up my tent and went to sleep. It snowed overnight. By morning, my tent was almost buried by several feet of snow, and white haze from the continuing snow storm gave everything an otherworldly aspect. Waking up to some animal sounds, I poked my head out through the flaps. I was surrounded by six cowboys mounted on enormous horses, all just staring at me. They might as well have been the ghost riders in the sky. The men all wore huge snow covered cowboy hats and well-worn dusters. The chin hairs and manes on the horses had various sizes of icicles hanging off them. The cowboys had the same hanging off their mustaches and beards. There was steam flowing from all their noses and mouths.

Their rifles were at the ready, but once they got a good look at me, they laughed. I'm sure they thought I was a greenhorn. I certainly wouldn't disagree. They turned out to be a friendly bunch and were a sheriff's posse out looking for someone. They also thought I might have frozen to death. I told them, not yet, but give me a day. They thought that worth a laugh. One of them said he figured I wasn't a fugitive from justice with a tent that could be spotted a mile away in a raging snowstorm. Soon after, they rode off in single file, disappearing one by one into the white haze, to continue their search.

Looking back, I thought it strange. They all were packing what looked to be single action Colt revolvers and lever action repeating rifles. I saw no cell phones or any other electronic equipment. Then there was the way they talked, which seemed to be from the Old West. They appeared perplexed by the material my tent was made of. I'd hate to be the guy they were looking for.

That was in the more distant past, That was a happier time. This particular trip, well, I made the journey for a specific purpose. I was doing it to forget. Because my whole life then was all about forgetting. It was working. That is, until I felt the tears. And my forgetting came to an abrupt end.

Most days now it seems like a long time ago. It wasn't so long ago when I was on that trail. What I was trying to forget was that I was married. That I had a family. We had a daughter, the most extraordinary, beautiful, vibrant, happiest, spirited, energetic child anyone could hope for. She was the center of our world. She was so eager to live life and met each day with the greatest joy and anticipation. My wife was beautiful and happy. We lived in a nice house in the suburbs. People would look at us and think we were a great, perfect family. I thought so. We didn't know, though. We didn't know that nothing stays perfect.

For a period of time, I would regularly pick our daughter up from an after-school girl scout meeting, since it was right on the way home. But, I was stuck in a court docket that day which would not end. I called my wife up, and she drove over and picked our daughter up. While driving back on the highway, an exhausted, over-the-road trucker, intent on making a deadline, was traveling in the opposite direction. He fell asleep, and his truck crossed the center line. It smashed into their car head-on. It was a horrendous collision. A highway patrol officer said they died instantaneously. I chose not to ask him how he would know.

It made no sense. How could such a thing happen? The days afterward were a blur. There is nothing on this planet more innocent than a ten-year-old girl. There was no one less deserving of such a fate than my wife. The funeral, I barely remember. It was impossible for me to accept. For the longest time I expected them to walk through the front door. I'd keep it unlocked in case they did. But, they never did. I'd save the last soda in the refrigerator for them. It's still there. I'd continue to lower the toilet seat and make up the bed so they wouldn't get mad. But, this happens a lot. In this country, all over the world. So I tell myself. In some sense I was insane, delusional, and it's no surprise I ended up on a frozen dirt trail in the middle of nowhere, in freezing weather, the day before New Year's.

I have a beautiful daughter who looks like golden
  flowers, beloved Kleis, for whom I would not take
  all Lydia or lovely . . . .
  Sappho, Fragment 132.

My daughter's life was just like Sappho's poem. There was just a fragment, and the rest was lost. I still wonder what our lives would have been like. I hope that, in another universe, another timeline, they didn't die and they lived a full life. Every time I've made it through a close call, dodged some near miss, I always wonder if I actually died, and that now I'm living in an alternate reality. So, I'm hoping in some other timeline, some other reality, the truck missed them, and life went on. But that didn't happen in the here and now. In this timeline, reality is cruel and heartless.

Is life worth living? There's an argument that every intelligent form of life in existence already answers that question by continually making a conscious decision each day to stay alive. I was told that when a person is depressed and suicidal, when one reaches a rational, logical conclusion to end it all, it is important for that person to understand this peculiar state of mind is actually more a reflection of his or her current chemical and neurotransmitter balance, than a result of any reasoning. Therefore, what he or she currently thinks is a rational, reasoned decision will not seem like one next week, or next month. I was waiting for next week, next month.

Around four o'clock I was several ridges past where I began, and I started looking for a campsite. Most of the snow had melted, or evaporated. Things were mostly all gray and brown again. I found an open spot, just off the trail. So, I took my backpack off and started setting up camp. Tarp, tent, sleeping bag. A lovely MRE dinner – beef stroganoff, heated by Sterno.

I brought along something I thought would be fun. I had a drone, a DJI Air 2, just an excellent piece of modern technology. The one I had came with a controller with its own video screen. I didn't have to connect my cell phone to it. So, before it got dark, I turned it on and got it going. Its GPS connected with twelve satellites and, using the control sticks, I had it go straight up about 250 feet. Looking at the video screen, which was fed a signal from the drone's camera, I checked out the forest. I took a few photos, using the buttons on the controller. Pushing the right control stick forward I had the drone fly forwards, at a good rate of speed. The video screen on the controller displays speed, altitude, and various other data. After about half a mile, I could see a small meadow surrounded by the forest. I stopped the drone above it and lowered the altitude a little. There were several deer in the meadow, grazing. I pushed the video record button.

After a few minutes, a very large animal walked into the meadow. The deer seemed rather disturbed by this, and they put some distance between themselves and this new creature. I realized I was viewing an elk. Elk look massive compared to deer. I've seen elk before, but this one was enormous. It had gargantuan antlers. They were not like deer antlers but more like huge, wide saucers, with antlers looking like a giant's fingers coming out of the saucers. It seemed almost like an impossible creature. How could any animal carry such huge antlers on its head? After a minute or so, I saw that it was looking straight up at the drone. The drone was at least 200 feet in the air and should not have been noticeable. Something about this was disturbing. I felt like it was staring directly at me. It was a frightening visage. Because of the frigid air, it seemed as if it was snorting steam through its nostrils. Icicles hug off the sides of its eyes, the cold weather making stalactites of its tears.

A wave of apprehension went through my body. It bellowed then. I saw it on the screen. I actually heard echoes of it where I was. Without even thinking, I quickly hit the Return Home button on the controller. The drone took off, making a beeline for my location.

That night I was in my tent, lying in the sleeping bag, wide awake. The phenomenally large elk bothered me. It put me on edge. It looked like drawings I've seen of Irish elk. I had no cell phone coverage, so no internet, and thus I was unable to pull up photos of what those animals looked like. At the time, it was just a very disconcerting mystery.

I believe that, like many people, when I've been alarmed or surprised by something, my senses become much more perceptive. I really didn't want that in the middle of the forest at night. Likewise, I didn't want to see a shadow or a blowing leaf out of the corner of my eye and, because of some heightened perception, then believe that it was actually some sort of fifth dimensional monstrosity. I'd rather not notice. I admit it, this is an adult version of the monster under the bed. I'm joking, more or less. Still, I attempted to just stay in my tent.

After two hours or so of staring at my wet socks dangling from the inside tent pole, I gave up. Screw it. I got up, put my clothes on, and crawled outside. I had a good flashlight. It had a red light option, which I used. They say red light doesn't interfere with a person's night vision. The stars were out, and so was a thin, crescent moon. It was a picture-perfect sight. It had to be a 1 on the Bortle Scale. So, I walked a little up the trail. It wasn't a stupid thing to do. I was camped right next to it and the trail was easy to see. I came to an overlook, where no trees were blocking the horizon. I didn't bring my compass, I'm not sure which direction I was looking. Clicking on my flashlight's regular beam, I pointed it down below. I wished I hadn't. I was on the edge of a cliff, and it was a great distance down there. Several sets of eyes down there reflected the light back. I had no idea what they were. But, again, I felt that wave of apprehension.

At that moment, this little nighttime walk turned bizarre. Out of nowhere, I felt a sudden urge to jump off. My knees became wobbly. It was a shockingly lurid, completely unexpected impulse. I kept on thinking it wouldn't look like suicide, not that it would matter. A quick and easy way to end the existential burden of mortality, to end the ongoing torture of remembrance. I mean, why not? Who cares?

I'm not sure what might have occurred had there not been a movement, a disturbance, in the sky to my right. Quickly looking there, I caught the stars disappearing. Surreptitiously moving across the sky, completely silent, a shadow was swallowing the points of light. My stomach tightened. It was about a thousand feet in the air. After focusing on it, the shape was unmistakable. A black triangle. It turned, and headed towards my location. It kept moving, and stopped over the campsite, a mere hundred yards away. It began rotating. I made myself small, crouching behind a tree. After a minute I peeked out, and it was no longer there.

Relieved, I stood up. I closed my eyes and took a deep breath. With my eyelids shut, I saw sparkles and light flashes. It occurred to me that this is phenomena that's experienced by people being exposed to radiation of some sort. I really did not want to, but I slowly looked straight up. Of course, the damn thing was directly above. Three bright lights switched on, at each corner of the triangle, lighting up the whole area. At first, I was paralyzed, but I quickly recovered my senses. I had to get out from under it. I knew what would happen otherwise. I would end up dead, and glowing in the dark. The only thing I could do was sprint into the woods, and that is exactly what I did.

———— ◆○◆ ————

In the morning, I woke up. In my tent. In my sleeping bag. I remember all that happened that night. I recalled everything as thoroughly as I could. After I ran into the woods, I headed towards a rock outcropping with a good deal of underbrush and I blindly dived into it. So, now I have this concern. Is there any missing time? I don't think so. I recall that, after an hour or so, I made my way back to the campsite. There was not much choice. My food, water, and everything else was there. I saw no more black triangles. It was infuriating. Whether it was something extraterrestrial, or some government-funded black project, I have no doubt it is extremely unhealthy to be directly under one. It's likely there would be some kind of electromagnetic, microwave, or gravitational emission coming out of it. I did not want to die a slow, agonizing death, glowing in the dark. Could you imagine me in whatever hospital I would end up at? At night every nurse, intern, and resident would drop by to check out the terminal patient who glows in the dark, who was zapped by aliens. Still, its timing was impeccable. There was an inexplicable feeling that had come over me while looking down from that cliff.

As far as I was concerned, my little winter vacation was over. When I took these trips, at least in warmer weather, I tried to make a week of it. Not this time. I packed up and headed back to my car. When I made it to the trailhead, it was unmolested. Again, one of the benefits of beat-up old cars.

Driving back, I began to question my recall. Maybe because I was now surrounded by the veneer of civilization, of normal reality - asphalt roads, billboards, traffic. Did all of it really happen? It was nighttime. Perhaps I just let my imagination get the better of me. Maybe it was merely a black helicopter, with a really good muffler. I don't know. Either way, I just wanted to go home.

About half an hour out of the small town of Eminence, I came to a stop sign where two state roads intersect. Three young women were standing at the other side of the intersection. They were apparently hitchhiking. They waved at me. So, I drove over there, rolled down the window, and asked if they needed a lift. One of them said they were headed to Springfield and would appreciate one. Springfield was on my way back. I think it was only another hour away at that point. So, I pulled over, got out, rearranged a bunch of stuff in my back seat and the passenger area to make room, and they all piled in.

An interesting conversation took place. They quickly found out I was a lawyer. Of course, one of them said she was considering law school, so we talked about practicing law. That carried on for a while. The woman next to her asked me, of all things, what I wanted out of life. I had a hard time answering. I should have considered my response more carefully. I finally said I wanted to know if it was worth living. I shouldn't have said that. She started crying. When we hit Springfield, they got out at Bass Pro Shops, a big tourist attraction there. They thanked me, giving me hugs even, which I realized I really needed. The girl who was interested in law school whispered to me that her friend who started crying, her dad had taken his own life the year before. So, I'm still processing all of that.

CHAPTER 8: THE PHAISTOS DISK PRISONER

Our office has an ancient fax machine in the reception area. No one uses it, so it was somewhat of a surprise when it came to life. It generated a great deal of noise and began spitting out dozens of pages, some floating to the floor. Several individuals walking by the front desk heard the commotion, looked at it, and laughed. Somebody was actually receiving a hard copy fax transmission.

At some time in the past, I asked our secretary why the office floor even has a fax machine. Everyone uses email or, rarely, an online fax service. Apparently, our office management company insists it stays there, for use by anyone in the building. They charge a dollar a page.

Regardless, the machine hadn't received a fax transmission for many months. The one being received turned out to be a hundred pages long. I had just made it back from my miserable winter trip. I wasn't working. Sitting in my office, I was just staring at the wall. I did manage to get up and open the door when I heard knocking.

"Essie, you received a fax transmission."

I was confused. "What are you talking about?"

Giving me a look that clearly indicated I shouldn't dare get mad at her, our secretary said, "It's a hundred pages."

I felt somewhat upset. I held it in. Well. Maybe I didn't. I'm sure she noticed a few veins appear on my face.

"Who in the hell would do that? I didn't ask for any damn fax."

"I didn't read it, but it's from the U.S. District Court. I couldn't exactly just turn off the machine."

Following her, I went up to the front desk and pulled the pages out of the tray, and picked up a few off the floor.

The first page I picked up was this:

IN THE UNITED STATES DISTRICT COURT
WESTERN DISTRICT OF MISSOURI

John Doe, Inmate

BOP Register No. 346672-46

Petitioner,

v.

Setiyun Osturs, Director

Federal Bureau of Prisons

and

Norman Goppert, Warden

United States Medical Center for Federal Prisoners

Springfield, Missouri,

Respondents.

APPOINTMENT OF COUNSEL FOR
PRO SE INMATE RE
PETITION FOR WRIT OF HABEAS CORPUS

This matter having come before the Court, and being fully advised in the premises, it is hereby Ordered that Esmond Kemp be and hereby is appointed as counsel for Petitioner.

IT IS SO ORDERED.

Lucas Briscoe Calhoun, Judge

Reading this put me into a state of panic. I just got appointed in a federal habeas corpus action! I didn't even know they did that.

I do not like federal court. I really work hard to stay away from it. I was surprised the judge, the Honorable Lucas Briscoe Calhoun, was still working. Or even alive. Known for a half century of eccentric behavior on the bench, he took senior status decades ago. Not only that, when he was active, his courtroom was in Springfield. What the hell was going on here?

I gathered all the paperwork, tried to organize it, and started to haul the stack back to my office. While doing so, I passed by Bill Hurley's office. The door was open, as most doors were on the floor. I looked in. He must have heard some of the conversation since he was hunched over, looking at some treatise. Except, judging by its cover, it was upside down.

Something occurred to me. Bill Hurley used to practice in front of Judge Calhoun. I recalled some of his old war stories of trials he had in Calhoun's courtroom. Bill Hurley would talk about all the screwball rulings, most in his favor. Occasionally, they went to lunch together. I began to put two and two together.

"Just what's going on here, Bill?"

"What? What do you mean?"

"Some clerk for a federal judge, the Honorable Lucas Briscoe Calhoun, faxed me a hundred pages of court files and an appointment in an indigent habeas corpus case."

"Oh really? I'm surprised they even used a fax machine. If I remember correctly, Judge Calhoun swore he would never use email. He said there is no real filing in a federal court without a physical document getting handed over to a clerk. So, his office never converts his orders into PDF files."

I read some newspaper story about this from many years ago. One of the many crazy stories about this judge. There's no electronic filing when it comes to this judge.

"As I recollect, you and he were tight. It seems to me that you might per chance know something about what all this is." I placed the pile of papers on his desk.

Bill leaned over, picked up a few, giving them a quick perusal. A somewhat suppressed grin appeared on his face.

"Well, Essie, looks like you're going to have to dive back into the practice of law."

I took a deep breath and then managed a polite response. "I don't especially want to dive into anything."

"How long has it been?"

We just stared at each other.

I whispered. "It might as well have been yesterday."

"Essie, it wasn't yesterday. It was at least a year ago. You'll never get rid of the pain. But, working as the smart, conscientious lawyer you are, you can squeeze it into a tiny ball. It's time to dive back in."

———————◦◦◦———————

Yeah, Bill Hurley and the Honorable Lucas Briscoe Calhoun were tight. In fact, they still go out to lunch. Every week. Even though he was on the bench in Springfield, Judge Calhoun was living in Kansas City. His children, all married, all with children, lived in Kansas City, or nearby in Overland Park and Lee's Summit. So, there was little hesitation on his part to move up here when he took senior status.

How does a ninety-year-old judge on senior status even get assigned a case? Well, he didn't. Many of the convoluted proceedings dealing with this particular inmate were previously heard in his courtroom. Fifty years ago. So the current Chief Judge, seeing the file, didn't bother to reassign it. She just sent it up from Springfield to the District Court Clerk in Kansas City. The relatively new United States Federal Courthouse in Kansas City, as far as courthouses go, is not too far removed from being a Taj Mahal. The rumor is the total cost to the taxpayer, including improvements and repairs, will be just shy of two hundred million dollars. So, it's no surprise that there are always a few spare courtrooms.

The last thing I would ever want would be an appointment in a federal court case. Most attorneys in the Kansas City area are appointed to represent parties in juvenile court proceedings. Those appointments can be nothing short of hellish nightmares. Being forced to represent monstrously abusive mothers in termination of parental rights cases. Or juveniles who were charged with any number of horrendous felonies. Some lawyers, some law firms, just pay out of pocket for other lawyers to cover those appointments.

I got my fair share of those. But, I didn't even know lawyers could be appointed in federal cases. Unless a lawyer signs up for it, I suspect they don't. Except for me. I suppose I'm just a lucky guy.

I visited the federal courthouse the next day, got a better and more complete copy of the court file, and gave the clerk my online fax number, my email address, and so on. Afterward, sitting in the courthouse's enormous lobby, with the half dozen U.S. Marshals watching over everything while running the metal detector, I was blown away by what I read. I should say I was blown away by what I didn't read. Because, almost all the records from the criminal trial, and the sentencing, were lost. They were burned up in a fire decades ago. There's another issue. The Federal Bureau of Prisons doesn't know their inmate's real name. They don't know his date of birth or how old he is. What they do have are some few records showing that John Doe, BOP Register No. 346672-46, was sentenced to life in prison. The prison records indicate the sentence was for homicide.

The Federal Bureau of Prisons operates a Medical Center in Springfield, Missouri. Part of the medical center is a psychiatric section. A very high security psychiatric section. It's where the most insane criminals, the uncontrollable homicidal maniacs, are sent from all over the country. John Doe was assigned to this psychiatric section.

Mr. Doe did not speak English. He spoke a language no one could recognize. At some point, he started writing down symbols on a piece of paper. The symbols were unidentifiable. Until one of the guards, who read a good deal on archaeology, realized that the paper writings they took from the prisoner had many symbols that were identical to those used in the Phaistos disk.

This disk was found in an archaeological dig in 1908. Some archaeologists considered the disk a hoax, but the unique symbols used in the disk were subsequently found time and time again in later archaeological digs in Crete. The disk is estimated to have been created sometime in the middle of the second millennium, B.C. 1400 B.C., give or take a couple centuries.

It gets better. It appears the Bureau of Prisons took custody of Mr. Doe in 1954. This habeas corpus petition was filed on his behalf by a fellow prisoner, a jailhouse lawyer who believes that John Doe is entitled to be free now. Why? Because he served his sentence. Yes, he's served his life sentence.

<hr />

There was no record of Inmate John Doe's sentence including, or not including, any possibility of parole. The one sentencing document they have doesn't mention it. But then, there's no actual section in that ancient document where parole, or no parole, would be set down. That would be in the court records, most of which have disappeared in fire, water damage, or just being lost.

I left the courthouse lobby, holding a box of court file copies, and headed to my car. Sliding into the front seat, and placing my hands on the steering wheel, I let out my breath. It seemed I was holding it in the entire time I was in the lobby, going through every single page.

Did I mention already how much I do not like federal court? The only case of consequence I had in federal court resulted in a judge issuing a ruling in complete derogation of the case law. And, he did it without even holding a hearing. My client was a widow, with small children, who was denied a life insurance payout because the federal judge ruled that suicide was a valid defense to payment. Except, the case law in Missouri was clear that it was not. Not if the policy wasn't purchased with that intent. The judge didn't care. He issued his ruling and didn't even bother to hold a hearing wherein he would have had to look at her.

There are many wonderful federal judges. I read about them. I hear about them. I didn't get any of them.

There's the little matter of my not knowing what the hell to do in a habeas corpus proceeding. I've never had one. I didn't even know where to begin. Other than reading the court file. And, perhaps, talking to the inmate and maybe the jailhouse lawyer who wrote the petition for him.

I wondered if this was going to be another case where the federal judge would not even hold a hearing, and will just issue a heartless ruling from the bench. Valid habeas corpus proceedings, by their very nature, require that a person be presented to the court. But courts can also just dismiss the petition arbitrarily, right from the bench, without any hearing.

When I got back to the office, our secretary told me I received another fax, the Writ of Habeas Corpus issued by the court, plus its return of service. According to the writ, the Respondents were ordered to produce John Doe before the judge, in Kansas City, in one week.

It's amazing the degree of consideration and deference given to federal judges. The witnesses, the Petitioner, the records, were all located in Springfield. That didn't matter. The judge was located in Kansas City. All the records were shipped up to the Kansas City courthouse. The Petitioner, and, at my request, the jailhouse lawyer, were also shipped up. They were flown up via a small government jet, accompanied by several U.S. Marshals. The inmates were housed in the Jackson County Detention Center, We just call it the Jackson County Jail. That's where federal detainees are held while court proceedings involving them are held in town. The local U.S. Attorney's office was not involved. A Special Assistant U.S. Attorney was flown in from Washington, D.C. Then, there's the psychologist. She was a full-time federal employee on staff at the psychiatric section of the Springfield medical center. She drove up here and was put up at some downtown hotel.

----•O•----

Since I was appointed only a week before the hearing, more as an afterthought, I suppose, I decided to call the court clerk and ask about a continuance. The clerk said to not even bother, it will just make the judge mad. The hearing date was solid. So, three days later, I paid a visit to John Doe, newly arrived at the Jackson County Jail.

The jail, or more correctly the detention center, is a twenty-story building right downtown. After passing through the metal detectors, I was given a pass and directed to a visitor elevator, which got me to the nineteenth floor. I got out, stood in front of a reinforced door, heard a buzzing and opened the same. I found myself in a room used for attorney-inmate conferences. I waited there a few minutes before Mr. John Doe walked in. He was not what I expected. Mr. Doe is an individual of indeterminate age. He did not look young. He did not look old. He was of small frame, and heavily muscled. His pupils were jet black, as was his hair, and he had a piercing gaze. He looked at me a long time before speaking.

When he spoke, I heard the emotion, and a hint of anger, in his voice. I couldn't understand a word he was saying. I did not recognize the language. I had a legal pad and pen. Mr. Doe reached his hands out towards them, looking at me. I pushed the pad over to him along with the pen. He proceeded to write down a number of symbols, none of which I could recognize. Some looking like small outlines of people. Another looked like the side profile of a punk rocker with a

Mohawk hair style. There was an outline of a bird, and a circle with multiple dots in it. He wrote them in a circle. I looked at him and shrugged. There were tears in his eyes. He reached into his pocket and pulled out a piece of paper. On it was written "Aurelio Viscuso, BOP 711424-91." That was the name of the jailhouse lawyer who wrote his petition for habeas corpus. I got up, walked over to the wall, where an intercom was, pushed the button, and asked that Mr. Viscuso come in too.

"I don't really have conversations with Doe-boy. That's what I call him. We were in a cell together for a while. But now, we just see each other during meals and when we go into the yard. I know what he wants. I know what he means when he talks. But I can't possibly translate it. Don't ask me how. One thing I do know. It's time for him to go home. He's served his time."

Aurelio Viscuso was a scary guy. I don't know if he was a made man in the Mafia. There was no way I was going to ask him that. But, as far as Sicilian tough guys go, he's on top of the heap.

"Do you have any idea of what he did to get sentenced to life?"

Viscuso's hair was completely gray. He had massive biceps. His chest was literally in the shape of a barrel.

He gave me a hard look. I held his gaze, thinking that's the safest thing to do.

"I don't know who he killed. Whoever it was, I know he had to do it. There was no choice but for him to do so. There was a vendetta he had to satisfy. I know all about vendettas. Knowing he fulfilled that got him through this far. Something else - it was important, really important for everyone that he did what he did."

"How could you possibly know this?"

"He talks to me, in my sleep. When I dream, he talks to me. After so many years, it doesn't even seem strange to me now."

"Do you know where he's from?"

"Don't you know? I think you do. He is from Crete."

I stood up and stretched my legs. They were an odd couple. But, both of them, hard as nails. There was a mystery here that I suspect I will never uncover. Regardless, that wasn't my job. My job was limited to getting him released from custody.

⊷◊⊶

"Why is he even in the psychiatric section?"

Elizabeth Dolson was the senior psychologist for the psychiatric section of the United States Medical Center for Federal Prisoners in Springfield, Missouri. A long time federal employee, she was tall and skinny, with long brown hair broken up by gray streaks. She had a great deal of nervous energy, something uncommon for psychologists and psychiatrists.

"Well, we diagnosed him as akinetic catatonic. He would continuously sit and stare at a wall. Occasionally, he would make facial expressions while doing so. The records I've reviewed document that this went on for decades. It stopped when Mr. Viscuso filed the Petition for Habeas Corpus on his behalf. Before that happened, the only other event noted was an incident that occurred in the yard years ago. Two inmates attacked him. He may be catatonic, but that didn't help the poor fools who decided he would be an easy target. He crippled one, and sent the other to a hospital for a month. These men were both big and tough. It did them no good. They were down on the ground in seconds, screaming. Mr. Doe can be a very dangerous man when his buttons are pushed. He makes his guards very nervous."

⊷◊⊶

Two days later, I was downtown again. I was meeting the assistant U.S. Attorney who flew into town to try this matter. He wanted to meet at a barbeque restaurant. For me, there are two barbeque restaurants downtown I go back and forth on. Gate's Barbeque, and then there's Arthur Bryant's. The restaurant Calvin

Trillin called "the single best restaurant in the world." When it comes to ribs, I always go to Gates. When it comes to everything else, I go to Arthur Bryant's.

There's an old joke about the place. Once, the restaurant had a grease fire. It burned up all the interior. The insurance payout was $10,500. It was only that amount because a $10,000 car parked right outside the front door also caught fire. There's nothing much inside Arthur Bryant's except old cheap 1950s kitchen tables and chairs. And, of course, the brick fire pit. But, the walls are covered with photos of every U.S. President since the 1940s eating there. Along with hundreds of celebrities. The place, after all these years, still has incredible brisket, burnt ends, even french fries.

So we met there. Augustus Haywood, III, is not a spring chicken. He walked with a cane. I saw him wearing a French beret. The only person I've ever seen wear one. He clerked at the Department of Justice while going to law school in Boston. After passing the bar, he worked a few years for the U.S. Attorney's Office in the Southern District of New York. After that, he spent the rest of his career at the Department of Justice in Washington. He handled the sensitive matters. He was loaned to the C.I.A., N.S.A., and other three letter agencies occasionally. He has been practicing law for sixty years. He handled some of the proceedings involving John Doe back in the 1960s. When he was first assigned the matter, he didn't believe what he was told by his predecessor. But, apparently it's all true.

"We didn't have the entire story until the late fifties. That's when one of the German scientists that we brought over disclosed it. During World War Two, the Germans invaded Crete. There, they conducted their one and only entirely airborne assault. They did it for some valid tactical reasons. But something that won't be found in the history books is that there was another compelling reason. They wanted to seize the Phaistos Disk. They were unsuccessful. Knowing it was at risk, partisans smuggled it off the island, and it, after several years, ended up in a visiting archaeologist's possession at Harvard. He was a federal employee of the Smithsonian, and working at Harvard on a joint project. He knew of the disk, and knew how to translate the symbols on it. This archaeologist determined that one of the symbols represented the bloom of a rare, perhaps extinct, plant, genus Narcissus tazetta, a subspecies of which is only found on Crete. Depictions of this rare plant are found on frescoes painted on the walls of ancient Minoan ruins. We believe it is a plant used in the Eleusinian Mystery ceremonies. There is some disagreement as far as that goes. But the German scientist, while living in Alabama, was moved by the warm welcome given him, and his family, by the people in Huntsville. He therefore warned us that the disk, when translated, and when instructions were followed, and words were spoken, endows an individual with certain abilities. The Nazis believed this, and it motivated the airborne assault. People in the C.I.A. were inclined to believe him."

"The agency attempted to track the disk down. They discovered that the Smithsonian archaeologist in possession of it had a hidden past. In Europe, before he immigrated, he was a Nazi. A true believer. We believe he was in Crete during the war. Regardless, he was murdered before he could translate all the symbols on the disk. Only a few days after he came into possession of the disk. Furthermore, the disk was taken from him. He was murdered by your client."

"What evidence do you have that my client did it?"

"At this point, we don't need any evidence. He's already convicted. But, we can offer a deal. We will not oppose this Petition for Habeas Corpus if he produces the disk."

"Wait a minute. Records I read in the court file mention that Mr. Doe wrote down symbols that were identical to what is found on the disk. So, I did some research on the disk. It never left Crete. In fact, it's on public display at the Heraklion Archaeological Museum in Heraklion, Greece. How can he produce something that's already in that museum?"

Augustus Haywood, III, looked up at me, finished a french fry saturated in barbeque sauce, and stated, "Have you seen a good photo of that disk? Do you notice anything unusual about it?"

"Yeah, my very first thought was that it looks brand new. The impressions, the symbols on it, are very sharp."

"Exactly. The real disk looks like it is three or four thousand years old. The one on display in Heraklion looks like it was made yesterday." Leaning back, and looking around, he said, "I can tell you something else. The symbols on the real one are different from what are found on the one at the museum."

Chapter 9: We Don't Dream Alone

"Are you sure/ That we are awake?
It seems to me/ That yet we sleep, we dream."
A Midsummer Night's Dream (4.1.189-191)

During the pandemic, I began to dream strangely. I still do. Even now, there are certain dreams I have that cause some consternation. What I find curious, even disturbing, about them is that they are vividly realistic, of a life, of events, of locations, that I have no experience of, that I haven't read about, nor viewed anything remotely similar in theater, television, or anything else. They're remarkably complex, and evoke emotions that I've long forgotten, or have never experienced before. Some dreams are so unbelievably imaginative that they could not possibly have been invented by me.

What is equally curious is that my mind fights with me to immediately hide them from my awareness when I awaken. Sometimes, though, I do manage to remember them. I then try to write down what I can recall.

Aren't these dreams, which we all have, evidence of something unseen by us, something extraordinary? Do we share our self-awareness, or our subconscious, and unknowingly receive the perceptions of others? Are we all, somehow, in a sense, connected to one another? The Roman poet Virgil thought so, and wrote of the "Soul of the World." Our dreams are like a nightly reminder that all is not as it seems, that there's something deeper, hidden, from our rational waking life. To me, it is inexplicable that I, and I understand others, on occasion, dream strangely.

Several months ago I came across *The Magic Mountain,* a novel written by Thomas Mann, one of the great writers of the twentieth century. In it, he wrote of a character who had an extraordinary dream that he was thoroughly mystified by, as it was completely outside his life experience. The character described so well what it is like.

But how is it a man can know all that and call it up ... Where did I get the beautiful bay with the islands, where the temple precincts, whither the eyes of that charming boy pointed me, as he stood there alone? Now I know that it is not out of our single souls we dream. We dream anonymously and communally, if each after his fashion. The great soul of which we are a part may dream through us, in our manner of dreaming, its own secret dreams, of its youth, its hope, its joy and peace – and its blood-sacrifice. Here I lie at my column and still feel in my body the actual remnant of my dream – the icy horror of the human sacrifice, but also the joy that had filled my heart to its very depths, born of the happiness and brave bearing of those human creatures in white

---

Across the Atlantic, Walt Whitman, the American poet who is required reading in high school, wrote of our universal communal nature in his poem *Song of Myself.*

I celebrate myself, and sing myself,

And what I assume, you shall assume,

For every atom belonging to me as good belongs to you.

...

And these tend inward to me, and I tend outward to them,

And such as it is to be of these more or less I am,

And of these one and all I weave the song of myself.

He goes on for a hundred verses or so reciting all the different people, in all the myriad of circumstances and occupations, he, and we, are.

Then there is Frederic Myers, who a century ago in his book, *Human Personality and Its Survival After Bodily Death,* wrote that dreams are evidence that some part of us survives death. Ralph Waldo Emerson and William James thought so too and called this the "Over-Soul." Perhaps, maybe, dreams are a hint, or even a promise, that there might be more.

So, now I think that when I dream, I'm not dreaming alone. Really, I'm fine with that.

Perhaps the very first song we are ever taught is *Row, Row, Row Your Boat.* Children singing this song don't realize that its final verse could well be true.

Chapter 10: The Habeas Corpus Trial

When a court issues a Writ of Habeas Corpus, it is an exercise of raw, unbridled, judicial power. It is a court's tour de force, its magnum opus. Presidents, generals, sheriffs, governors, jailers, all must comply with the writ. Historians trace its roots back to the Magna Carta in the thirteenth century. Contumacious English barons insisted on its inclusion, as a counter to the king's divine right to incarcerate his subjects.

I hate trials. Until they start. Then, they are exhilarating, life affirming. You've got the tiger by the tail. You can't let go until it's over. You don't sleep. You can't eat. You are totally immersed in the moment. Bill Hurley knows this. That's why the son of a bitch got me appointed in this matter. He knew there'd be a trial. He knew I needed to wake up. Speaking of Bill, I spotted him, in the back row, watching.

"All rise. Court is now in session."

The bailiff, looking like a retired U.S. Marshal halfway through a second career, scanned the courtroom looking for threats. He gave my client a second glance. Thankfully, Aurelio Viscuso was not in the courtroom. As a witness, he was waiting in the hallway, in handcuffs, guarded by a marshal. U.S. Marshals seem to be everywhere in federal courthouses.

The Honorable Lucas Briscoe Calhoun strolled in. Wearing his black robe, it was difficult to tell, but he appeared to be wiry, very wiry. He looked so lean, one could reasonably conclude he did not weigh more than a hundred pounds. Yet, he was at least six feet tall.

With a sly grin, he spoke. "Don't just stand there. Sit down!"

We sat down. True to his reputation, this judge still had a crazy sense of humor.

Looking at the docket sheet, he stated, "John Doe versus Setiyun Osturs, Director, Federal Bureau of Prisons, and Norman Goppert, Warden, United States Medical Center for Federal Prisoners, Springfield, Missouri. Please make your appearances."

I stood up. "The Petitioner appears in person and by counsel, Esmond Kemp."

Augustus Haywood, III, stood up and spoke. "Setiyun Osturs, Director, Federal Bureau of Prisons, and Norman Goppert, Warden, United States Medical Center for Federal Prisoners, Springfield, Missouri, appear by counsel, Augustus Haywood, III, Assistant U.S. Attorney, Department of Justice, Washington, D .C."

Judge Calhoun asked. "Mr. Haywood. It's been a long time. Are you a Missouri licensed attorney this time?"

Smiling, Mr. Haywood responded. "Yes, your Honor, I am now a full member of the Missouri bar. They even gave me a bar card."

"I won't ask that you show me. Mr. Kemp. I know you're a local attorney. Do you understand the nature of these proceedings?"

"Yes, your Honor. My client wants to get out of jail. The government wants to keep him in jail. We believe the law requires that Mr. John Doe be released from incarceration."

"Well, that, perhaps inelegantly, but succinctly, sums it up. So, we're going to have a trial then?"

"It would seem so."

"Before we begin. Mr. Haywood, has the U.S. government, with all its vast resources, still not determined Mr. Doe's true name?"

"No, your Honor."

"Jesus Christ. Alright, Mr. Kemp, call your first witness."

"Your Honor. Initially, I ask that the court take judicial notice of the court file, and all the documents therein."

"Any objections, Mr. Haywood?"

"No sir. Well, except that, if there is extraneous material in the file."

Mr. Haywood, have you had occasion to go through the file?"

"Yes, your Honor."

"Did you find anything extraneous?"

"Well, not offhand, I can't think of anything."

"The court takes judicial notice of its own file. I'm not sure I even have to do that. Proceed, Mr. Kemp."

"The Petitioner calls Margaret Cooper."

Mr. Haywood promptly stood up. "Objection, your Honor. Ms. Cooper is the District's Court Clerk. There's no reason for her to be called."

"Mr. Kemp?"

"Actually, your Honor, technically, her title is Court Executive. Her testimony is entirely relevant."

"Okay, proceed then."

Ms. Cooper was duly sworn in, and took her place on the witness stand.

"Ms. Cooper, have you occasion to review the court file in this matter?"

"Yes, when it was transferred up here, I reviewed the same."

"Did you also review any electronic versions of this court file?"

"Yes, I did."

"Did you discover anything that varied from the hard copies transferred up here?"

"Yes, I did."

"What did you discover?"

"I discovered an intake form from the Bureau of Prisons dated November 11, 1954."

Augustus Haywood, III, quickly stood up. "Objection, your Honor. Whatever this document is, it has not been provided to me."

"Your Honor, if I may respond. It's part of the court file. It was just discovered by Ms. Cooper this morning. I can ask her a few more questions to better explain this."

Judge Lucas Briscoe Calhoun looked at everyone in the courtroom with barely controlled amusement. Obviously, he was really enjoying this. He did something odd. Leaning back, he pulled an apple out of his pocket. He took a penknife out of another pocket, and started peeling it. We all just stood there watching him.

After a few more minutes, without even looking up, he spoke. "Alright, let's hear what the story is on this document."

"Ms. Cooper, did you make a copy of this intake form?"

"Yes."

"I'm handing you what is marked as Petitioner's Exhibit 1. Is this a true and correct copy of this intake form?"

"Yes."

"And, it is part of the actual court file, which the court has taken judicial notice of?"

"Yes."

"When did you discover it?"

"This morning, while collecting the file. It was folded in half and stuck to the back of one of the folders."

"Your Honor, I offer Petitioner's Exhibit 1 into evidence."

"Objection, your Honor."

"I'll take your objection under advisement. Mr. Kemp, what is it about this form you want to draw attention to?"

"Your Honor, two thirds down, on the sentencing data, there's a line for the sentence, and the eligibility for parole. There's also a specific line for no possibility of parole for homicide convictions, which is blank."

"Objection, your Honor, this is hearsay."

Looking up at Mr. Haywood, with a grin on his face, Judge Calhoun stated, "Strictly speaking, court files mostly consist of hearsay. The Federal Rules of Evidence still allow for the court to take judicial notice of what is contained therein, and I have done so."

The judge continued. "Mr. Kemp, do you have anything else?"

"Yes, your Honor. I call Elizabeth Dolson to the stand."

Ms. Dolson was duly sworn in and took her place in the witness chair. After asking her the preliminaries, her position, her education, I got to the point.

"Ms. Dolson, are you familiar with John Doe's incarceration history?"

"Yes."

"He does not speak English, does he?"

"We don't know. He really does not speak much at all."

"Is there anyone who communicates with him?"

"Yes, I believe inmate Aurelio Viscuso does."

"How do you know?"

"Well, for several reasons. He has told me he does. Also, many times he would recite some requests from, or information about, Mr. Doe, and they would invariably prove to be correct."

"How long have you seen this?"

"Around ten years."

"Have you known John Doe to be a dangerous person?"

"No."

We took a short break. Elizabeth Dolson was not cross-examined. I thought this odd. She had essentially testified that Aurelio Viscuso had accurate communications with John Doe. Her testimony to that effect probably would not have held up under any sort of scrutiny. Yet, no objections were made.

———◄○►———

I called Aurelio Viscuso to the stand.

"Yes, I been convicted of a number of murders." Mr. Viscuso was not shy about his history.

"You've been an inmate at the Springfield psychiatric facility, correct?"

"Yeah."

"How well do you know John Doe?"

"Know him? Not really. If you're asking am I very familiar with him, yes."

"Does he communicate with you?"

"Yup."

"What does he communicate about?"

"He warns me about inmates trying to shiv me, like a day beforehand. I'd tell the guards, who say bullshit. Then everyone watches it happen just like John Doe let me know it would. Who would do it, when, where, even what the shank was made out of. And things like this happened over and over."

"We're here because you hand wrote out on a form a Petition for Writ of Habeas Corpus. You wrote that out on his behalf?"

"Yeah, he let me know it was time to do that."

"There's an "X" on the signature line. Is that his?"

"Yeah."

"There are three signature lines for three witnesses. Did all of them watch him make his mark all together in the same room, and sign the witness lines themselves?"

"Yeah. Believe me, we all know exactly how to do that the right way, after so many of us fucked up doing it the wrong way over the years."

Looking around the courtroom, he turned back to the female court reporter, blushed, and said, "Sorry."

"Did you have occasion to determine why he wanted this Petition filed now?"

"Yeah, he's served his life sentence. He wants to go home."

Augustus Haywood, III, stood up and spoke. "Objection, your Honor. That answer was non-responsive to the question. Additionally, at this point, I must make a general objection to further testimony from this witness regarding any sort of 'so called' communication with the Petitioner. There's no testimony that the Petitioner has uttered a single word to him."

The Honorable Lucas Briscoe Calhoun, his mouth full from eating another quarter slice of his apple, looked at me, looked at Mr. Haywood, turned his attention to his legal pad, and jotted down something.

Immediately after that, he looked up, and turning to me, he said, "Don't just stand there, Mr. Kemp, respond to this objection."

My apologies, your Honor. I thought perhaps you were going to summarily overrule the objection, and I didn't want to deflect from that.

Judge Calhoun stared at me for a few seconds. "If you are not going to respond to this objection, I will sustain it."

"Judge, my apologies. Let me address the objection by rephrasing the question."

"I was going to say, hurry up, we don't have all frickin day. But then I remembered. I'm on senior status. We do have all day. Well, when I say we, I mean me. But I'm the judge here so, that's all that matters."

Turning to the court reporter, he said, "Don't put that down. It's not part of the record."

I figured I'd better proceed, rather than allow for any more awkward pauses. "Mr. Viscuso, did the Petitioner want this habeas corpus action filed?"

"Yeah."

"Tell the court how you know this."

"He told me."

"Thank you."

At the same time I said "Thank you," Mr. Haywood stood up and, in a strident voice, objected again.

"No foundation. No foundation for the witness to make this statement. Your Honor, he gets these messages in his dreams! None of these claims that he told him, or communicated with him, are verifiable, are in any way admissible here."

Aurelio Viscuso turned and looked at him, his face flushed with anger. With a loud voice, charged with emotion, with tears on his cheeks, he stated, "They were good enough for you! You told me to write down every dream and get it to you! You said it was important! That they are real! That this is how he communicates! You put me in there with him! He knew the minute I walked into his cell that I was supposed to rat on him! He told me not to worry about it! In my dreams! He said everything was cool. He's a good man. He's more than a good man. He deserves to get out. He had done nuthin wrong. That man he killed was a Nazi. A monster. He wanted to rule the world. With some crazy thing you and your friends want now. That's why you keep him locked up. That's why his records were burned. Doe-boy wants to go home. He deserves to go home. He's no murderer. He's a hero. I don't care what you do to me. I ain't playing your games nomore."

We all were frozen by this outburst. Mr. Haywood, the Special Assistant U.S. Attorney flown in from Washington, D.C., was literally sputtering, unable to speak. All of this was obviously not intended to be disclosed to the court, or to me.

For the first time, I saw the Honorable Lucas Briscoe Calhoun in a rage, with his eyes glaring at the special assistant attorney general. Red-faced, eyes bulging, pencil size veins throbbing up and down his neck. For a ninety-year-old man, it was a very dangerous state.

"Is this the truth, Mr. Augustus Haywood, III?" Judge Calhoun, his voice barely under control, asked.

But, before Mr. Haywood could respond, not that he was physically able to at the time, it got even wilder. The judge asked a follow-up question.

"Mr. Haywood, is there an undisclosed party to this proceeding? Are you here, not only for the Bureau of Prisons, but acting on behalf of the Central Intelligence Agency? Is that the real party in interest here?"

Mr. Haywood looked like he had seen a ghost, a ghost that had just ripped his liver out. Unintentionally, he turned his head to look behind, at the gallery where the public sits to observe the proceedings. Bill Hurley was sitting on one side. But, Mr. Haywood did not look at him. He looked towards the other side. One man, in what appeared to be a bespoke suit from Savile Row, was sitting there. We all turned around to look at him.

The man quickly stood up and tried to make his way to the door.

"Stop that man!"

This being a federal courthouse, the U.S. Courthouse for the Western District of Missouri, when a U.S. District Court judge yells, U.S. Marshals come out of the woodwork. The courtroom was flooded with them, men and women, with their guns drawn.

One of the marshals approached the bench. He tendered to the judge the man's wallet. In it was official identification. He had a title. "Deputy Chief of Operations, Central Intelligence Agency, United States of America."

There was a one-hour recess. Then, court was called to order.

⸻ ◆ ⸻

Judge Calhoun spoke. Reading from the written order he prepared during recess, this is what he said:

"In every jurisdiction in this country, in state and federal courts, in civil and criminal proceedings, attorneys have an absolute duty of full candor to the court. I find that duty has been grossly violated in this instance. It is ironic. The C.I.A.'s involvement should have been fully disclosed. But then, if it was disclosed, it would have revealed the Agency's entirely improper scheme, its illegal plot, to incarcerate Mr. John Doe forever, not because of the crime he was convicted of, but to coerce him into revealing the location of this mysterious disk."

"Furthermore, it has acted, not in a foreign country, but within the borders of the United States, in gross violation of the National Security Act of 1947 and the C.I.A. Act of 1949. All of this is clearly relevant to the Petition for Writ of Habeas

Corpus that is before the court today. All of this was intentionally hidden from the court."

"After reviewing what we have of the Bureau of Prisons records, and whatever else that has found its way into the court file, I find that Mr. Doe is not a threat to the public, that his Petition for Writ of Habeas Corpus is well-founded, that the government has no argument for continuing to incarcerate him. I further find that Mr. Haywood has acted in gross violation of the Federal Rules governing the conduct of attorneys, and subsequent inquiries will be made in that regard."

"The relief prayed for in the Petition for Writ of Habeas Corpus is granted. I ORDER that Mr. John Doe be released from custody of the Bureau of Prisons. Furthermore, I ORDER that no conditions of parole shall be imposed."

"IT IS SO ORDERED."

———◦———

That is not the end of the story. Elizabeth Dolson, the psychologist, after talking with Bill Hurley, decided to put Mr. John Doe up at a local downtown hotel, the Hotel Muehlebach. So, they did that, and began to think about how to help him adjust. But figuring that out was for later, not then.

Late at night, in the hotel room, John Doe woke up. At first, not knowing where he was, he was disoriented. Slowly, he grew aware of his circumstances. Sitting up, he placed his feet on the floor, and his head in his hands. Whereupon, Mr. Doe contemplated how his life would change. He wanted to go home. Now realizing too much time has passed, and he could not, his pain was almost unbearable.

Like many rooms late at night, there was a corner of the room in shadow. A sound, a whisper, emanated from there, startling him.

"Son of Rhadamanthys." It was a woman's voice, barely perceptible. It was a beautiful voice, with a melodious accent.

Recognizing the language the words were spoken in, he smiled and turned his head to the corner.

"Son of Rhadamanthys. I see you have followed in your father's footsteps. He is proud of you. Still, it was enough for you to retrieve the disk. You did not need to kill that man, though he was evil."

He replied. "The man was a Nazi. They did not know. He took many innocent lives across the ocean. Some of whom I did know. In the future, he would have taken many more. And you know, the future was dark with the disk in his hands."

"Regardless, you've served your sentence. A punishment you accepted and imposed on yourself. Now, you can go home."

"I can't go home. It's too late. Now my home is in the past."

"I understand it is in the past."

John Doe, confused, tilted his head, attempting to get a better look at the person in the shadow.

She stepped forward. She wore a tunic. She was very beautiful, and had silver in her eyes.

He recognized her, and experienced a wave of trepidation.

"Son of Rhadamanthys, you can take the disk with you, but, it will be found again. If you wish, you may leave it in our care."

"I can think of no safer place for it than with the immortal ones."

She held out her hand to him.

<hr>

Elizabeth Dolson was very upset. No one could find John Doe. She always cared for him, recognizing an old soul when she sees one. Bill Hurley comforted her, offering assurances that he found his way home.

Chapter II: Anti-Gravity

What happened at Monkey Mountain was a mystery I found myself constantly thinking about. In the middle of the week I had some free time, so I engaged in some research.

In the 1950s, the successful development of anti-gravity propulsion became the holy grail scientists and engineers sought after. Universities, research institutes, and government laboratories all started programs and spent significant sums of money to unlock the secret, at locations all around the country. The impetus started in the 1940s with the observations of incredible objects floating in the air, traveling at extraordinary speeds, with no visible means of propulsion, and making impossibly sharp turns. Applying the conventional laws of physics, as understood even now, meant that any biological entity inside such craft would turn into slush because of the enormous g forces created by such maneuvers. For that matter, scientists who have expertise in the field of material science are still unaware of any substance that would not disintegrate at the g forces observed. G-force, which is shorthand for the gravitational force equivalent, is a measure of the force imposed by acceleration upon matter, 1g being the gravitational force imposed on matter on the surface of the Earth.

Scientific observation of these objects in the sky, and study of the reports made by those individuals who have observed them, caused scientists to come to the unavoidable conclusion that somehow the force of gravity was suspended by these craft. Their acceleration and extreme maneuvers were simply impossible otherwise. The physical nature of the objects was confirmed multiple times by radar and also, in certain instances, by the objects leaving a condensation trail or distorting a cloud formation. Previously, Einstein's General Theory of General Relativity, confirmed on every level, was thought to rule out the creation of anti-gravity fields.

An interesting aspect of gravitational force is that gravity alone has no impact on physical objects, its force is only felt when that object is facing resistance by another mass. Without an opposing mass, the object is in free fall.

Most Americans are still unaware of the Twining Memorandum, originally classified as Secret until declassified and released under the Freedom of Information Act many years ago. It was drafted by General Nathan F. Twining, United States Air Force, and dated September 23, 1947 (The United States Air Force was officially created on September 18, 1947). When it was written, General Twining was the Commanding Officer of the U.S. Air Force Air Material Command. Several years later, he would be appointed as Chief of Staff, U.S. Air Force, the senior officer commanding this service, and as such served as a member of the Joint Chiefs of Staff. In this memorandum, General Twining stated, regarding flying saucers, which he referred to as "flying discs" that "The phenomenon reported is something real and not visionary or fictitious. ... There are objects approximating the shape of a disc, of such appreciable size as to appear to be as large as man-made aircraft." The memorandum describes their remarkable flight characteristics – an absence of any atmospheric trail, metallic and circular in appearance, sometimes flying in formation with others and producing no sound.

The first Director of the Central Intelligence Agency, Vice Admiral Roscoe H. Hillenkoetter, after retirement, became a board member of the National Investigations Committee on Aerial Phenomena (NICAP). In 1960, he wrote a letter to the U.S. Congress stating in part "Behind the scenes, high-ranking Air Force officers are soberly concerned about UFOs. But through official secrecy and ridicule, many citizens are led to believe the unknown flying objects are nonsense."

Throughout the first part of the 1950s many popular magazines, newspapers, and respected scientific publications described the ongoing research into anti-gravity propulsion, also known as "field-dependent propulsion," and some of the accomplishments made in that regard. Several publications reported that experiments were able to cause small objects to rise, sometimes shooting upwards at a significant velocity. This includes nonmetallic objects floating in the air, such as blocks of wood, and even one report of half-melted ice cream shooting upwards. Then, in the latter half of the 1950s, there were no more articles, either in the popular magazines of the time or in any of the scientific journals. Many journalists and researchers believed this was because there may have been a breakthrough, and the government decided to make all the research highly classified. Others believe they gave up in frustration. The contrast in reporting and information concerning the field of anti-gravity research between the first half and the second half of the 1950s is remarkable.

More recently, it was reported that a university scientist, based in Huntsville, Alabama, had some success in this area. But then, nothing more was heard of that. Even more recently, a scientist working for one of the U.S. Navy research laboratories applied for, and was awarded, patents on mechanisms he developed that would create an anti-gravity field. The patents described plans for a "high frequency gravitational wave generator," a "high temperature superconductor," an "inertial mass reduction device," and other mechanisms. As with what happened in the 1950s, once the initial reports of these breakthroughs became known, nothing more was heard of them.

What little details that were shared about these inventions included descriptions of spinning ceramics, rotating from 5000 to 25000 revolutions per minute, generation of magnetic torsion fields, and possible time-bending effects. *The Hunt for Zero Point,* a book published several years ago by Nick Cook, who at the time was Aviation Editor for *Jane's Defense Weekly,* describes all of the above, as well as his frustrated search for answers to this mystery.

Some of the leading physicists of the time joined these research projects in the 1950s, and nothing more was heard of their work in this area.

———————◄O►———————

Gravity is a mystery, just like magnetism. Scientists describe magnetic fields and draw diagrams of the magnetic force, showing the field poles. Physicists describe how mass attracts other masses through gravity. They say mass creates a curvature of space and that what we sense is an illusion. But, really, every single treatise, every single paper, about gravity, or magnetism, does not actually tell us what they really are. When a cheap magnet sticks to a refrigerator door, that fact is described, it is measured, but really, how does it actually work? No one has explained that. It is the same with gravity. What is actually physically keeping us from flying off? How do these fields, physically, push or pull matter? One would ask scientists this question, and they would invariably describe a field, or that a gravity well is created, and so on. But that doesn't answer the question. It merely describes the effect and how to predict and measure it. Nothing I know of describes how magnetism actually works, or how gravity actually works, what the actual thing is that reaches out and grabs an object and either pulls or pushes it.

These are exactly the same questions a five-year-old would have. You know, when a child gets an answer, and the child responds with a how or a why. Then, when another answer is given, the child asks another how or why. Eventually, the adult has to admit that he or she simply does not know. From my perspective, these questions remain unanswered.

After I wrote the above, I wondered if I'd just documented how unintelligent I am. Then, I received one of the blessings of having good friends. Ray Langstaff dropped by. He wanted to read this. So, rather sheepishly, I let him. After a few minutes, he looked up at me and laughed.

"Essie, what you've written here is exactly what the great men of science, the giants of physics, have stated. Exactly the same thing."

I was dubious. My reply, of course, was, "Bullshit!"

Ray laughed some more. "What you've described has a name. In physics, it's called 'Action at a Distance.' It remains one of science's mysteries."

"I thought scientists always say they've got it all figured out."

"They, do, but when they say that what they are really saying is that they've got mathematical models to predict the effects. The absolute why, which you've just written of, remains a mystery. Let me pull up some quotes."

Ray proceeded to get on my computer, and, I have to admit, he pulled up some pretty damn impressive ones.

⎯⎯⎯⎯⎯⎯⎯◦O◦⎯⎯⎯⎯⎯⎯⎯

Richard Feynman:

"The problem was, what makes the planets go around? (In those days, one of the theories proposed was that the planets went around because behind them were invisible angels, beating their wings and driving the planets forward. You will see that this theory is now modified! It turns out that in order to keep the planets going around, the invisible angels must fly in a different direction and they have no wings. Otherwise, it is a somewhat similar theory!) ...

But is this such a simple law? What about the machinery of it? All we have done is to describe how the earth moves around the sun, but we have not said what makes it go. Newton made no hypotheses about this; he was satisfied to find what it did without getting into the machinery of it. No one has since given any machinery. ...

Why can we use mathematics to describe nature without a mechanism behind it? No one knows."

Sir Isaac Newton:

"It is inconceivable that inanimate brute matter should, without the mediation of something else which is not material, operate upon and affect other matter without mutual contact, as it must be, if gravitation in the sense of Epicurus, be essential and inherent in it. And this is one reason why I desired you would not ascribe innate gravity to me. That gravity should be innate, inherent, and essential to matter, so that one body may act upon another at a distance through a vacuum, without the mediation of anything else, by and through which their action and force may be conveyed from one to another, is to me so great an absurdity that I believe no man who has in philosophical matters a competent faculty of thinking can ever fall into it."

For most of the twentieth century, Western Electric Company was at the cutting edge of technological innovation. In 1949, President Harry Truman requested that Western Electric take over the operation and management of Sandia National Laboratories, located in Albuquerque, New Mexico, as an "opportunity to render an exceptional service in the national interest." Sandia was the location of several black projects involving research on anti-gravity. Several of Western Electric's senior executives, some from their enormous operation in Lee's Summit, subsequently moved to Albuquerque to do so. More recently, Honeywell took over Sandia's management.

Kansas City is the location of the Honeywell Kansas City National Security Campus, formerly known as the Bendix Atomic Energy Commission facility. Throughout its history, it has always worked closely with Sandia, Los Alamos, and Lawrence Livermore National Laboratories. Their staff regularly travel back and forth. Among the staff are material scientists, mechanical engineers, computer scientists, laser scientists, and physicists, who collaborate in physically fabricating any equipment and mechanisms designed in those laboratories. It has unique expertise and capabilities in creating extraordinarily sophisticated mechanisms, one of a kind electronic and mechanical devices, from extremely hard, exotic metals. Using a variety of methods, including the use of high temperatures combined with extreme pressure, their extraordinarily skilled operators and machinists use computer controlled equipment to bond together and shape disparate metals, minerals, and plastics, producing parts made of composite materials once thought impossible to create. These meta-materials and extremely high temperature alloys are analyzed and tested utilizing several methodologies, including X-ray scattering and supercomputers with simulation software. It's been reported that the complex has a milling machine the size of a house, which is capable of such precise tolerances that the phases of the moon are factored in when programming it.

The nearby Western Electric operation, making use of its clean rooms, manufactured, tested, and supplied the government with extremely sensitive gyroscopes, electronic vacuum tubes, and other made-to-order, specialized electronic equipment. In the 1980s, before it was closed, Western Electric fabricated memory chips and integrated circuits.

So, why am I even bringing all this up? This is why. Nowhere else in the country, or the world for that matter, is there gathered together in one location such an extraordinarily unique combination of expertise, skills, and scientific know-how along with such sophisticated, cutting edge, technical manufacturing capabilities. If the government wanted to create a revolutionary, technically demanding, groundbreaking experimental propulsion system in a top secret facility that had advanced manufacturing capabilities, it would be here.

———————◄O►———————

All the scientists engaged in the many research projects around the country attempting to create an anti-gravity effect, either from theory, from measuring the emissions of the mysterious craft that were the subject of the Twining memo, and even, allegedly, by attempting to reverse engineer some crashed craft, give little consideration to what might happen if they succeed. How would a hostile and paranoid world change when nuclear warheads can be delivered by craft traveling at extraordinary speeds, that can go up to space and return to the ground in seconds, that can reverse direction instantaneously while doing so? This is not their area of expertise. But, other people, other groups, are immensely concerned. And this, in fact, was, and is, their area of expertise.

CHAPTER 12: MAJOR COLLINS, USAF

I'll try to recreate this conversation as best as I can recall. There is an Air Force base not too far from Lee's Summit. Whiteman AFB. They have lots of nuclear bombs. Along with a dozen B-2 bombers to drop them from. It's a large base with many different types of units located there. Some of the airmen and officers have families in Lee's Summit, even though it's a good hour's drive away. Apparently, they just visit their families on weekends. Some couples really like that arrangement. One of the officers is Randall Collins, a major who graduated from the Air Force Academy fifteen years ago. He attended the old Lee's Summit High School before going to the academy. He did not have perfect vision, so he did not fly. He ended up in Air Force Intelligence. He is on the list for Lieutenant Colonel and has rotated through a number of commands. He and his wife were very happy he got an assignment to Whiteman. Both their extended families live in Lee's Summit. She teaches at one of the Lee's Summit high schools. During the weekend, they were invited to a party at a friend's house in a Lee's Summit neighborhood. I was also there. An interesting conversation took place.

I was standing in the corner of the main room, nursing a bottle of beer. It was a good-sized living room, with a high ceiling and a large fireplace. Lots of people were conversing, so there was some difficulty in hearing what people were saying. It was a Friday evening and Collins apparently just made it into town and picked up his wife before coming over. He was still wearing his uniform, which caught my eye. While saying hi to the host, he heard I was a lawyer, so he made his way over to get some legal question answered. People invariably do that.

I was conversing with a local teacher about UFOs and alien life, not an uncommon topic in recent years.

Collins interjected. "Well, this is always an interesting conversation topic."

We looked at him, smiled, said hi, and introduced ourselves. I said something like, "This is Larry, and Larry, I can't remember your last name."

Larry laughed. "No one does. It's Findley."

Collins said, "Well, good to meet you. UFOs are always fun to speculate on. No one really knows what the heck is going on there."

Larry responded. "Well, if you don't know, we are in deep shit."

We all laughed.

I asked, "I follow this stuff too. Are there any new things that have popped up?"

Collins said, "Nothing that I can say and not have to go shoot you afterward."

Again, being polite, we all laughed. At this point, I maybe blabbed when I shouldn't have.

"I was going to tell Larry that the newest thing I heard is what's been uncovered about Skylab. It had some encounter with a black satellite. It punched a hole in one of its solar panels."

Collins was a bit taken aback. He had been briefed on this years ago and understood it was a very classified, hidden incident. How did this guy know about it?

"So, where did you come across this news?"

I looked at him and realized that this was information that I perhaps should not be passing on to complete strangers.

"Well, it's something I picked up on Reddit or somewhere."

Collins, of course, thought that unlikely. "But seriously, was it really the internet or someone you know who passed it on?"

I looked at him sideways. "So, you don't work for the government, do you?"

Again, we all laughed.

"Just curious."

Later on in the evening, after the usual talking, drinking, laughs and all Collins was walking out and, serendipitously, I was too. It led to a somewhat more involved conversation.

Me - "So what the heck do you think it was?"

Collins - "Like you said, it had to be an extraterrestrial satellite that monitors the planet."

Me - "How would anyone know?'

Collins – "How does anyone know anything? I just do. Just like you know what you know."

Collins decided to up the stakes. "So, you seem to have some inside knowledge. You know of persons who had some interaction with nonhuman intelligence, by chance?"

I just stared at the ground at that point, trying to decide what to say. "Well, I'm a lawyer, There's a lot I know that I don't want to talk about. Pretty much like anyone. I am convinced of a number of things. Some things I'm convinced of, and I don't even know why I'm convinced. But I do believe this. There's a great number of things hidden from the public. And the people doing the hiding are finding it more and more difficult to continue the hiding. And they are worried about what the impact of their failure to do so will have on our society."

Collins shot back, "Like what?"

Me - "Don't laugh, but I think extraordinary people live among us. Whether they are aliens, super-humans, extraterrestrial humans, or whatever, I believe they're here, have always been, and we all may be in for a rather shocking realization at some point. By the way, what exactly do you do in the Air Force?"

"Well, they wouldn't let me fly, so I do intelligence."

"Oh, really? You know, part of this story that I heard was that there was some sort of beam that was emitted, and that it blanketed all over Missouri, or at least the northwest part."

"Yeah. Some of what you talked about rings a bell. You know, that part you said about a special kind of human living among us, have you run into any?"

At that point, we both noticed a quiet man who seemed to be moving a bit closer to hear us.

"Look Major. I think we should call it quits for now. But, are you aware of these interesting people that I mentioned?"

He looked at me with a big grin. "Can't rightly say."

Chapter 13: My Client Spills the Beans

After socializing at my friend's house where I had the conversation with the Air Force major, I became even more unsettled over things. The whole episode with Monkey Mountain was intensely disturbing, and I was trying to deal with it, figuratively of course, by what I always did - putting a big curtain around all of it and what it could mean. I tried to simply not think about it. Denial ain't just a river in Egypt. It wasn't working.

I believe it was two days later. It did not start off well. It was one of those days when everyone seemed to be in a foul mood at the same time. Commuting to work, it quickly became obvious this was the case. Everyone was having a bad day. I wish we were given a heads-up when these days occur, so we all can just sleep in. At any rate, between every driver honking and traffic continuously stopping and starting, I was thankful to make it to my office in one piece.

Sitting at my desk I took a few moments to do absolutely nothing. Still, I knew I was stressing out from recent events. I decided to call up Ray Langstaff, my engineer friend. He picked up right away. I told him interesting things have been happening, and that I've met a couple of unusual people. I added that I can't help but think they're perhaps telepathic. He insisted on coming over, and so we got together at my office right after lunch.

Turns out, Ray conveniently forgot to tell me some things about his background when I was representing him. It's somewhat extraordinary. I knew he was an engineer, but it turns out his *curriculum vitae* is a bit more substantial. It should have been disclosed during the divorce proceedings, but that river has been crossed. In his defense, he stated that a security protocol Sandia and Honeywell follow, and the DOE audits, is to restrict disclosure of just where all their physicists are located. If it is disclosed publicly, or in professional literature, that information could be used to uncover locations of special access or other restricted research and development activities.

When he showed up, I went out to the lobby to meet him and we both went back to my office. I'm sure I didn't look great. I had a headache, probably from high blood pressure. He picked up on it.

"Essie, I want to share some things but . . . man, you don't look all that great right now, even for a lawyer!"

"Ha, very funny! Yeah, I had a bad night, what can I say?"

"Essie, there are a few things I never got around to telling you and I suppose I better now. I do unusual research for the government, I mean really unusual research. More than I let on before. I know I told you I'm an engineer. I am, but that was my undergraduate degree. Several years later, I somehow got into graduate school at Stanford, and, eventually, I obtained a doctorate in physics. The government got interested in some of the work I did. I subsequently did my postdoc and was awarded fellowships at both the national laboratories in New Mexico, Sandia, and Los Alamos. Essie, my work is, well, straight out of science fiction. They had me put together a special access program which tracks down certain phenomena. Phenomena that by measuring it, I became convinced we just might have sufficient insight to duplicate it to some extent. After some success, the Department of Energy had Honeywell move most of us up here because, as it turns out, there's been a longstanding program the DOE runs here, with occasional assistance from the old Western Electric complex in Lee's Summit. Most people don't know, but it was connected to Sandia National Laboratories. Apparently, Harry Truman had something to do with these programs being based here. While working here, we've uncovered a bit more than we were expecting."

Ray stopped. He closed his eyes for a second, apparently contemplating just how much to reveal to me, and then he said, "You have to keep this confidential. Okay?"

"No problem. My lips are sealed." There was no way I didn't want to hear what he was about to say.

Ray continued. "I was briefed on a group of people who have resided here in the past. They've attracted some interest from our intelligence services. There is some confusion as to what degree different elements of the government are aware of them."

I picked up on it immediately. "Ray, I ran into this Air Force guy the other night who seemed to already know that, and he knew about the satellite thing. And, well, I've had some unusual experiences."

I told him everything. It was a huge relief, a surprisingly emotional decompression. I related the whole Monkey Mountain experience. I told him about that after-work get-together at the house with Aggie and Zoe Eliades, and I described the crazy exchange I had with Zoe in the grocery store.

Ray said something very surprising.

"Records I've seen show that, in the past, our Defense Support Program satellites have picked up some unusual activity over this area. What you've seen may be the anomalous objects those satellites picked up. Just like at Skinwalker Ranch. The D.I.A.'s interest in that location was only partly because of some book one of their scientists read during his downtime. DSP and I think SBIRS satellites detected anomalies there, just like in this area."

"Maybe I'm not insane. That's always good to know. Ray, I think it would be fair to say Zoe is remarkably attractive. In conversations with her, I sure am led to believe she's telepathic. Her brother seemed to go out of his way to talk to me. Things are weird."

"This has to be the family I was briefed on. But, I don't believe she has a brother. Do you know her brother's name?"

"Well, it's Aggie. I think his full name is Aegeus."

"Essie, if I remember correctly, I think that's her dad."

"What?"

"What can I say?"

"They look the same age."

"That was commented on in the briefing."

We both just paused for a while thinking about what this might mean.

"Okay, look, maybe I shouldn't be telling you this, or maybe I should. I think I already crossed the Rubicon on this anyway. You may be dealing with trans-humans, or whatever. We don't think they are aliens. They could be. Who knows? Still, they just seem too human. At the very least, they've been in this area since Harry Truman was president. Hell, the records we've retrieved from Western Electric and Bendix indicate some of them had meetings with him. All the files I've seen, at least, indicate they are not threatening and have committed no crimes. Regardless, the general public, absolutely and completely, no matter what detail, simply can't be informed about any of this though. Right?"

"Okay"

"I should mention this - the senior DOE and CIA people who've been handed down all this information have speculated that there appears to be some formal or informal understanding between different visitors to our world. There appears to be a solid desire to leave us alone. The Air Force and the few agencies that are in on this, over the decades, have picked up some knowledge about different species visiting us. Our smartest people who have been brought in, exo-anthro-pologists, sociologists, and political scientists, hell, we've even got consultations from science fiction writers, all concur on this, independently no less. With so many different cultures, species, and whatever else there is out there, logically, Earth should have been overrun or colonized hundreds, thousands of years ago.

Well, it hasn't been. The only plausible reason why it hasn't been is that our planet is off-limits. Protected by an agreement or understanding among all the extraordinary extraterrestrial visitors, the craft of which we detect every month or so. They enter our atmosphere all over the place, at phenomenal speed, with no interaction with our atmosphere. No sonic boom, radical course changes. I think you know what that implies"

Ray stopped, took a breath, and continued. "As the guy on TV says, 'Wait, there's more.' This I can vouch for. Some of the craft we detect seem to be, at some locations, on regular schedules. That makes it easier to set up instruments to detect their emissions. Hell, their teenagers probably come here for their senior trip, while ours visit Florence."

I interjected. "So, what you're saying is there is superluminal travel, there are extraterrestrial civilizations, they visit us. Some maybe live here with us?"

"Well, yup."

I have to admit, there's something incongruous, and absolutely hilarious, about a nuclear weapon scientist, who had fellowships at Sandia and Los Alamos National Laboratories, a Ph.D. from Stanford, and an engineering degree from Princeton, saying "Well, yup."

CHAPTER 14: I NEED SOME METAPHYSICS

"The first thing I do every morning is pick up the paper and turn to the obituary page. If I'm not in it then I get ready for work." This phrase, or something like it, has been attributed to Benjamin Franklin, George Burns, and various other illustrious characters. I don't do that. It's the 21st century. I look at my Google Calendar. In fact, I look at the current day's schedule and also several weeks ahead each morning. I check for events like hospital admissions, date of death, funeral, and so on. So, my thinking is this would be a sensible, less traumatic way for the Angel of Death to inform me of my demise, that I've croaked, and I'm on my way to the Great Beyond. I hope it won't be a text message – too tacky. Also, it would be confusing if the entry type was a Reminder, instead of an Event. Humorous, yes, but also somewhat empowering. Like, God is worried I might forget to die.

No such entries today. I'll go take a shower. After my conversation with Ray Langstaff, I need to.

While in the shower, I contemplate my life. Things get better. Then, they get worse. That's just the way life is. Our civilization functions through the exchange of money, and most people experience its ebb and flow. Our sense of happiness follows right along with our bank account.

Last year things were not great for me. Besides all the other trauma, I was broke. I'm certainly better off now. It seems like it is always feast or famine. Perhaps it is foolish for someone who still has his or her health to have these ups and downs. Maybe, but this is what bothers me. It's metaphysics. That is, the absence thereof. What I mean is that I could really use some transcendental experiences, religious miracles, or mystical occurrences in my life. After everything that happened, life seems rather futile, dull, and sterile without that. Of course, our everyday consciousness itself is an amazing thing. I suppose experiencing that all day and night my entire life has me taking it for granted. I need to do better.

I think, though, that there's at least one thing which transcends our everyday reality, that's a transformative experience. I suppose most people would agree that when you meet and bond with someone it, in a sense, transforms you. You feel like a different person. Your self-identity changes. You simply cannot think of yourself without also thinking of that person. The person you love, and you, are in some crazy way the same. It's also synergistic. Something becomes greater than the sum of its parts. When this happens, and it is a too rare event, life becomes very surprising and unexpected, and you treasure every second of it. Life is worth living when this occurs. It towers over all other experiences. Tolstoy said it makes the world anew. I'll settle for that.

This woman I've run into has somehow changed my reality. After my wife and daughter died, I was cynical about life, I was suicidal, and I grew exhausted with my law practice. I compartmentalized everything. Really, I couldn't do otherwise. Years ago, I wasn't like that. After meeting this woman, maybe, I hope, there can be a new beginning. I know nothing about her, but it sure seems like maybe I did at some time. Things are, well, I suppose the word is spooky and, yes, meta-physical. Is she connected to the weirdness I went through at Monkey Mountain? Does she have some type of supernatural ability? Am I being manipulated? Do I even care? I've seen many bad dealings between people in past years. The results are predictably ugly. If there is bad faith or ill intent involved here, I will at some point uncover it. Still, to be perfectly honest with myself, when it comes to her, I don't care!

However, I still need to find some answers, some resolution to what has been swirling around. I know where I could at least go look for some.

Chapter 15: A Field Trip to the Local Museum

Most towns, even very small towns, have a historical society, which invariably operates a museum of some sort. Lee's Summit, because it has grown so much over the last few decades, has a good-sized one, with a large group of people, mostly retired, who operate it. Many of them have lived in the town all their lives. I've visited it before. In fact, I've visited several of these museums in the small towns surrounding Kansas City. They are fascinating. They are depositories of lost history, filled with artifacts from a different time. There are fossils, relics from Native Americans, fur traders, and pioneer families, contraband from town residents coming home from wars, and just a huge number of idiosyncratic items. I had a specific task in mind. I was interested in old telephone books, school yearbooks, and the local newspaper from back then. I don't think any of the information contained in these can be found on the Internet. I've tried the Internet already. Lawyers have certain databases to check out people with. I pulled up *Lexis-Nexis*, which is supposed to have almost every news article ever printed, and did a search. It came up with nothing. I pulled up a Missouri court database, which has records on most legal actions in Missouri, and nothing. So, I decided to do this the old-fashioned way.

These museums have irregular hours, so I made sure it was actually open before I drove to its downtown Lee's Summit location. After parking in front, I strolled in. There was a large open room with maybe twenty, twenty-five exhibits, most in glass showcases. There were a few side rooms, one of which was apparently the office. A woman standing behind a counter there was watching me. It was apparent I was the only visitor. I walked over and introduced myself.

I told her what I was looking for, and she directed me to one of the other rooms. She stated that the local library probably has the town newspaper on microfiche, but there are bound originals in the next room. She was pretty adamant about having me fill out the visitor log.

Walking back there, I passed an exhibit on the town's fire department. Some old equipment was on display. I saw an oxygen mask, helmet, ax, and several photos of some of the town's big fires. There were some very major fires. Somehow, people picked up the pieces and carried on.

I noticed the next display over. It was about Jesse James, his local relatives here, and the James-Younger gang. This, of all things, brought back certain childhood memories. Consequently, lightning struck! Metaphorically, of course. I remembered her. I recalled this extraordinarily kind, beautiful girl - Zoe Eliades. We were young, children, but still, I don't understand how I could have ever forgotten her. An unexpected wave of happiness and sadness passed through me.

When I was a kid, people made fun of my name. My nickname. No one called me Esmond. I was called Essie. Some kids thought that was a girl's name, and started calling me a girl. Except there was a girl, a very cute girl, named Zoe, who told them they really shouldn't do that. She said my name was just like Jesse James. Except no "J." She told them that no one ever called Jesse James a girl, not ever, because bad things would happen to them. All of them shut up. How could I have forgotten that? We became best friends. We were inseparable. It was pretty dusty in that part of the place, and I felt some tears. I wiped them away.

I spent about an hour in the back room, rummaging around. It was dusty, and my eyes grew itchy. But I figured out a way to narrow down what to look for. The phone books. In the 1956 book I saw a listing for the Elades family. That spelling was close enough. However, the address was a rural route. My understanding is that could include dozens of houses on a mailman's daily delivery route. Anyway, I took finding that as a good omen and turned my attention to the bound newspaper archives. I started with 1956, then 1955. Nothing caught my eye. Turning to the 1954 newspapers, I came across an interesting article.

GREEK FAMILY WELCOMED TO TOWN

Aegeus and Helena Elades, sponsored by the U.S. State Department, have relocated here, having escaped Communist aggression in northern Greece. They will be residing with the Hurley family until they find their own house. Mr. Elades, formerly a professor at the University of Athens, has secured employment with Bendix.

That's all it said. There was a photo. The man looked like he could be Aegeus Eliades. The woman? Even in this fuzzy black and white newspaper page, she just radiated strength and beauty. Was she a Greek goddess? Well, there are none, right? Still, she could pass for one at a costume party.

Bendix was the corporation that operated the Kansas City Atomic Energy Commission facility before Honeywell took it over. It was thereafter renamed the Kansas City National Security Campus, which is the place Ray works. That's interesting.

CHAPTER 16: THE ICE SKATING RINK

I decided to take a quick break, to figure out what to do about all this. I guess I needed a time-out. One of the suburban towns surrounding Kansas City has a very nice, upscale shopping area that, all winter long, puts in an ice skating rink. It brings in all the holiday and post-holiday shopping. It's not too far away from my place, if I take the interstate. I like it because it's cheerful and uplifting. There are always tons of people there, both during the day and during the evening.

I got it in my mind to go there, for the above reasons, and to think things through. It's always good to go to a place and wander around in the middle of a bunch of happy folks.

So I hopped in my car and drove over there. The place was stuffed with winter holiday decorations, red and green and blue. All the lamp posts were covered in fake icicles. Even the sidewalk trashcans were covered in gift wrapping and ribbons. Outdoor speakers played all those holiday songs that are so awesome for the first two weeks, before they begin to slowly drive you nuts. There are these poles with open flames coming out of their tops, more for the atmosphere than to create any warmth. It's an upper, upper-middle class shopping experience. I was thankful to be wearing a suit and tie, so I didn't appear too out of place.

There's a central open area, which is where the ice rink is. I suppose this is why I enjoy going there – entire families skating together. They are all so perfect.

Beautiful clothing, perfect children. They're all holding hands together as they skate in a circle around the rink. I mean, isn't this the thing we're all going for? I was perfectly happy watching all this. When I get married, I'm moving here, so we can be perfect like them.

I listened to a sermon one time by a Methodist minister who said that all those neighborhood families you think are perfect, that nothing but awesome things happen to them? Well, he said that, as the minister for this very large church, he was in a position to know, and he said, "They don't exist. These perfect families just don't exist. Believe me, I absolutely know."

I believed him at the time. He was a full-time minister for twenty years or so, at various medium and very large churches. He did the weddings, the funerals, the counseling, the heartbreaks. He would know.

That's what I thought. Until I started going to this place. Everyone in these families has perfect teeth. They don't even go to the dentist. Their children don't get arrested and never go to juvenile court. They never develop substance abuse problems. They don't shoplift. They don't vandalize. The girls don't get pregnant out of wedlock. They don't get kicked out of school. They're always in the National Honor Society. They go to law school, they go to medical school. The moms don't work, unless they want to. They never argue. There's no domestic violence. The fathers make tons, tons of money. Their houses are bigger than European castles. That minister was never a minister at a church in this part of town. No, I then concluded that he was just plain wrong. There are perfect families. They just hide from everyone else. And they go to this ice skating rink during the winter. When I get married, we're going to move here and be a perfect family. And socialize with all the other perfect families.

Out of the corner of my eye, I noticed a group of children waiting in a line. I walked a bit around the rink, and I see it's a line to talk to Santa. Apparently, they have Santa all winter. He's sitting on a throne, surrounded by elves and cameras. I observed a ten or eleven-year-old girl there, standing in line, a girl who probably will not wait in line next year to see Santa again because she will be too grown up then. She reminded me of someone. I was a good distance away, but she turned around and looked in my direction, like she was looking for her mom. Or her dad. And God help me, she looked just like my daughter.

I turned around and walked off. I remembered. I was married before. I had a perfect family before. And that minister was damn right. Bad things, horrible things, happen to perfect families.

———◆○◆———

It was time to go. I squeezed by a large man standing behind me and walked down the street. I turned around and spotted him looking my way. It occurred to me that I'd noticed him before earlier in the day. He was also watching me then. He wore a camel hair overcoat, which is why I remembered him. He turned away and walked in the opposite direction. I thereupon realized I was being tailed, followed. Why? I walked a block down the street. In his book, *Journey to Ixtlan*, Carlos Castaneda wrote about a time he was told by Don Juan, a Yaqui shaman, that, if one quickly looks over his left shoulder, sometimes he would see his death waiting for him, biding its time. So, while still walking, I quickly glanced over my left shoulder. I saw death walking behind me, and he wore a camel hair overcoat.

Chapter 17: I Find Out Everything

Taking every back road I could think of, I made it back home. I drove past it a dozen times, looking for strange vehicles. Nothing seemed suspicious. Still, I took the precaution of taking the house number down from the front. Kind of a silly thing to do, I admit.

Things were getting out of hand, I realized. I think our sanity, our sense of what's real, actually depends on what the consensus is among the people you share that with. Yet, when strange, crazy things occur, sometimes their nature is so bizarre you just can't share them with the people you share your reality with, because they would look at you with suspicion. Then, things get really weird. So, that's where I believed I was.

I decided to call up Bill Hurley and ask for the phone number for the Eliades house. He found it. He mentioned that Aggie Eliades called him on the day of that fundraiser and asked if he was going. Eliades then said that Bill should get me to come along too. I suppose it's good to feel wanted.

The next day I got up early. I couldn't sleep. I thought about calling them. I can't help but think they wanted me to contact them anyway. Why do this? I still found the whole alien thing a little too outlandish, and it was hard to believe these people are trans-human, or extraterrestrial, or whatever the best term may be. I knew Zoe in grade school! Anyway, it was still way too early to call. But I was in hyper-mode and I needed to do something to help resolve all this. I looked outside, hoping there wasn't some strange car parked out there, with people inside spying on me. Seeing nothing, I hopped in my car and drove over to their neighborhood.

It was a hilly section of town, and the dips were shaded by large old trees, which I'm sure are remnants of the original old-growth forest. There was a morning fog at the bottom of the hills, a sure sign that it was way too early to be up and about. Some of the trees were huge. I recalled the formula for estimating tree ages – for most types determine the diameter of the trunk in inches and multiply that by 4, 5, or 6, depending on the species. So I was looking at trees three, four hundred years old. Wow.

Driving by the front entrance, I noted two columns made of rocks cemented together, with a metal gate hung between them. Really, pretty unremarkable for the area. I passed it by and drove some more down the road. It started to go up again, and I saw a paved side road on the left. I turned into that and drove some more. I came up to a trailhead with a small parking area and pulled into it.

I love to go hiking. It is a grounding thing. Here was a trail that I hadn't been on before, and it was the perfect thing to do this morning. So, I stepped out of my vehicle, locked the doors, and started down the trail. Crisp sun beams were cutting through the last of the fog, silhouetting the bare tree branches. They reached out from both sides of the trail, merging and creating a beautiful tunnel of sorts, fracturing the morning light. I heard song birds, an odd thing for this time of year. I turned a corner and was surprised to see one of the beams made its way through the forest roof to illuminate a woman, like a spotlight from above. She was bent over, in a jogging suit, looking to have just finished up a run. She raised her head, saw me, and stood up. It was her, Zoe.

"Serendipity is strong in you," she said.

Apparently, she's right. "Yeah, that's my middle name now."

She actually laughed at that. I noticed her hair, bound in a ponytail, long, black, shiny, reflecting the sunlight. She smiled, and her smile was just glorious. It melted my heart. What struck me, gazing at her in the sunlight, was that she seemed completely, one hundred percent genuine. No guile, no hidden personality. She wore no makeup, no manicured, painted, glittered nails. Her eyes, I saw them again, there was definitely a silver sparkle there. I couldn't help but doubt what Major Collins suggested. Alien? Ha!

And then, it happened again.

She tilted her head, and with a mischievous look said, "How many aliens do you know who go jogging on trails at seven in the morning?"

She began running again, but turned around, and running backward, yelled, "Come by the house around noon time, if you want. Some friends are coming over."

—◆O◆—

Close to noon, and I'm pulling into the driveway. The gate was open, and it was a hundred yards or so of driveway until circle parking in front of the house. There were lots of oak trees, and fir trees that looked planted on the land fronting the road. There were enough fir trees so even in winter none of the yard or the house are visible. I have to admit, it's a beautiful residence. I didn't notice the English Manor architecture when I dropped by for that reception, fundraiser, or whatever it was. It was too dark by then. So many suburban houses in America now are more or less interchangeable. I think the word is McMansion. This place obviously was built long before the suburbs moved in. Privacy is certainly a strong attribute of the current landscaping. If there wasn't a gate with stone pillars, no one would even notice the driveway. But then, there are lots of houses like this hidden away all over the country. No one wants to advertise their wealth to the general public.

The cars parked around the circle drive were impressive. Several Teslas, a Land Rover Defender, and a Mercedes. There were a couple of older Buicks for those who, I assume, did not wish to flaunt their wealth. I parked behind a Jeep, a very nice one with, I'm guessing, tires maybe costing fifteen hundred each. I think to myself, well, that's probably too rough a ride anyway, but I suspect the springs and shocks were upgraded along with everything else on that monster.

Aegeus Eliades greeted me at the door and shook my hand. I'm a tall man, and we are more or less the same height. Weird thing about that. When I meet someone my height, I have some degree of bonding with him or her right off the bat. We've all shared too many small seats and low overheads. When I thought that, it occurred to me he would now say, "I know." I'm glad he didn't. Too much of this mental telepathy lately for me.

Inside, in the great room, there were maybe twenty men and women standing up and conversing and a few sitting down. Some took surreptitious glances at me as I entered.

Have you ever been walking around in public and seen someone strolling by who surprisingly looked familiar? Like someone you may have known in the past? I do, on rare occasions. Of course, they turn out to be total strangers. My thinking is that there are only so many ways people can look, and this phenomenon is merely because of that.

Anyway, a few folks there looked familiar. Not familiar enough to approach and slap on the back. Still, their characteristics sure seemed to ring a bell.

I turned around and spotted Zoe walking into the room from the kitchen area. I felt my face blushing because, well, she is very fascinating, and alluring. There seemed to be little doubt that, when she and I look at each other, she knows pretty much what I'm thinking. What is going on with that?

"Well, you showed up. I'm glad. Want a drink?"

"I never drink before the sun goes down."

"You know, I mean coke or tea or just water. We have the very best water."

"You do? I'm very picky about water."

"I'll get you some water."

She turned around and strolled back to the kitchen, stopped by the sink, held a glass under the faucet and filled it up with tap water. Walking back and handing it to me, she was the picture of innocence.

I laughed. "Gee, Thanks."

"Only the best."

I really, really like her.

We sat down in a corner and began talking. Whereupon, time slowed down for us. We became oblivious to everything else. We talked, we joked, and we laughed for the longest time. It felt like many hours. We were in our own world, and it was as if all the many years we were apart melted away.

At some point then and there I became convinced that Zoe Eliades is one of those people. What do I mean by that? There's this notion, this belief, I have. I want it to be true. It could be true. It's that there are certain people who are so overflowing with life, so vibrant and exuberant, and the force of their personality so strong, it seems impossible that at some time in the future they will grow old, pass on, and no longer exist. Meeting them, knowing them, one is forced to question the finality of death. Looking into her green eyes, I saw a spirit that was just eternal, that could not be bound by time or death.

She smiled back at me, and that smile, and the warmth, and the love, that it reflected electrified me. I almost wanted to cry. That would have been difficult to explain.

She looked at me in silence. I gazed at her, her hair, her eyes, her lips. I thought back to when I saw her at the grocery store. I thought then she was the most beautiful woman in the world. I was right.

We continued our conversation. She brought up what I do for a living. That led to this amusing exchange:

"Essie, I can trust you, right? There are things I'd really like you to know. As long as you're a lawyer, whatever I or Aggie might discuss with you would be protected by this attorney-client privilege, right? I suppose there are some legal issues involved. Okay?"

"So, Aggie's your brother?"

She scratched the side of her head and smiled. "Well, that's something that we should discuss."

Switching to my lawyer mode, I stated, "Look, for this to be a legally protected conversation, there has to be an actual attorney-client relationship established. What do you want to retain me for?"

"Okay, well then. Let me think. How about this? It may be that some people here are illegal aliens. Would that work?"

Seriously? I started to laugh. I held it in.

Looking at me in a way that was both mischievous and innocent, she continued. "What can I say? Now I have to pay you some money too, I think, right? So, here's a dollar. Don't spend it all in one place."

She shrugged her shoulders and looked at me with a straight face. Though, it did seem like she strained to keep it. Her brother, or dad, who knows, was just a few feet away and probably heard some of this. I suspect he thought it might be impolite to be overhearing the conversation, because he got up, turned around, mumbled something to himself, and started walking away.

I found all of this hilarious, but I still kept it together.

"Well, then, I suppose I can keep a secret."

"Okay Essie, I'll take you at your word. Hold onto your balls then, because I've really got something to show you."

We stood up, and I noticed Aggie making eye contact with Zoe as I followed her. Oddly, he was holding a bag of popcorn.

We walked outside, through the front door, and headed towards one of the barns, a hundred yards or so away.

Zoe reached for and held my hand, gripping it tightly.

I looked at her, grinning. "Are you expecting me to run away?"

She had that sly but innocent look on her face again. Responding, she said, "You might. But, I don't think you'll want to."

So she certainly engaged my curiosity. We reached the front of the barn. The barn door had, of all things, an eye scanner. She looked into the lens and it popped open. We walked in. The barn was very large. The interior space was impressive, and mostly empty. There were some boxes stored at the far end. There was a car parked against one side.

"Look, I know you have talked to Raymond. Aggie wants to talk to him. And, he's my dad. No one would believe that, looking at him. Raymond's a very smart man. That's created a dilemma."

"Really, because of what he's told me?"

She stopped and turned around to face me. "No. I'm not quite sure what he told you. I suspect he might have said my family and my friends are not from around here. If so, well, he's right, and also wrong."

She paused. For a minute or so, we just stared at each other. I thought to myself how remarkably beautiful she was. She smiled.

"You remember when we were kids? That seems so long ago. We had so much fun together. Some of those men you just saw in the front room, Essie, they were engineers at Western Electric and Bendix. So was my dad."

Well, that hit me. Holy shit. Western Electric, the enormous manufacturing and engineering company that was part of the old A.T.&T. conglomerate. It built and operated the giant plant in Lee's Summit, which employed thousands of people. In the sixties, seventies, and eighties it manufactured gyroscopes, telephones, electron tubes, and all manner of telecommunication equipment for A.T.&T. A federal judge split up the entire Bell system monopoly in the 1980s. The whole Lee's Summit operation then shut down. Parts of the complex, including the clean rooms, were occasionally leased to various small companies. As it turned out, back then Western Electric also operated Sandia National Laboratories in New Mexico, and along with Sandia it also did work for the old Atomic Energy Commission.

Boy Scouts has always been hit or miss. Still, it was different back then, before online video games, three hundred cable television channels, the internet, Facebook, TikTok, and everything else we have now. In some towns and neighborhoods, it was a bigger thing. In other places, not so much. What I remember was that my old scout troop was a good one, and it was run by men who worked as engineers at the Bendix Atomic Energy Commission complex and also at Western Electric. I've long lost track of them.

Those faces I thought I recognized in the house. They were those men. From my scout troop. Except, they were not as old as they should have been, just like Zoe's dad. In fact, they didn't seem to have aged at all. They should have been much older.

She saw it on my face. She knew what I just realized. It worried her, and she held my hand again. "They occasionally get involved in certain projects which require them to travel a great distance. We, um, have a different concept of time."

"But, then, it's all true," I stuttered.

She smiled at me. "Whatever you're thinking is probably close to it. Anyway, I wanted you to see this." She pointed towards the far wall. Before, where there was just a vacant area, there was ... a vacant area.

"What? I don't see anything."

Zoe looked around, then, strangely, turned her head and looked straight up. Shrugging her shoulders, she said, "Well, crap. I was going to show you something. Oh well, let's go back to the house."

I began to wonder about this. Maybe I was being taken for a ride. We turned and went back to the door. I opened it for her, and we walked back outside and headed for the house. I realized that it was rather overcast. Before, it was bright and sunny.

I looked up. That's when I saw it, a couple of hundred feet above us. An immense, football field-sized, seamless, rivet-less, perfectly symmetrical pitch-black egg. It was floating in the air. It was completely silent. There was no buzz, no hum, no sound from it at all. It was shocking, astonishing. I looked at Zoe.

"Hi Essie."

I looked up again. It just talked to me!

Zoe, smiling, nodded her head towards it.

"There she is. Sorry about that. Eleni has a mind of her own. Really, she does. We've known each other since I was sixteen."

The craft is a she? Named Eleni? This was crazy.

As if all this was not crazy enough, this extraordinary craft's surface began morphing into a stunning, luminescent silver metal, and while doing so it began to rotate. Its shape gradually flattened, and it transformed into a disk, with strange symbols manifesting along its circumference. It was hard for my mind to accept this amazing object right above us. But, there it was. Right there.

"Essie, I know this must seem crazy to you, but there are craft of all sorts around the globe. Several are somewhere in the Indian Ocean, miles deep. Some come by here every week or so. There are studies, and various undertakings, that involve a number of us. This is our home, Essie, but we don't spend all our time on our planet."

I was going pale, and my arms of their own volition were stretching around for a pole or wall to lean against. Ontological shock is a real thing.

She looked at me with some concern.

"Essie, now, don't freak out! Just take deep breaths. Why don't we head back to the house? I just wanted you to meet Eleni, so you know we're not insane, or you. It wasn't my intent to cause a nervous breakdown."

Chapter 18: I Make a Decision

So we walked back, in the shade. As we approached the front door, Aggie, Aegeus Eliades, stood there, waiting for us. He looked at Zoe. She nodded at him, then at me, and walked past him, entering the house.

Aggie Eliades is a fearsome, formidable man. His eyes drilled into me. It seemed he was considering whether to let me keep on living. He stared at me for a few seconds, then his expression appeared to lighten.

"Let's go for a walk," he said.

We strolled towards a path leading to the surrounding woods. Looking over at me, he said, "Our world here is an almost infinite place in itself, filled with countless mysteries people have never known, or heard of. Then, there are other mysteries, arising from outside our planet. People hypothesize about extraterrestrial life, whether it exists, whether it has ever visited our world. Either there is extraterrestrial life, or there isn't, right? For all intents and purposes, the universe is so limitless, with so many different planets, moons, and stars, that it would be extraordinarily unlikely that intelligent, extraterrestrial life did not exist. So, given that there is intelligent, extraterrestrial life, again, it would seem that, given the age of the universe, and the age of the Earth, it would border on the impossible that Earth has not been visited."

We walked along the treeline. I looked up and saw that extraordinary craft miles high in the sky. It was flying around in circles. After strolling another minute or so, Aggie talked some more. It seemed as if he was reminiscing.

"Seven thousand years ago, the world was a much different place. There existed many different peoples, of varied ethnicities and lineages. Where the Black Sea is now, an adventurous, curious people developed a distinct culture. Some of us trace our ancestry to them. Those ancestors encountered an extraterrestrial exploratory group that found itself in some degree of distress. Our ancestors possessed several unique qualities, one of which was an ability to sense their presence when they thought they were hidden. They are humanoid. It is a remarkable thing. Convergent evolution is widespread, given similar planets. That encounter was fortuitous for both our groups. We assisted them. Without hesitation. We were extraordinarily comfortable with each other, even though we evolved on different planets. Several of our ancestors agreed to visit their home planet. Afterward, when they returned, they discovered the Black Sea had inundated our homeland, and our families that stayed behind were scattered. Our extraterrestrial friends, whom we call the Filoi, were stricken with guilt. Ever since, they have always assisted us. A certain number of us reside on their home planet. We travel the galaxy with them. They have promised to us that whenever we travel with them, Earth, and our homes, will be here when we return."

He stopped and looked at me. "Do you believe this?"

I looked at him, and turned my head to the sky to look at that remarkable craft. I thought about Zoe.

"Yes, I do. How can I not?"

We strolled some more.

"Certain things changed in 1945. With the Trinity explosion, and subsequently with Hiroshima and Nagasaki. The Soviets detonated an enormous thermo-nuclear device, shocking the world. It became obvious to the Filoi, and us, that we had to keep a closer watch on our world. Our extraterrestrial friends demanded it. In 1952 Harry Truman met an individual, not from his neighborhood, as he said it, in Key West. He didn't initially know what to think when she introduced herself to him and said there was a concern over the growing and long-term human ability to exterminate itself. He didn't take it seriously because, well, it was Key West, and he was on vacation. Key West even back then had that reputation. She said her people would put on a demonstration in Washington later after he got back if there was some doubt. Harry said sure, knock yourselves out."

Aggie stopped for a moment, looked around, and we continued walking. "In late July of that year, Harry and everyone else watched as a rather amazing flying saucer air show on successive weekends confounded the Air Force and everyone else over the city. On successive weekends that month there were remarkable demonstrations of unbelievable craft performing impossible things. As General John Samford famously said in a press conference then, 'Reports ... have been made by credible observers of relatively incredible things.' That was an understatement. After that, we re-engaged and got along extremely well. We wanted a very low profile, so we asked for an understanding that we would have a continuous presence in an innocuous location. Truman suggested a small town he was familiar with. It worked out well because no one looks for aliens in Lee's Summit. At least back then. It seems the details of this arrangement just weren't passed on completely from Administration to Administration. The incoming Republican administration thought that the exiting Democratic officials were trying to make fools of them. The paper records are there, but the whole matter just seemed preposterous on its face."

We started strolling back to the house. "Many of us have families. Families with children to raise. It's better for our children to grow up here. At least in their early years. Again, Lee's Summit was ideal. It seems our children are more than happy to grow up here and explore the Universe when they get older. There are regular transits between Earth and other locations, planets, moons, and what can best be described as space stations. So, how do we stand with each other now?"

We were back in front of the house. He was looking at me, expecting me to either accept all this or laugh it off. I wasn't going to laugh.

"Everything you've said, logically, is entirely plausible. I believe you."

He smiled. He looked to the front door. "So, you can leave now. Your car is right over there. Or, you can follow me and we'll walk inside. But, if you walk inside with me, there is no going back."

With that, he turned around and started walking inside. I hesitated for, maybe, one second, and I joined him.

Chapter 19: 1952

March

An older gentleman with a cane, wearing a wide-brimmed golf hat, white pants, and a wild tropical shirt, briskly strolled down Front Street in Key West, taking in the bright light and warm ocean breeze. His thick wire rim glasses somehow gave him a no-nonsense, all-business appearance. He was intent on walking to the nearby beach for his morning swim. There were two other gentlemen following in his wake, several yards away. A small puppy ran down the sidewalk to him, happy to be free of its leash, and excited to meet a new human. The man bent over and let the dog sniff his hand, and then he scratched its neck. The puppy was ecstatic. It made a new friend.

A few seconds later, an attractive woman in a bright blue sundress, with long, black, braided hair, appeared and saw them together.

"Mr. President, I am so sorry. He got away from me."

Harry Truman looked at her, noting her remarkable beauty, and smiled. "Well, I'm glad he has an owner, and a beautiful one at that."

"If only all men thought so. Thank you for the compliment."

"Miss, please tell me your name."

"I am Helena Eliades, and I've just arrived in your wonderful country."

They started strolling down the sidewalk together, the two men following them seeing nothing to alarm them.

"Are you from Greece? Your accent sounds Greek."

"My family is from Greece, and I was raised there. After that we traveled a long distance to other places."

"Oh really, where have you traveled?"

"Mr. President, I know you are a historian, and you know of the ancient Greek history."

"Yes, I've read Homer, and many of the Greek philosophers and historians."

"Well, my family's history predates all of them, as great as they are."

Harry Truman grew more interested, and also somewhat suspicious.

"There are not too many historical documents preceding those, unless you mean the Epic of Gilgamesh and a few others."

"Yes, we are from a time before that. Mr. President, the beginnings of my family and my people are not in any historical documents, though we have been a part of Greek history in all its recorded time."

"Okay, Miss Eliades. I wasn't born yesterday. And as much as I enjoy talking to a beautiful woman like yourself, I ask that you tell me your purpose in being here."

"Mr. President, you are an extraordinarily intelligent man, and the country is blessed to have you as its President. You are no doubt aware of certain anomalous events occurring throughout the country, and the world, involving unusual flying objects, correct?"

"Oh, that's all a bunch of hogwash. People see things in the sky all the time."

"You know better. Most of those objects are not ours, but they are observing this world closely because there is a fear of a global catastrophe."

"How so?"

"The Soviets have several atomic bombs. By next year, they will have the hydrogen bomb. After that, in ten years, those bombs will be placed in missiles that can cross the oceans. All this time, your country and the Soviet Union will grow in distrust and animosity. It is plain to see."

"I appreciate your foresight. But history has a way of moving on in unpredictable ways, with not much any of us can do about it at times."

"Mr. President, my foresight is impeccable."

Harry Truman looked over at her and was unsettled by the silver sparkles in her eyes. A strange feeling came over him, like he was in the presence of someone more than human.

Helena looked at him and smiled. "Mr. President, this world is also our world. We live here too. We do not wish to see it burn up in atomic fire. Which it will, if no one intervenes."

"Alright, Miss Eliades, just who will intervene?"

"That is why we've returned. We will intervene, if need be."

"Okay, just who are you, And just where did you return from?"

———◄O►———

July

". . . The operators called the Airport tower, a quarter of a mile away. The excited response was that the radar there showed the identical pattern. Andrews Field, the Air Force base across the Potomac in Maryland, was queried. The worried reply was that the radars there showed seven blips. With three 'fixes' like that, the operators were able to compute that one of the UFOs was directly over the Capitol, while two hovered over the White House, many thousands of feet in the air, but visible to observers in the tower." *The American Weekly*, November 22, 1953.

Washington, D.C. in July is a hot, muggy place. In 1952, there was no air conditioning. A large part of the city, mostly along the Potomac River, is at sea level. Before it was drained, it was swampland. Some say it's never been completely drained.

It was one of those days that made Sergeant Finnian O'Sullivan ever so grateful that he was a member of the U.S. Park Police Horse Mounted Patrol. He did not have to walk the National Mall. He rode up and down the mall on his horse, along with two other members of the patrol. Because of the heat, they were intent on not working their horses too hard. Also, they saw to it that the horses had plenty of water. That is why, when they reached the north side of their route, along E Street, NW, they stopped at the Butt-Millet Memorial Fountain. All three horses, with their riders still mounted, surrounded it, and the horses greatly enjoyed drinking water from the fountain, with the spray cooling their heads at the same time.

Something odd happened while this was going on. The horses stopped drinking, lifted their heads to the side, and stared at the sky above the mall. The Park Police officers thought this odd, so they also looked up at where the horses were gazing. They saw nothing.

After a few minutes, they resumed their patrol. While riding east on E Street, Sergeant O'Sullivan looked to his left, at the South Lawn of the White House. To his surprise, a woman appeared out of thin air near one side of the lawn, and started walking over to the south portico of the White House. He blinked his eyes a couple of times, and noticed a large area of blurriness just to her left. Then he realized it was just his cataracts. He knew he needed to go schedule that eye doctor appointment. So the Mounted Patrol continued on its route.

Walking on the freshly manicured grass, Helena Eliades thought to herself how ironic it was that most Americans say they would never believe in flying saucers until one landed on the White House lawn.

— ◆ —

"I want to know what the hell they are, and if they keep on flying over us, then I want them shot down!" He slammed the phone down. "Temperature inversion, my ass!"

President Truman looked around the Oval Office, his face beet red. "God-dammit, two weekends in a row. We can't even control our own airspace over the capital, and the whole world is watching."

Bob Lovett, the Secretary of Defense, remarked, "These things have incredible speed and maneuverability. Radar has them at Mach three, and our pilots report seeing them make instantaneous ninety-degree turns at that speed. They acceler-ate and shoot up into the stratosphere and beyond. Our radar doesn't even reach objects that high. The physics are impossible."

"The whole country is in an uproar. Have you seen these headlines?"

Clark Clifford, who happened to be dropping by, said, "Yes. It's unbelievable. Everyone's gone flying saucer stir crazy."

"Are these the same things they found at Roswell? It hardly seems possible."

The intercom beeped. "Mr. President, a Miss Eliades to see you."

"What? That's not on my schedule."

The door opened and in strolled a breathtaking, stunningly attractive woman, wearing a bright blue, double-breasted pencil dress. She had long, wavy, black hair and was wearing a thin golden necklace. The men stood there, dumbfounded. They sensed there was something extraordinary about this woman.

She spoke. "No, they aren't what crashed at Roswell. The objects navigating the airspace above this city are ours. They have never crashed. Here ... or any-where."

Harry Truman stared at her, stunned. "We've met before. I recall you, Miss Eliades. I didn't know what to think talking with you. Everyone in Key West is crazy."

With a serious expression, she responded. "I've driven men insane before, yes, but not in Key West."

The three men standing there heard this and were speechless. They realized she was telling the truth. They were certain of it.

Helena smiled. "Mr. President, are you going to introduce me?"

CHAPTER 20: ALIENS, EVERYWHERE

S o we walked back into the Eliades house. I already felt changed by the talk I had with Aggie. I proceeded to listen to remarkable, extraordinary, conversations. In the great room, there was a meeting in progress. We found some chairs, sat down, and listened. There are times in one's life when a person's understanding of the world shifts. When you discover there is a life outside high school, when you visit a foreign country for the first time, when you join the military, when someone you love dies, when you struggle through a divorce, when, as a child, you experience blatant prejudice and hatred, even when you fall in love with someone. These things are transformative, they change your reality. On that day, something like that happened. We live in a far different universe than we know.

In the distant past, various extraterrestrial intelligences, certainly the ones that have communicated with each other, arrived at an informal consensus that humans, and human civilizations, are rather unique and that overt contact with human society shouldn't occur. Through long experience it is understood that any culture's drive to invent, improve, and overcome will likely dissipate once the existence of more technologically advanced civilizations becomes widely known.

Still, many different expeditions, scientific in nature, have traveled to Earth. A common objective was to study how humans independently invent new technologies in unexpected ways, how they experiment, successfully and unsuccessfully, with all manner of social government and engineering, how they arrive at new and imaginative mathematical theorems, and create unique works of art and literature; many of which have, to varying degrees, not occurred to other intelligent species. These expeditions are all regularly surprised at the unique cases of seemingly obvious discoveries made by humans that were overlooked by their scientists and their artificial intelligence systems.

In one sense, the human race, and human knowledge and experience, are used as a counterbalance to their widespread reliance on A.I. Except, in their languages, they don't commonly use that term. Several use a term similar to Q.I., since their artificial intelligence is based on quantum computing parsing enormous databases, grown over thousands of years. Many extremely advanced technological cultures concluded that their long term reliance on artificial intelligence unavoidably leads to a loss of skills and knowledge in areas as diverse as music, mathematics, literature, engineering, biology, even fundamental physics. The knowledge, experience and data obtained by their observations and study of human culture and science, it is believed, alleviates this to some extent. Humans, through history, have demonstrated extraordinary problem-solving abilities.

After hearing this, I couldn't help but think of something that modern American truthsayer and podcaster Joe Rogan said one time on his popular show. He speculated that aliens visit the Earth and would almost certainly find humans interesting because, after all, who wouldn't want to watch a bunch of crazy apes with thermonuclear weapons?

In retrospect, all this seems obvious. The human race is not in bondage, It is not colonized by an alien empire. There are no extraterrestrial embassies or consulates issuing passports or work visas anywhere. None of this has happened now or in any documented history of the human race. Given the fact that intelligent extraterrestrial life exists, and can travel here, the above is a logical explanation of why this is true.

Physicist Enrico Fermi once asked, "Where are they?" But, that famous question assumes a fact that isn't true. "They" in fact were already here. They have always been here. Even more so, Enrico Fermi and his fellow scientists must have known. When he reportedly asked that question at Los Alamos in 1950, people in New Mexico and the rest of the country were sighting glowing disks, flying saucers, and green comets traveling alone and in formations across the sky at thousands of miles per hour. In 1950, there were front-page newspaper accounts of flying saucer armadas flying over hundreds of witnesses in Farmington, New Mexico. Farmington is located a mere 110 miles northwest of Los Alamos.

The extraterrestrial scientific, educational, and surveillance missions and expeditions that increased after the Trinity fission explosion started decreasing in numbers after 1952, and became more surreptitious, when their unwanted effect became more obvious. No one wanted humans to stop being human.

I looked around for Zoe. I'm sure I had the appearance of someone in shock after hearing all the above. I spotted a pitcher of mint tea. While pouring some into my glass, she came over and whispered, perhaps facetiously, "That could be kykeon. Don't drink too much. You might start seeing things."

I thought, *Yeah, right. Like I'm not seeing things already!*

One woman, apparently a professor, mentioned that several of her students enrolled in various European history postgraduate courses. Apparently, they believed the study of how so many different countries living so closely together, with different languages, religions, and cultures, manage to somehow coexist has much merit. She said they believe the intense competition between the different states led to amazing human progress and see historical similarities to interplanetary relationships. Her students are not from around here. So, I suppose it's really true. Aliens do walk among us.

Aggie Eliades spoke up. Everyone in the room stopped to hear what he had to say. He looked at me.

"Essie, your acquaintance, Raymond Langstaff, and the group he is leading, have conducted some anti-gravity trials. They were successful enough that one of our orbitals detected it. This is one of several reasons we are here today."

This was fascinating, and also confusing. I replied. "Wouldn't this be a good thing?"

"Essie, if only it were. Unfortunately, the way it stands now, such an extraordinary advance, once known, logically creates an irresistible urge for a nuclear power to conduct a first strike, and results in annihilation of all life on the planet, by any number of scenarios. It destroys the logic underlying the Mutual Assured Destruction doctrine, which has forestalled a nuclear exchange the past seventy years. A propulsion system that allows for almost instantaneous delivery of a nuclear warhead, with an adversary having no opportunity to launch a retaliatory strike, gives an overwhelming tactical and strategic advantage to the adversary that strikes first. Furthermore, it gives an adversary absolutely no time to verify if the detection of an attack is actually a false alarm."

"We think he likely figured it out by using magnetic field and particle detectors and monitoring the pulse rhythms of some craft traveling through the atmosphere. To the best of our knowledge, nowhere else on the planet do we currently have this issue. We simply have to forestall the development of this technology given the existence of thousands of thermonuclear warheads and the present state of affairs."

One of the men who looked familiar spoke up. "Essie, life is full of surprises, isn't it? You knew some of us from a long time ago, back when we worked with Western Electric and the old A.E.C. nuclear facility in Kansas City, when it was operated by Bendix. It's good to run into you again."

Stupefied was a good word for my state of mind. I eyed that bronze sword on the back wall again.

Aggie asked me a strange question. "Essie, have you ever encountered, for want of a better term, a Third Man?"

Initially, I was confused by this. "I'm not sure what you mean. Which man?"

"Have you ever felt the presence of someone or something else when you are alone?"

I recalled something I read years ago. "I think you're talking Ernest Shackleton, 1917, that Antarctic expedition. I've read about him. Well, I've had experiences like that. I just don't know if it's a third man."

The Third Man is what Sir Ernest Shackleton called an entity he claimed saved his life in Antarctica in 1917, when he was close to death. I thought it odd, even striking, that he would bring this up, because, for a while, it was a subject of some concern with me. This is why. I had an experience years ago, when I was completely alone, swimming in the middle of a lake. Somehow, I inhaled at the wrong time, and a slug of water got into my lungs. Choking, I went under. Someone grabbed me and pulled me out. But, there was no one around, anywhere, when I reached the shore. It was something of a near-death experience, and like so many other things, I've built a wall around it and hidden it from myself.

Aggie looked at me a bit more intensely. "What do you mean?"

"Well, I don't know, but maybe there's a distinct, an identifiable, subconscious mind that surfaces in extreme circumstances and takes charge. Sometimes."

This was a strange moment. Some of the people there looked at each other and smiled.

I barely overheard someone whisper, "We'll see."

One of the men in back spoke up. "Essie, we went camping quite often in those days. Do you recall a winter survival camp-out, back when you were thirteen or fourteen, when you were wandering around in the middle of the night, and perhaps seeing something unusual?"

This question really surprised me because I did in fact have, well, not a memory, but a dream of something I saw then. The dream was of me getting up sometime during the night during this camp-out. In the middle of a forest here in western Missouri. I recall it being frigid in the extreme, like twenty below. I tried for as long as I could, but I eventually had to slide out of my sleeping bag and go outside into the arctic night air to find some place to relieve myself. While doing so, I spotted a silver glint in the tree tops a little further away. Keeping an eye on my footprints in the snow, still half asleep, I walked towards it, curious about just what it was. From what I seem to remember, it was a brilliant metallic object of some sort, just floating between the trees. There seemed to be no shape to it, but it was very large and silhouetted the bare tree branches. I heard someone call out, "Essie, go back to your tent. You're hallucinating." A different voice said, "or not," followed by laughter. Retracing my footprints in the snow, I went back to my tent. It was a strange dream. Was it actually a memory?

Those guys really enjoyed camping in fairly remote forests. We undertook camping trips at least once a month. We did extreme things. People did that stuff a lot more back then. It doesn't seem that long ago now. We'd go on trips and do things our parents would never have allowed if they knew. I'm sure those guys running the scout troop were more than happy that so many of the parents just did not bother to get involved.

On that same trip, in the morning, I recall watching a dozen people clustered around a wooden box trap. Sometime during the night a possum managed to get itself caught in it. As I remember it, a number of us surrounded the box, armed with frying pans, bats, and shovels, anticipating eating this thing for our next meal. When the box was lifted, there was a sudden and unexpected reversal of roles. The possum, in a furious state, showing its enormous fangs, bolted out and commenced to chase everyone, grown men and teenage boys, through the campsite. People were diving into their tents and climbing up trees. It was a madcap, chaotic scene. At some point, the roles reversed again, and the possum, true to its nature, decided to stop, roll over, and play dead. It was a bad decision. I'm sorry to say it in fact did end up as our lunch. After all, this was a winter survival camp-out. It tasted somewhat like chicken, but perhaps a little too greasy. Maybe it is not so crazy that I possess an indelible memory of the possum, but I dismiss the silver object up in the tree branches as merely a dream.

So I answered his question. "Yeah, now that you mention it, I do. But, really, how unusual was that compared to eating a possum for lunch?"

Some of them, grinning, looked at each other. So, I think this was an informal evaluation of whether I could fit in. I think I passed. I remember most of these guys. We all looked up to them. To me, they were incredible, just by being normal. But, seeing them here and now, they apparently aren't so normal after all. Life is crazy. I turned my head and glanced at Zoe. She was looking at me and beaming.

Chapter 21: I Have a Midnight Encounter

"There is the heat of Love,
the pulsing rush of Longing,
the lover's whisper.
Irresistible – magic to make the
sanest man go mad." Homer

It was late at night and I couldn't sleep. All the recent events, everything I've been told, the things I've seen, they all take some processing. I was just staring at the ceiling. And, I was thinking about Zoe. She seemed to be everywhere in my mind. But, she seemed so beyond me. Zoe Eliades is just such an extraordinarily beautiful woman. How is it that I could even have a chance with her? Finally, I gave up. I rolled out of bed and splashed some water on my face.

I was worried and agitated. I dug around in my dresser and came up with an old diary. Alright, an old journal. I wrote in it long ago. I found what I was looking for - an entry I wrote down many years ago about falling for a beautiful woman, and the emotional trauma that results when it doesn't work out. Reading it made me afraid all of that might happen again. Once it became apparent that she had no interest, nothing but misery followed. I had such high hopes, only to be crushed by a tidal wave of hopelessness and despair when it became obvious it was not to be. I remember, she was not disdainful or contemptuous, just the opposite. Yet, I found it so difficult to go on. Afterward, life was so dull and pale in her absence, and I felt like it was going to stay that way forever. I just didn't want that to happen all over again.

The fear of rejection is very real for men. Overcoming that fear, only to be rejected by a beautiful woman, brings on so much despair, and Zoe Eliades is the most beautiful woman I've ever met. It seems crazy I would even have a chance. But, no matter how hard I tried, she was all I could think of. It seemed impossible to get her out of my mind.

I grabbed my keys, hopped in my car, and began driving around randomly. It was just before midnight. People drive unconsciously all the time. We get in our cars and most of the things we do while driving are seemingly automatic. I remember many times getting in my car to go somewhere, becoming absorbed in something else, and consequently I'd be surprised that I arrived at whatever place I wanted to get to. It happens a lot.

So, somehow, I realized I had just passed by the street that the trailhead was on where I bumped into Zoe. The weather was not too bad. I have several good flashlights in my car. I just couldn't sleep. So, what the hell, I turned around and drove up to the trailhead. I parked, grabbed a flashlight, and started walking the trail. Weird, I know, but I do this kind of thing now and then.

I recalled when I spotted her there before. I wondered about whether she was an alien and she, somehow, knew what I was thinking. The thought of her being partly alien is intriguing, I have to admit. The moon was out, and the trail was easy to follow. The moonlight created a world in black and white, and all the shades in between.

I strolled down the path a few hundred feet. Turning a corner I saw, standing next to a tree, the shape of someone, or something, in shadow. Stopping to observe it more closely, I saw the shape separate itself from the tree. Silhouetted by the moonlight, Zoe Eliades stood there, in silence, gazing at me. Her hair filtered the light, creating an aura around her head. She wore a tunic, and was wrapped in a cloak, which was completely baffling. Turning around, she walked away. While walking, she glanced back at me.

I followed her. I couldn't help myself. My heart was racing. After twenty or thirty feet, she turned off and strolled down a side path. Coming up to it, I turned and followed her. The wind picked up and the rustling of the trees was a premonition. After a few steps, I spotted her again. She was leaning against an enormous tree trunk, staring at me, intensely, with the silver in her green eyes flashing in the moonlight. Among the tree branches above her, and all through the forest, tiny fairy lights darted about. Time stood still. I walked up to her and our faces were inches apart. The silver flecks in her eyes were whirlpools, then galaxies. They drew me in, and I gladly went. We wrapped our arms around each other. She gripped my hair, whispered into my ear, and we went down to the moss-covered ground. In the cold air, she was shockingly warm.

The entire forest was alive, with every animal observing us. It seemed her mortal veil was put aside, and there was a transfiguration. Beauty, love, and desire, they all manifested in her. Our bodies merged, and it was far beyond any intimate encounter that we can imagine. It was a pure, mystical ecstasy. I was engulfed, overwhelmed, by her. She had transformed into a primordial force, and I became strong, glorious, magnificent in her presence. How could I not be? I was making love to a Greek goddess. We knew each other, and there were no defenses, absolutely none. It was an annihilation of any sense of self.

Beams of the morning sun eventually found their way through the forest roof and returned us to this plane of existence. But they were too late because time has no power over her, and we had already lain together for an eternity.

CHAPTER 22: AFTERWARD

The next day I was in my office, reflecting on the strangeness, the unpredictability of one's life. A while ago I had wished for something metaphysical. I suppose I got what I wished for. What occurred last night seemed surreal. It left me with the impression, no, the certainty, that Zoe Eliades is much, much more than human, much more than any extraterrestrial. We live in a cold technological society, but there still is magic. For me, I found it. I'll never understand how I could be remotely deserving enough to be near her. But, perhaps that's not a consideration. It must not be, because when we had our encounter, she didn't turn away. Now, I believe, I hope, we are destined to be with each other. If I can help it, nothing on Earth is going to stop that.

I am so far away from what my dismal reality was not too long ago, and how it is possible, I don't know. In this life, as it turns out, there are miracles. I know it now, because she loves me. I have no doubt that she does, none. I don't understand how or why, but my life has completely changed.

She seems to be a goddess. How can that be? I knew her when we were kids. Extraterrestrials and flying saucers, that is one kind of thing. Our rational minds can more easily handle that. It is advanced physics. Right? But, what I experienced seemed to go way beyond that, and no explanation can be found in our rational view of the world. It was a theophany, in its purest, classical sense. It was a magical, metaphysical mystery. Unexplainable in any other way.

No, it wasn't a drug induced experience. There were no drugs involved at all. It was real, even though what happened seemed to be an affront to what we believe reality is.

I believe there is some scientific thinking about this. I should say, some scientific speculating. If gods exist, it may be that they are derived from humanity's group consciousness, physical manifestations of Carl Jung's collective unconscious. Our desires, our beliefs, somehow taking physical form with certain individuals. Our subliminal mind superimposing our need for the supernatural, the metaphysical, upon a certain few. Or, perhaps, there could be something built into us, perhaps inherent in our genetic makeup, which causes us to perceive them as such. Would it give our species a Darwinian advantage? Who knows? Really, none of this is very scientific. If they are real, it seems they are not bound by our present understanding of the laws of physics. I know, that one argument - even what we do in our present time would surely seem like magic to people just a hundred years ago. But, no. For me, that's not an explanation for what I experienced. It was too real.

I recalled something disquieting. Years ago, while visiting the Nelson-Atkins Museum in Kansas City, I came across a beautiful bronze statue of Aphrodite. Next to it were a few lines from the *Homeric Hymn to Aphrodite*. They were so powerful that I later found and read the entire hymn. It recited a time when Aphrodite made love to a mortal shepherd. I looked it up again. It is lengthy. Here are the parts of it that concerned me:

<hr />

Muse, tell me the deeds of golden Aphrodite the Cyprian, who stirs up sweet passion in the gods and subdues the tribes of mortal men and birds that fly in air and all the many creatures.

When laughter-loving Aphrodite saw him, she loved him, and terrible desire seized her in her heart.

And she put on all her rich clothes, and when she had decked herself with gold, she found him alone in the homestead.

And Anchises was seized with love, and said to her: "Hail, lady, whoever of the blessed ones you are that are come to this house."

The goddess put sweet desire in his heart. And Anchises was seized with love.

Then by the will of the gods and destiny he lay with her, a mortal man with an immortal goddess, not clearly knowing what he did.

After he awoke in a moment and saw the neck and lovely eyes of Aphrodite, he was afraid and turned his eyes aside, hiding his face with his cloak.

Then he uttered winged words and entreated her: "I beseech you, leave me not to lead a palsied life among men, but have pity on me; for he who lies with a deathless goddess is no hale man afterward."

Then Aphrodite, the daughter of Zeus, answered him: "Anchises, most glorious of mortal men, take courage and be not too fearful in your heart. You need fear no harm from me, nor from the other blessed ones, for you are dear to the gods:

But, if you tell all and foolishly boast that you lay with rich-crowned Aphrodite, Zeus will smite you in his anger with a smoking thunderbolt.

Now I have told you all. Take heed: refrain and name me not, but have regard to the anger of the gods."

When the goddess had so spoken, she soared up to windy heaven.

———————◄O►———————

So, I'm not telling anyone what happened last night. And, I'm hoping that Aegeus Eliades, whoever he really is, doesn't find out. After all, I'm a mere mortal.

CHAPTER 23: ONE MORE SECRET

There were many things to think about. A slight understatement, I admit. Those folks I knew from decades ago. They haven't aged, much. That night I saw the metallic object back then. It turns out to be real, I suppose. We went on many camp-outs, in very remote locations. I wonder how many were rendezvous of some kind. I remember they made such an impression on me back then, mostly by simply being normal. Boy, if I only knew. My dad was a horrible alcoholic. He was a decent man sober. But, he was rarely sober. Now, as an adult, I question whether he ever had the ability to control his drinking. It was not a great family life. Anyway, I'm sure they suspected what was going on. I recall they all worked at Western Electric, or the Bendix Atomic Energy Commission complex. The Bendix complex has since been taken over by Honeywell. Now it's a National Security Campus for the National Nuclear Security Administration, whatever that is. I always thought they just made bomb parts. They make much more.

I decided to give Ray a call about all this. When his voicemail kicked in, I left a message. We found out later that my office was bugged. And it wasn't bugged by the good guys.

An hour later, my secretary buzzed me, "Ray is here asking for you."

I wasn't expecting him to come over. I went out to the reception area and escorted him back to my office. Ray appeared to be disturbed about something.

"Ray, you didn't need to come."

"Hey, you're my lawyer and I need advice."

"Tell me what's bothering you."

"Okay. Well, I guess I should just tell you. I think I have to at this point. Essie, I actually do a bit more than what I've told you about at Honeywell. My ex-wife doesn't even know this. That Special Access Program. Well, there's something included in it that's very unusual. And, this is where I need your help."

Ray stopped and looked around. "No one can hear us in here, right?"

"The walls are soundproofed. At least that's what the contractors told us. Still, just don't talk too loud."

I went over and closed the office door. Ray looked stressed.

"Essie, I've run into a lot of weirdness, and some disturbing events. Let me give you an idea of what's going on here. We've stumbled upon a certain semi-super-conducting alloy that, with extremely high current running through it, rotating at a couple of thousand rpm, produces an unusual effect. Anti-gravity."

Once more Ray managed to get my full attention.

"There's more to it than just that, though. There has to be at least two, or three, of these devices we've created. The electromagnetic fields they create, once they interact with each other, a distortion field is generated, a zero gravity bubble. That's the gist of it. The details get very complicated. My problem is that I think, I'm almost positive, my group has been compromised. I'm certainly being watched. I think my cell phone and certainly our office phones are monitored. There's an FBI agent assigned to our office, and I think he's spying on us. And, I don't think he's doing it for the good guys. I think there are multiple dangers here, and I'll bet that the special access program security here has been turned."

"Oh boy. That's not good. Ray, tell me what I can do. Anything I can do to help you, you know I will."

Ray lowered his voice. "Look, your office phone can't be bugged, right? I understand it takes a court order, but I've read that judges won't issue one for an attorney's phone. Thirty years ago, that's supposedly how the mob ran its business out of Vegas. They'd go to their lawyer's offices and call Chicago, or Kansas City.

The feds could not get a wiretapping order on their attorney's phone. So I'm thinking it's safer for you, as an attorney to make a call, to Lawrence Livermore. Dr. Peter Dennett is a Senior Scientist and manager at that location. I did part of my postdoc there. He was my advisor. Also, the agents at the FBI unit there I know and still trust, and I don't think they've been transferred. There's a thumb drive with the data I've described, out in the car. I'll get it to you. That's the backup I want you to have in case I disappear."

Ray continued. "Essie, I'm really worried about disappearing. If that happens, get the thumb drive to Dr. Dennett. He'll understand what it is. If you know someone in the FBI, that you trust, well, I'll leave that up to your discretion. But don't trust the local security officers here at the Kansas City plant. I'm pretty sure I came across one guy going through my office. I guess, I'm asking you to get it to someone you can trust in case something happens to me here. Also, this is weird, but I do not even want my own group to look at this data, as crazy as that sounds. One or more of them might be compromised, but mainly I think that whatever data they have will be pilfered from them, the way it seems it's been attempted with me."

"Okay, Ray, you know I'll do whatever I can to help you. But, there's something you should know. Yeah, you're right, the FBI and the CIA can't bug our phones, or place listening devices in our homes and offices without a wiretapping order signed by a federal judge, who must find probable cause. There are exceptions to this. But, we're talking about the real world here. Have you read about the CIA giving German and French law enforcement heads up on terrorist attacks that were going to happen in their countries? How did they know? Because they, by what they call 'national technical means,' and plain old wiretapping, uncovered this information, in those countries, in violation of the criminal and privacy laws in those countries. Now, I think it is naive to assume that those countries do not return the favor. Our agencies probably know this, but maybe go to some lengths to 'not know.' So if they've seen you come here before, then I might be bugged, and I'd have no way of detecting it. Also, Ray, some guy was following me a couple of days ago. It was pretty damn intimidating. I'm on someone's radar."

I took a deep breath. I thought of another possibility. "If we're talking about a crooked agent here, it's good to remember that the local FBI had a new high-tech headquarters built north of downtown. The story is that the building's basement is a communications hub, similar to a telephone system's wire center, and the equipment there has the ability to intercept every single landline and cell tower in Missouri and Kansas. They don't even have to leave the building. A.T.&T., Verizon, and other telecommunication companies were required to give this equipment access to their systems. Agents no longer have to find a substation or switchboard and physically connect wires to a phone line, and have to sit and listen for days. I'm sure the older agents are pissed that the new agents don't have to go through that miserable assignment. Now, telephone lines are recorded automatically, with the recorded voices saved to hard drives and burnt onto DVDs. Artificial intelligence monitors conversations for certain keywords and phrases. This is supposed to only occur when a federal judge issues an order allowing the same. But, Ray, the problem is the equipment is there, in their own basement, with no padlock on it, so to speak."

"Essie, I don't know what to do then."

"Okay, I understand. We'll figure out some way to make a secure call. I can go to the other side of town and use my old partners' phone there. Or, the easiest, we'll just buy a burner phone."

"Also, Ray. You know, that family, that group of people we discussed? They're certainly not from around here, I'll put it like that."

Ray looked at me with interest. "They're human, aren't they?"

"Maybe, maybe not. But, they're certainly Greek! I guess you can say they are old school. Um, they know you by name. They are worried about what you've figured out."

"Oh, my God."

"That's what I thought. It gets even crazier. As it turns out, I know several of them from when I was a kid. They've been here in town that long. They worked at the old Bendix A.E.C. nuclear operation before Honeywell took it over, and it relocated to south Kansas City."

"Essie, this may explain some of the mystery that surrounds all of this. I've looked at the old research data from Bendix. It is still highly classified. It is not common knowledge, almost nobody knew, but some theoretical anti-gravity drive equipment was built, with electron tubes no less, at Western Electric and Bendix. The gyroscope mechanisms that Western Electric made were especially important. The different magnetic fields intersect at precise, specified angles, which change with the voltage and gauss strength. This, theoretically, controls the vehicle movement through every axis. If one field's gauss strength is lowered or increased compared to the other field or fields, or the angles of field intersection change, the vehicle vector is altered. Oddly, those attempts went nowhere. This was before transistors were commonplace. It was almost like they went out of their way to go the wrong direction ... well, shit!"

"The computing power needed to figure out all the vectors to keep it from crashing probably wasn't available at the time anyway. But then, I'm just a lawyer. What do I know? Ray, think about this. I remember these people. They were just really decent to me back then. That's how they come across. They said stuff that makes eminent sense. This type of technology, once it's out, is impossible to keep to one group. It allows for an almost immediate, successful first nuclear strike. The attacked nation has no time to launch a counter-attack. The first nation that initiates an attack wins. The extraordinary speed and maneuverability afforded by the technology makes defense against nuclear attack impossible. Thus, the logic underlying the Mutually Assured Destruction doctrine, which some argue has kept this planet free of nuclear war for seventy years, becomes obsolete. I listened to them talking about other civilizations imploding within years of discovering this technology, if they've got nukes. Apparently, that's one of the reasons they're here."

Ray was speechless, and his mouth was wide open. He slammed his hands into his face, groaned, and bent forward. "Oh, fuck."

We sat in silence for a while.

Ray stood up. "Anyway, first things first. Let's go out to my car, and I'll hand over this USB stick to you. Find some place safe for it. Also, I need to get back to the office. Yeah, what you just said is a real possibility. I have to admit, I've thought about that, too."

There was a black Mercedes parked outside at one end of the parking lot. It arrived along with a van with mirrored windows that parked on the other side. Inside, three men listened to our entire conversation. It was not good.

CHAPTER 24: RUSSIANS

My office is on the second floor of a four-story office building. We walked down the stairs and exited out the front door. Ray had an SUV, a Honda Pilot. We walked to its rear, he popped open the rear hatch and reached in.

"Here it is, and also here's Peter Dennett's card. Both his phone numbers are there. His office number is secure, and it's okay to leave a phone message. But please call from your lawyer's office phone, or better, a burner phone, in case everything blows up."

We didn't notice the Mercedes pulling up. Something slammed into my back and my head smashed against the Pilot's hatch. I saw a man grab the USB thumb drive. The van pulled up. Ray had a bag thrown over his head, and two men threw him into the van, jumping after him. The man who slammed me pulled out a gun. I don't remember much, but I knew he was going to shoot me dead on the spot. I was certain. He was wearing a camel hair overcoat.

I spotted a tire iron just inside the Pilot. I groaned, bent forward, and allowed my torso to fall into the SUV. Grabbing the tire iron, I turned and swung as fast as I could. It made contact with his hand and the gun went flying. The men in the Mercedes got out. I took off and ran along the front of the building. Turning the corner, I saw my car. Thank God I had my keys. I unlocked it remotely with the key, hopped in, and backed up. The guy I hit screamed at me, and the Mercedes pulled up alongside him. Someone in the car was yelling at him. I saw the van take off out of the lot at high speed. Ray was in that van. I took off after it. After a block, I could not see it. I stopped at a light and was rammed by the Mercedes. One of the men started to get out. I hit the gas, ran the red light, and got on I-470.

At any other time, the Highway Patrol or the city police would be parked somewhere on this stretch. Not this time. Looking down at my speedometer, I saw I was reaching 90. I almost rammed a semi in front and weaved to the left. In my rear view mirror, I saw the Mercedes. I got to the I-70 intersection. West towards Kansas City looked like a traffic jam. I turned right and got on I-70 East. I was still being followed. It dawned on me that they shouted at each other in what sounded like Russian. They were Russians!

There was a loud thud. Looking back, I saw a chunk of my bumper falling on the highway. The bastards were shooting at me on I-70. There are still no police around. My cell phone was back at my office. Then I got a gut punch. The fuel light turned on. I was maybe running on fumes.

The next exit was Grain Valley. I had to turn off and do something. If I ran out of gas on the highway, I was dead. I had to lose them.

Chapter 25: Return to Monkey Mountain

It comes to me. Monkey Mountain. If I can't lose them in the car, I think I can get to Monkey Mountain, park next to the south trail, and sprint into the woods. There's not much else I can do.

I take the exit and make the turns. At one point, the car dies, and starts up again after I weave back and forth, shaking what is left of the gas into the fuel line. Finally, I spot the gravel parking lot just as the car engine dies. I coast into the lot. I jump out and run like hell. I spot the Mercedes pulling up. Three men quickly exit. One of them opens the trunk and, looking back, I see two rifles handed out. Oh, Christ.

I head into the woods, get off the trail, which was too exposed, and head up the hill to some bluffs. I hear them, and seconds later hear a bullet smash into the brush near me. I duck and head into an opening between the rocky bluffs. It's all uphill for a few minutes and I'm starting to feel it. Looking back, these guys are nonstop. At one point, I think they don't see me any longer. I certainly don't see them. Then, it occurs to me. They've split up. Sure enough, I see one to my left and another guy maybe twenty, thirty yards to my right. The third guy, I don't know. I presume he's behind me. There is nowhere to go but straight forward. I sprint ahead, only to get a shock. The way is blocked by tree branches. Covered with hundreds of huge thorns. There are Black Locust trees right in front of me. They form a wall of vicious, evil thorns that look like they're made of obsidian. Some more rounds are fired, and I jump from an impact to a limb right overhead. There really is no option. I can hear someone coming up the hill behind me. Okay, if it's going to be this way, so be it.

I stand up, lean forward, and sprint into the branches, ramming my way forward, making headway through them. I feel thorns stabbing into my scalp, my cheek, my shoulders, my legs. This infuriates me. I become enraged at the whole damn situation. I hear screaming. It's me. I break into the open and there's tall brown grass in the open field straight ahead, all dead winter grass but a good three or four feet high. I run into it trying to keep as low as possible. There's blood flowing into my eyes. I stepped on some of the thorns, and now my feet are sloshing in my shoes from my own blood. I look around, and I don't see any of them. I hear someone speaking Russian. I get maybe twenty yards into this field and one of them opens up. A good ten rounds. I hit the ground and get as low as I possibly can. They are random shots. I hear one of them approach, and he passes by my left. There are shadows moving across the ground. I look up, and I see swirling indigo clouds, roiling with energy. The whole field is darkened.

I am covered in blood. But, strangely, that's okay, I've been covered in blood before. I feel an all-consuming rage come over me, and an immense clarity arrives with that. These sons of bitches, these bastards. It occurs to me, they don't know where I am. Three of them, separated, and one of them passed by and is in front of me. It's dark enough and the grass high enough that none of them quite know where the others are. I know exactly. They are walking forward, pushing through the grass, and they're in a horizontal line. I'm behind them. I could, if I chose, just backtrack, head home, and forget this, forget all of it.

No, that's not going to happen.

I feel it. Aggie knew it all along. It's the third man. He's here. His presence is unmistakable. I smile to myself. These poor bastards. They don't have a chance.

I crawl forward and find what I want. A rock, about softball size. I rise a foot, from prone to kneeling position, and hurl it ahead of me, slamming the Russian to my front. He grunts and stumbles. The man to the left opens up, thinking it's me. A half dozen rounds, maybe three hitting him. They are 5.56 military. It would have only taken one of those. He falls to the ground. The man to the right is in the direction of fire and screams something in Russian at the other bastard, who stops, not wanting to hit him.

I sprint through the grass hunched over, and almost immediately stumble over the dead man. Who, serendipitously, left his rifle for me. It's an AR. I pick it up, not bothering with the safety or with chambering it. I assume it's good to go, and I aim and shoot three or four rounds toward the Russian to the left, who I can't really see too well now. I hear the impacts. I take off sprinting, but suddenly the man who was to my right slams into me, and the rifle goes flying. I elbow into his temple as hard as I can and manage to stand up and get away from him. Looking over the grass, I'm able to see the far tree line, a good distance away. I see a woman there. She's dressed in white, and she's watching all of this.

I look behind, over my left shoulder, and I spot the Russian bastard. With my blood on him, ruining his camel hair overcoat. He gets up and walks towards me, with murder in his eyes. I can see he's built like a tank. From under his belt, he pulls out a handgun. A blur, an amorphous black shadow, rushes in from the right, slams into him, knocking him to the ground. I see something metallic in the dead grass, and I think it's the rifle. I dive toward it. But, it's not the rifle. It's a sword, a short bronze sword, thrust into the ground. I grab it. It looks familiar. The Russian gets up, smirks, and reaches down to pick up his gun. I look at him and smile. As he raises his gun, I swing my sword.

CHAPTER 26: KIDNAPPED

Raymond Langstaff wakes up. He looks around, and he sees he's in a van. With a couple of men. One of them is wearing a suit. He recognizes him. He's the FBI liaison at the Kansas City National Security Campus. Initially, he's relieved. He's been rescued. Then he sees he's still hog-tied. In the van with the men who grabbed him.

He tries to talk, but he's gagged.

The FBI guy looks over at him. "Just behave yourself, or these gentlemen will not take it kindly. Also, thanks for what we've been trying to get for a year."

Ray looks at him holding up the USB thumb drive that he made for Essie.

One of the men says something in Russian. The FBI guy turns and looks at him, and talks back. In perfect Russian. *Oh God, I fucked up,* Ray thought. He did. Someone put a bag over his head.

The van heads to the Lee's Summit airport. It began as a little strip for puddle jumpers forty years ago. As the area grew, along with other Kansas City suburbs, it doubled in size and then tripled. Now it takes small commercial jet traffic.

The van drives past the gate and heads to a hangar on the far end. It pulls up to a Cessna Citation parked there, which is warming up. Cessna Citations have a 3500-mile range.

The two men grab Ray, pull him out, and drag him up the stairs to the jet's interior. He's no longer hogtied, but his hands are duct-taped together and so are his ankles. There are two other men inside, presumably the pilots. None of them look friendly.

The door slams shut, the two turbines rev up, and the jet taxis out of the hanger and heads to the south end of the longer runway. In a few minutes, it's airborne.

Ray hears some more talking. Someone pulls off his hood. His gag is cut off. The FBI guy says, "You've got a decision to make. We're headed for a place that is not going to be too friendly to you if you don't cooperate. There's no way things change now. My advice is to not cause any trouble with anyone you will be dealing with from now on."

Ray Langstaff breathes deeply for the first time since he was thrown into the van. "Where are we going?"

"Well, there's nothing you can do about it. We're headed for Cuba. And soon after to other parts."

"I can't believe that you're doing this. You're FBI, for God's sake."

The FBI guy laughs and looks at the other men. "I'm not FBI. I was the company's FBI liaison. I'm Russian. Everyone here is Russian."

Without even thinking, Ray yells out, "Fuck you. Fuck all of you."

The guy backhands him. Things get blurry.

About an hour later, Ray hears a bunch of laughter. He looks up and sees everyone giving each other high-fives.

The "not FBI" guy looks over at him and sneers. "We're outside of U.S. territory and fifteen minutes to Havana. By the time the F.A.A. controllers notice we've deviated from the flight plan, we'll be landing. I can't think of a better reason to shut everything down and head home."

He holds up the thumb drive. "Thanks for putting everything on this. Very convenient. We won't have to pull your teeth out. Yet."

Ray closes his eyes. He tilts his head back and tries to figure out what to do. But there isn't anything.

Life is full of surprises. One is coming your way.

Ray Langstaff jolts upright. No one is looking at him, and nobody onboard said anything. But he heard a voice. It seemed like it was Essie Kemp's voice. Ray thinks he's hallucinating. *Is the oxygen low? Did they drug me?*

He hears some loud voices and looks forward. The pilot is yelling. All the men rush up and look outside the cockpit window.

Ray is able to scoot over a seat and look up the aisle to the cockpit. He sees it. There's a bright light out there. They all see it. The light is jumping up, sideways, down. It goes below the view from the window. About a mile in front, an immense black ball rises in front of them. The pilot, copilot, not FBI guy, and the other men are all yelling. The pilot uses both his hands and grabs the yoke, taking the plane out of autopilot. He makes a hard turn to starboard, and the plane's nose tilts and turns right. Whatever the thing is, it stays in front of the plane. But, it is changing. The black surface is undulating and looks alive. There's a glowing, a morphing of shape, and it becomes so luminous it's hard to see. Now it's an immensely brilliant gold. It gets even bigger. It covers all the cockpit window view. There is nothing but overwhelmingly brilliant golden light. The pilot screams.

Chapter 27: Keeping the Secret

From the 1950s to this decade, there's been a top-secret, special access program in Albuquerque, Kansas City and Lee's Summit. Very few people knew there was a network of deep tunnels at the Bendix plant in Kansas City. Bendix was contracted by the Atomic Energy Commission for numerous undertakings. In those tunnels, a parade of scientists and engineers endured repeated frustration attempting to create an anti-gravity propulsion drive that they absolutely knew existed elsewhere. No matter how it was approached, nothing ever came of it. That effort included the old Western Electric plant in nearby Lee's Summit, which had its own tunnels no one in town knew of.

The program was partly located in Kansas City and Lee's Summit because of a certain U.S. President who wanted to bring some economic benefits to the people who kept on voting for him ever since he first ran for a county judge position. Eventually, Honeywell took over the operation, along with its special access program and other top secret projects, that were first contracted for in the 1940s by the old Atomic Energy Commission. It was renamed the Kansas City National Security Campus.

Harry Truman wanted to make sure that any discoveries made would be in the hands of civilian scientists and not a certain few of the military generals and admirals he dealt with. Eventually, the A.E.C. was rolled into the newly created U.S.

Department of Energy in 1977. The National Nuclear Security Administration is an agency under the Department of Energy, and the operations of what is now called the Kansas City National Security Campus moved to a new facility located at the far south end of the Kansas City metropolitan area. This facility, state of the art, also has a complex of underground tunnels and rooms. I remember, there was actually a moving sale. I saw a Cray computer listed. I've always regretted not buying it.

The special access program group, set up by ARPA-E (Advanced Research Projects Agency-Energy), was holding a meeting in one of the underground rooms. The issue was how to go forward towards creating an anti-gravity effect. One member of the group, a well-known string physicist who flew in from Boston for this meeting, spoke up.

"I was very disappointed by the experiment run over the weekend. Going over the printouts, everything was done correctly, 150,000 gauss rotating fields initially at ninety-degree angles. The emissions and particle profile are somewhat similar to what we are detecting from the operations of these vehicles, yet no go. I can't think of what we've done wrong."

A gentleman from Sandia Laboratories, who flew in from Albuquerque, stood up and spoke. "I've been advocating for a Z-Pinch plasma technique, using our Z Machine. With the extraordinary magnetic fields it creates, it might get the effect we're looking for, without rotating the fields."

Several others gave their inputs.

"I agree." Everyone stopped. They turned around to look at the speaker. It was Raymond Langstaff.

"I think the methodology suggested by the Sandia group is the best way. Our experiments over the last weekend show conclusively that the high voltage rotating magnetic fields approach, even at 150,000 gauss, is a dead end. There's nothing there."

The string physicist responded. "I'm looking at the report. Maybe there's another approach we can take on what was done last week. Dr. Langstaff, you've got the final say, what do you think?"

"Looking at the records from the past fifty years, I see every variation of that approach was tried. The clean room at the old Western Electric plant had ideal conditions for the experiment but no luck. We thought with the increase in voltage provided by superconductivity, the results would change, but no luck there either. Therefore, as the director, I'll get a draft together with new timelines, deliverables, and goalposts and get it to everyone by the secure mail system. I've got to get a report over to the Secretary later today. I'm sorry we hit the wall here. I'm just happy that all of you still have your day jobs. As always, it's good to see all of you again, and with that I've got to run. Bye."

Dr. Raymond Langstaff picked up his briefcase and exited the room. He headed to the nearest elevator, walked in, and pushed the button for 10B, the very lowest floor. It occurred to him that, despite the Q-Level 4 security clearance he possessed, he had never been to this floor.

There was a high-security entrance outside the elevator door at 10B, including an eye scan, fingerprint, and voice recognition. "Raymond Langstaff," the automated voice said, "Welcome Dr. Langstaff."

Raymond Langstaff walked through the entrance, down the hallway, and came to a door. There was a sign on it with the words "National Nuclear Security Administration - Counter-Proliferation." He knocked, opened the door and walked in. He spotted a man sitting behind a large desk, who stood up, walked over, and shook hands with him.

The tall man smiled and his eyes, with silver in them, made contact.

"Hi, Ray. How did it go?"

"I really had to think about how to do it. It isn't the easiest thing to do, to spike the voltage on the superconducting electromagnet, and then feed a false reading to the Tesla meter. But I did."

"Did the group have any suspicions?"

"No, on the contrary, the Sandia representative was obviously happy. He will be able to run his own trials in New Mexico and not have to do the KC trips anymore."

"Doesn't he like barbeque?"

"Oh, God no. He's vegan now. Completely. No dairy even."

"He must have been going to the wrong restaurants. Vegetarian barbeque is big in Kansas City at the moment."

"Oh, well."

Both Raymond Langstaff and Aegeus Eliades chuckled.

"You know, this has been an insane two weeks. No one will ever believe this. I made perhaps the greatest physics discovery of all time, only to be kidnapped by the FBI and the Russians, get hogtied, and flown halfway to Havana. Then the cavalry comes out of nowhere."

Aggie replied, "We had some help. They never had a chance. If a nuclear power on this planet got hold of that thumb drive, and the technical information on it gets out, well, every analysis anyone's done says it leads to a cataclysm."

"I know Esmond talked to me about this. It's like a no-brainer now. Those goons reinforced that. I was convinced that I would never see the light of day again. I'm still not quite sure what happened, but I'm glad it did."

"We're getting together tonight. Essie's going off-world, with Zoe. They'll be gone a while."

"Oh really? Maybe someday I can make that trip."

"Count on it. Some of our friends have a few ideas to bounce off you. But, anyway, come on by tonight. We have a friend who'd love to discuss classical physics with you. She's Greek, and she's from out of town."

Ray hesitated for a moment, then smiled. "Okay."

Ray looked around the office. "Aggie, just what exactly do you do?"

"Funny thing. I'm engaged in a number of endeavors here and there, but I've always been a 'Special Assistant' to the Under Secretary of Energy for Nuclear Security - Counter-Proliferation. A position not listed anywhere. Obviously, I keep a low profile."

"Jesus, how did that come about?"

"Harry Truman was the first to arrange it, back when it was the Atomic Energy Commission. As you've probably figured out, I've been around for a while. President Truman took some convincing, but after everyone started exploding thermonuclear devices like firecrackers, and after what he saw over Washington, D.C. in 1952, he changed his mind. He previously asked Western Electric to take over Sandia National Laboratories back in 1949, which in turn shared management with the predecessor to the Kansas City National Security Campus. That old saying is just as true now as in the past - it's good to have connections in high places."

Ray said, "Sometime in the future, historians will have a field day researching all this."

"As the title says, counter-proliferation is what we do. Except, we don't just limit ourselves to nuclear materials. We have the assets to detect, and we surreptitiously halt, any progress in anti-gravity technology, anywhere in the world. By doing that, without any doubt, for seventy years, we've prevented what would almost certainly be a nuclear apocalypse. It's a rather serendipitous arrangement, don't you think?"

PART TWO

"I know not what the truth may be,
I tell the tale as twas told to me." Herodotus

"Don't believe everything you read." Ross Myers

CHAPTER 28: A PSYCHIATRIC EVALUATION

MISSOURI-KANSAS PSYCHIATRIC
& COUNSELING SERVICES, L.L.C.

Franklin P. Rew, M.D.

Board Certified – Psychiatry & Neurology

Diplomate - Carl Jung Institute - Zurich

2144 Bering Medical Building

Kansas City, Missouri 64112

Office Number (816) 229-04XX

Facsimile (816) 229-04XX

INITIAL PSYCHIATRIC EVALUATION

Name: Esmond (Essie) Kemp

Patient Number: XXXX772

Date of Examination: XXXXXXXX

Gender: Male

Education: Postgraduate

History: Patient is male attorney referred for evaluation by the Missouri Bar's Lawyer Assistance & Intervention Program. According to Program Manager, patient self-reported to their hot line two days ago. Patient recites a history of amnesia. He asserts he has no recall of the previous five months. He reports his personal calendar contains no information for this time period, except for certain court dates he apparently attended, but does not recall. Patient further reports a sense of overwhelming loss and extreme frustration over inability to understand his status. Patient non-responsive to inquiry regarding suicidal ideation. Patient reports death of wife and ten year old daughter in automobile accident. Finally, patient reports lucid dreams of unusual nature.

Drug & Alcohol Use: Drug use denied. Alcohol consumed socially on rare occasions.

Prior Treatment: None reported.

Present Medications: None reported.

Family History: Patient reports father was alcoholic. He is unaware of other family mental health history.

Examination: Patient presents as a tall, well-developed male. Speech is normal, coherent and perhaps lower in volume than normal. When asked, he admits to difficulty sleeping. When he does sleep, he reports strange dreams of a silver disc above him, running in a forest while being chased by Russian spies. When pressed, patient admits he is dissatisfied with his life, does not wish to continue his law practice. He reports no significant relationships and very little social life. Patient admits to deep depression and anger in regard to his memory loss.

When asked if he has hallucinations, patient was hesitant to respond. He apologized and said he wasn't sure but, if he did, it was long ago. When asked to clarify, he said it was likely lucid dreaming.

Advised patient that under no circumstances was he to be prescribed Ambien by anyone. Melatonin, over the counter, is permissible if he feels need for sleep aid.

Patient symptoms seem to include some indicia of delusions and hallucinations, yet there is no incoherence or agitation.

Memory loss is a known symptom of major depressive episode, as well as a coping mechanism for post-traumatic stress disorder. Patient is aware of his name, location, calendar date. Unresolved grief/repressed memories of prior events may be a factor here. However, the memory loss relates to a more recent time period.

Jungian Analysis: I briefly discussed Jungian Analysis with patient. I advised him that, according to Carl Jung, the unconscious mind communicates with the conscious mind by the dreams he or she experiences. The issue for analysis is just what exactly the messages in the dreams are. Patient reports dreams are vivid and do not fade from memory upon awakening. Classic analysis of dreams where someone is fleeing could result in several interpretations. I advised him it would take subsequent sessions to determine just what the most likely one is. I advised patient of Carl Jung's theory of the "collective unconscious." I noted Carl Jung had previously written of flying saucers. Jung hypothesized that the same were products of the collective unconscious, reflected humanity's anxiety with the modern world, and served as a modern day myth. If Jung were alive today, no doubt he would say the same. The patient inquired whether the collective unconscious, the group mind, could have something to do with a person's belief in or encounter with someone from mythology. I responded that it would be consistent with Jung, since Jung believed flying saucers could be a product of collective belief in myth. I asked him if he encountered such a person and, also, that it would be important for me to know. The patient looked up and responded, stating that if he replied in the affirmative, by definition, he would be admitting to a delusion, and he would be diagnosed as delusional. After that, he could be subject to a 96-hour involuntary psychiatric hold, with a hearing in front of a circuit court judge afterward. He stated he's had conflicts with several judges, and he would rather just not go down this path. We agreed to move on to the Roschach test.

Roschach Test-Series 10: Patient cooperated and responded to the complete series of inkblots. Scoring may be inapplicable to this situation in that, while he did report animals and humans, he stated almost every inkblot was representative of what he saw or experienced in his lucid dreams. Patient experienced a sudden feeling of extreme suffocation when viewing one inkblot. Another he said could be a goddess in the forest, and a third reminded him of a flying saucer. These unique responses are not listed in the scoring manual. By themselves they are concerning and indicative of delusion, but the Roschach Test is never used for diagnosis by itself.

Diagnosis: F32.2 296.23 Major depressive disorder, severe, without psychotic episode

F44.0 300.12 Dissociative amnesia

Treatment/Plan: Twice weekly group loss therapy for four weeks.

Celexa 20 mg x 30 days #30

Klonopin 0.25 mg PO TID x 30 days #90

Melatonin 10 mg (OTC)

Further Treatment: Schedule follow-up appointment in thirty days.

I found myself at home, alone. I'd catch myself staring off into the distance, or looking at my face in the mirror, and experience an inexplicable wave of uneasiness. Something was missing. Something was very wrong with me. Whatever it was, I couldn't figure it out. There was a mental wall blocking my reasoning. It was maddening. I kept on trying to force myself to remember what I didn't know. It was so odd. Perhaps a good analogy is attempting to remember what it was like before you were born. Good luck with that. Still, there had to be a revelation hidden somewhere. Eventually, I grew mentally exhausted and I called for help.

The psychiatrist actually did help. I believed that I may have been delusional. I couldn't tell him that, or some other things. I had these dreams of amazing occurrences. They seemed so real. But they were just dreams. I mean, it is ridiculous. If it were a novel, no literary agent or editor would touch it as it is such a common trope, such a pedestrian theme and plot. I mean, who would buy a story like that? This amnesia I have - after the visit with the psychiatrist, I think the real diagnosis for it is this - my life sucks. Quite frankly, I lead a very dull life. Nothing exciting happens. I believe my mind somehow decided to erase my tiresome, everyday life and replace it with the vivid dreams I've been having. According to the psychiatrist, using Jungian Analysis, it is likely my subconscious sending a message to my conscious mind to do something exciting, to make my life less boring.

I already knew I was extremely depressed. The psychiatrist said major depressive disorder causes memory loss. So, it all fits together. Both the memory loss and the lucid dreaming. That explains it. Of course, I'm getting even more depressed now, because it was in fact all just my imagination. My life really, actually, is unbearably mundane. Nothing happens.

I was in bed, asleep. My window was open. It was pitch black. I woke up to a fog horn in the distance, as if ships at sea were being warned of dangerous shoals. It created some confusion for me. I felt that I was in a different place, a different time. Then, I realized it was merely a train, many miles away, crossing an intersection, or going through town. At night, when everything is closed, and people are asleep, sounds seem to travel remarkable distances. But, the feeling of dislocation, of lost time, persisted.

In the morning, with the sun just rising, I crawled out of bed. I made my way downstairs, to scrounge around for something to drink. I found an energy drink and some leftover, cold coffee. So, I mixed them together and drank it. It's a concoction I don't recommend, but it helped. Next, I checked my Google calendar. I wanted to see if something was scheduled I wasn't aware of, like, you know, a funeral. Nope.

I stepped outside the front door and spotted a number of crows waiting for me. There's around forty of these rather large black birds just perched in the oak tree in the front yard. A murder of crows. I turned around, went inside, quickly grabbed a handful of trail mix, went back out, and tossed it on the driveway.

Sitting down on the front steps, I watched as they glided down one by one, then two by two, to pick over the selection. A larger one definitely preferred M&Ms, which was curious. A crow with a sweet tooth. I wondered if it preferred the red ones or the green ones. I tossed my one slice of bread into the air, spinning it like a Frisbee. A crow dived off a tree branch and effortlessly latched onto it with its claws. Watching all of them in my front yard, it occurred to me that it was rather odd. They were all just looking at me.

I forgot to ask the psychiatrist if there was any possibility I was drugged. He wanted to know if I had an accident. If there was, I sure didn't remember. I still felt a tremendous sense of loss. I wondered if this is how honey bees, or ants, go through life. With no awareness of time passing, no recall of how they arrived where they were, or why they were doing what they were doing. Like robots, they would just respond to an impulse, a genetic imperative, to perform tasks. I think those creatures do not possess any curiosity about their state, or about missing time. I did.

It occurred to me that I had the benefit of the latest artificial intelligence to assist me in resolving this, even though I think I've got it figured out. My own personal A.I. I might as well make use of it. I walked into the living room where the Google Hub with Home Assistant was. It would know.

"Okay, Google. Why am I suffering from amnesia?"

In its female Australian voice, utilizing the sum total of human A.I. computing power, along with its incomparable access to big data, it replied. "I don't know, but I found these results on search."

I rolled my eyes. "Okay, Google. How do I clear up my brain fog?"

"I don't know, but I found these results on search."

I attempted to be more specific. "Okay, Google. What would cause memory loss?"

"I don't know, but I found these results on search."

Thereupon, I told Google something that is probably told to it more often than anything else it gets.

"Okay, Google. Go fuck yourself."

"I don't know, but I found these results on search."

Out of curiosity, I checked those search results. I won't list them here.

Chapter 29: Dragons Dream

E leni is visible to anyone who knows where to look. If one only gazes in the right direction, he or she will see her as a silver glint in the bright sunlight, as she darts from cloud to cloud above mid-Missouri on this sunlit June day.

It surprises me to feel such cold air on a day like this. The sun warms me, though. I let its rays slide around me, but I still feel its warmth. Down below, there's a magnificent, enormous lake extending across the middle of the state. Its main body weaves and undulates north and south as it makes its way across. From my vantage point, it looks like a colossal, mythological dragon. It's the weekend, so thousands of boaters are cruising every section of it, and their wakes make white dashes covering the entirety of the lake. This perspective brings back some old memories. There were several times I encountered enormous dragons. Once, I did so accompanied by a not quite sixteen-year-old girl. It was long ago.

Zoe Eliades was tired, and bored. She spent several hours a day taking lessons on speaking and writing various Filoi languages. She knew there were translating machines and software programs to make such an effort unnecessary. Zoe wanted to explore this new world, informally called Magna Graecia, and its people. Instead, she found herself in a classroom, outside a sparkling city she could not visit. But, there were boys, and she saw them outside playing. And the school was beautiful. It was designed and built like a temple, with a large covered terrace, and Doric columns supporting a tiled roof. The tiles were composed of a synthetic material, a concession to modern construction methods. It was situated high up on a ridge, overlooking a deep valley, bordered by snow capped mountains.

The morning fog was violet, with the shadows of the distant mountains barely visible. Her mother was there. Despite the boredom of the lessons, Zoe loved spending time with her, and Helena Eliades cherished every moment with her daughter. They were seated in front of a large antique mirror, made of highly polished copper. Zoe watched in the mirror as her mother braided her long black hair in a complex weave, with one part going around her head, and the remainder of her woven hair falling down below her shoulders. It made her feel like a princess.

"Zoe, it is much easier to do than it seems. We braid all your hair to begin with, then the upper part you simply wrap around your head and fasten with these silver pins. It is the way I was taught so long ago in Greece."

"Mother, I've never been to Greece. Will we go sometime, all of us?"

"Zoe, if you wish. Your birthday is this week. Perhaps a trip there can be part of that."

"I would like that. And I believe you would want to go back, wouldn't you?"

"Well, Zoe. I have a secret. I have been back there, several times."

"You should have taken me!"

"Ha, I will next time."

"Mother, why do the Filoi boys follow me around? I say hello to them and some greet me in return, but then they run away. I want to practice my lessons with them."

Helena Eliades laughed. "Zoe, you are almost sixteen. You'll soon understand all too clearly the answer to that question. For now, it's just as well they do run away."

Zoe turned her head to look at her mother, who raised one of her eyebrows, and they both laughed for a long time.

In the afternoon, Zoe finished her lesson on several Filoi dialects, arising from the different planets that host their population centers. She turned off her laptop computer, and the holographic images projected by it. The tutor, an elderly man who had the kindness of a saint, asked Zoe how she was enjoying her summer.

"Mr. Lambros, I am fascinated by everything I see and learn here. But, the more I see and learn, the more I feel trapped in this beautiful place. The city I see nearby looks so interesting, and the different worlds I learn of are places I feel I have to visit sometime."

"Well, that is certainly understandable. Zoe, I talked to your mother earlier. She suggested a place that you might wish to visit. It is far away from our world, but there is a ship that can quickly transport you there. The ship's name is Eleni, and she has visited this place several times. She has friends there, and would be happy to return there with you."

Excited, Zoe quickly asked. "When can we go? What kind of place is this?"

"Your mother knows of this world. She has visited it before also. Zoe, it is a place of dragons."

— ◆O◆ —

The next day, Zoe was bursting with excitement. She was standing outside, with her backpack, in the field the boys would play their games at. She saw it approach. A golden spot on the horizon, growing larger as it approached. It stopped directly above the field, hovered, and slowly descended. When it reached the ground, an opening appeared. Zoe turned to her mother and hugged her.

Helena, while hugging her daughter, whispered. "Zoe, there are many hidden things in life. I believe you will find some of them on this trip. Always remember who you are, and know that, for you especially, it really is true - love is the greatest strength of all."

As I approached the field I saw a lone child, with her backpack, accompanied by her mother. Landing on the field, I realized this was an unusual situation. Helena Eliades is whispered of throughout the Filoi worlds. I have traveled with her before. Her daughter would be the only one traveling with me on this voyage. She sensed my apprehension. So, she spoke to me.

"Eleni, I understand your unease. Please understand, this visit to the dragons is something my daughter must do. Just as you have taken others, I ask that you take her on this journey."

Ms. Eliades, I consider it a great honor to do so. The dragons though, they live their lives in a different realm. I cannot protect her at all times.

I understand. Eleni, I trust you. All I ask is that you do your best. The rest, that is in the hands of the fates, and the dragons.

Zoe gave her mother one final hug, picked up her backpack, and walked inside.

"Hello, Zoe. I am Eleni. I am so happy to have you on board. Our trip will not be too long, though we will be going to another arm of the galaxy."

"Hi, Eleni. Thank you so much for having me with you. I'm really excited about seeing dragons. I was getting rather bored here, as beautiful as it is."

We took off and gained altitude. It would take a day to get to Chihetu, a Jovian planet, a gas giant, if we travel safely. With Zoe Eliades on board, I would travel no other way.

Helena Eliades watched Eleni, with her daughter onboard, rapidly gain altitude, gain speed, and disappear. There was a wistful look on her face, and tears in her eyes.

Several hours later, Eleni thought it wise to discuss the planet, and its inhabitants, with her passenger.

"Zoe, has anyone talked to you about the dragons, or the planet where they live, Chihetu?"

"My mother did. She said that she's visited the dragons before, but she did not want to tell me too much because I need to find out the rest on my own. I thought that strange. I tried to look it up, but there were no entries in any of the databases I checked."

"I'm not surprised. Zoe, these are rare creatures. They are unique, to my understanding. And I have access to the entirety of Filoi knowledge. The Dragons of Chihetu are very friendly, and very trusting. In a sense, they do not believe in evil. The dragons are always hungry for new knowledge. They always welcome visitors. They seek out memories, and they seek out dreams. And, they share their own."

"What do they look like?"

"There are thousands of them floating through the planet's multi-layered atmosphere. Some are a mile or more in length. Many have spots of different types on their long bodies. They do not have scales, they have skin, similar to yours. They are far, far longer than they are wide. They mostly communicate telepathically, but everything, their thoughts, their emotions, their physical feelings, and their dreams, can be merged with those they have physical contact with."

"Zoe, if you choose to have contact with them, be prepared. You could feel you have physically merged with them in some aspects, and the mental and emotional connections, if any, could be very unexpected. It is an amazing sight to see them in contact with each other, to see these mile long creatures become intertwined. They do this in flight, in a layer of the planet's atmosphere. So, I wanted to prepare you for this. It is an unusual experience."

"Eleni, have you merged with them?"

"I have, several times. The experiences have helped me become more alive, to sense how it is to be Filoi, and human. For me, it was, and is, an ongoing revelation."

Zoe found a place to sit, and then lay down. She brought some books with her, touching upon aspects of Filoi dialects. Gradually she became tired, and fell asleep.

So, this was the first time I met Zoe Eliades. I am not human. I am not Filoi. But, I am alive. I sensed it somehow. I felt it. There was a hint of something beautiful, a spark of something divine, manifested in her, apart from her simply being a young girl. I recall suspecting it could be something extraordinary. I doubted that she was even aware of this.

After a day of traveling, we arrived in the star system. The sun is a large, stable, red star, and the gas giant, Chihetu, is in a safe orbit. Several layers of Chihetu's atmosphere protect it from ultraviolet and cosmic rays. Some layers of the atmosphere host immense quantities of plankton-like organisms. Exobiologists call them aeroplankton. They are the main food source for the dragons. There are no predators in the ecosystem, apart from the dragons consuming the aeroplankton. Perhaps that explains the friendliness and openness of the dragons on Chihetu. Though there has not been a hint of any danger to them, the Filoi, ever since they were first encountered, protect and guard the system. Many suspect the Chihetu dragons must have encountered hostile life forms at some point in their development, and likely have some unknown defense mechanism. The Filoi hope to never have reason to discover what it is.

"Wow, what a beautiful planet. There are so many colors. Are there storms, like Jupiter has?"

"Good morning, Zoe. I thought you would appreciate this live projection, to wake up to. Yes, there are several areas that have cyclonic activity. There's heat coming from the planet's core, due to its great mass, along with the heat from their sun. That and the planet's rotation result in many active weather patterns. The colors are real, I haven't changed them, except to brighten them a little, and I had to dampen the red somewhat. It is a beautiful planet."

———————◆O◆———————

Eleni, with her passenger, approached the planet and entered an orbit just touching the upper reaches of the atmosphere. She could feel the presence of many dragons. She recognized several of them. Soon, Eleni's presence was known to all of them.

———————◆O◆———————

Eleni, welcome back. You are not alone. You brought someone with you.

Ouron, the Filoi send greetings. I was asked by a mutual friend to visit you and I, of course, immediately accepted. I do have a passenger. Do you remember Helena Eliades?

Yes, indeed. She told us her daughter would visit in the future. Is she your passenger?

Yes. She is here. She is a young girl, and I believe there is much that is still hidden from her. Her name is Zoe. Zoe Eliades.

This is a great honor. To be visited by the daughter of Aegeus and Helena Eliades. Will she dream with us?

I don't know. She does wish to meet, though.

Good. We welcome you and Zoe Eliades.

———————◆O◆———————

"Zoe, they've welcomed us and invite us to come meet them. This is your decision. We can simply orbit the planet, or we can enter the lower layers of the atmosphere, and then meet and talk with them. Perhaps you would enjoy riding with them through their atmosphere. I believe they would be happy to do that with you. There is protective clothing for you to wear that keeps a breathable atmosphere around you."

"Eleni, thank you. I've worn those before, and yes, I really want to see them. If I can ride a dragon, that would be the most extraordinary, the most amazing thing ever."

———◦———

Zoe recalled what that day was like.

I remember looking at my hands, because they were shaking. I grabbed onto some protrusions of skin and there was a depression I sat in, and it formed around me like a saddle. Eleni had traveled down, through several layers of the atmosphere, and Ouron came right up to the ship. I simply stepped out of the door and sat down on Ouron's neck. Looking down below, it was like the ocean, a deep, translucent, cobalt blue.

I felt Ouron's presence as soon as I sat down. Eleni was right. I felt so safe. There was this sense of great concern from Ouron, like he was holding an egg. Yet, I was riding this massive, powerful, enormous, creature. It was just an incredible feeling. He was moving under me. I could feel him pulsing, and his muscles were moving in different directions. I had a surprising realization. Ouron is a creature of immeasurable wisdom and immense power, completely apart from his physical size.

We took off, like a rocket, and the saddle depression pushed up and supported my back. I was on the most remarkable roller coaster ride in the entire galaxy. Traveling in and out of the mist, I spotted other dragons, and other creatures of various shapes. I saw a manta ray creature bigger than a house, but it was minuscule compared to Ouron. As we twisted and turned, I noticed the undulating motion of a dragon's tail, and I realized it was Ouron's. We dived, and went through clouds and mists of green, white, and blue. My hair flew up and down, and I realized why my mother braided it. Of course, she knew!

Zoe, all of us are so happy you are here to visit.

I am happy too. This is just so amazing to be here, and fly through the air with you.

I saw a white and black dragon come closer, and for a while it traveled alongside us. Then, slowly, it rubbed against Ouron's middle section, and though I did not see it, I felt its tail wrap around Ouron's. Its main body went up over us, and it wrapped completely around us! I felt all of it. I felt its warmth, its skin pressing against and rubbing along their entire length. Now I sensed and felt both of the dragons, their bodies, and their minds. They loved each other. I felt they loved me. Then, I understood the great comfort, and the joy, that comes from no longer being separate, no longer being just one lonely soul.

I looked to my left and I saw the new dragon's head right next to me.

Zoe, do you have any dreams?

Yes, I do. But I really hardly ever remember them. I'm sure my dreams are not interesting. I'm just turning sixteen.

Look to your left, Zoe.

I was unsure what that meant. I looked to my left, at the incredible dragon and its very large head. I saw its right eye, looking at me. I saw myself reflected in it.

Both the dragons, together, flew upwards, almost vertically. Then, together, they curved down and dived. We went faster and faster through layers of atmosphere, with different clouds, densities, colors, and temperatures.

I looked to my left once more. I saw myself reflected in the dragon's eye, again. But, something was off. I was wearing different clothes. I was wearing a tunic. My hair wasn't braided – it was in a ponytail. And, I was looking straight ahead. Was that me? How could that be?

CHAPTER 30: COLONEL TRAVINSKY

Colonel Igor Travinsky, on special assignment from the Russian Aerospace Forces, was sweating profusely. The command's radar, a phased array Voronezh-VP, detected a clear object flying over Russian territory at over Mach 3. No IFF response. Over the last thirty minutes, its altitude changed drastically, back and forth, from 25,000 meters to below the radar's coverage. He knew what it was, and it was not the Americans. He was hoping it would go away, disappear. It didn't. So he gave the order to shoot it down. The order was given and a special Mig-29 Fulcrum was ordered into action. It was armed with two Vympel R-37 hypersonic air-to-air missiles, one attached to a pylon on each wing. The pilot, Sergei Shaskovich, has practiced this scenario before. He would go up to 18,000 meters, get a radar lock on the target, and fire both missiles simultaneously.

Fifteen minutes later, Major Shaskovich, Russian Aerospace Forces, contacted the controller at the radar base. "Vector requested, at 10,000 meters and climbing. Heading is 075 degrees."

With Colonel Travinsky watching over his shoulder the radar operator, Sergeant Ivan Yeltsei responded. "Target 30 degrees left of your current heading, come to new course 045. Range 20 kilometers. Altitude 15,500 meters."

Several minutes passed. Major Shaskovich reported in. "Target detected. Missiles locked."

Colonel Travinsky, hoping he would not regret it, gave the order. "Destroy target."

Major Shaskovich never heard it. There was a brilliant flash of light for a fraction of a second. His plane suddenly jumped up in altitude, as if a hand grabbed it and yanked it up. The red light on his missile control panel lit up. He flipped the toggle switch back and forth. It stayed red. It was like he had no missiles at all. His peripheral vision noticed a small shadow, a dot that passed by. When he turned his head, he lost his breath. A black oval, a fifty-meter-long egg, was flying right off his wing, keeping formation with him. He blinked, not trusting his vision. When he looked again, he saw it travel, at an unimaginable speed, to the horizon, and disappear. Only then did he hear desperate voices on his radio, demanding a response.

CHAPTER 31: I GO DOWNTOWN

I needed to do something, anything, to break up the mind-numbing routine I was stuck in. The medication I was prescribed did nothing for me. I felt like any sense of purpose in me had evaporated. Quite suddenly, I felt old. Well, I suppose I am old, but not ridiculously old. There's a difference. Right? I want to believe there's a difference. I suppose people in their twenties will disagree and snicker. I'm sure I would in my twenties. I know I haven't made much difference in life. I haven't changed history. My name won't be found in history books. It certainly is not in Wikipedia. I pondered whether my mood was an accurate reflection of reality, or merely the result of too many of those energy drinks. Probably both. If I had enough motivation I would have long ago closed up shop, sold, just plain give away all my stuff, it's junk anyway, and traveled far and wide. It would make so much sense to do that. Why didn't I? Maybe being just lazy, and too comfortable. But, it's more than that. It seemed like I was trapped in an almost robotic routine.

Years ago I attended a Catholic mass with a friend who dragged me along. The Jesuit priest performing the service talked about suffering in the world. He said that, of course, life is not a rose garden, but it was never intended to be. We are here on Earth to overcome hardship, disability, and be challenged by the obstacles we encounter. We're not supposed to stay at home and avoid the world. We are expected to, and we are obligated to, go out into the world and meet it head-on, and we should expect to suffer while doing so.

That memory came back to me. I think it is the complete opposite of what is known in the evangelical community as the "Prosperity Gospel." I think I'd go with the Jesuits if I had to choose between the two. One, the Jesuits, invariably, are extremely well-educated. Two, it's right there in Genesis. God kicked Adam and Eve out of the Garden of Eden, to make life miserable for them. He outright told them that. How do those who push the Prosperity Gospel explain that away? Are they going to argue with God?

The same day, and this is strangely serendipitous, I came across a speech by Teddy Roosevelt. Apparently, it's a well-known, celebrated speech. I think I've got to start reading more often because I never came across it before:

> "It is not the critic who counts: not the man who points out how the strong man stumbles or where the doer of deeds could have done better. The credit belongs to the man who is actually in the arena, whose face is marred by dust and sweat and blood, who strives valiantly, who errs and comes up short again and again, because there is no effort without error or shortcoming, but who knows the great enthusiasms, the great devotions, who spends himself in a worthy cause; who, at the best, knows, in the end, the triumph of high achievement, and who, at the worst, if he fails, at least he fails while daring greatly, so that his place shall never be with those cold and timid souls who knew neither victory nor defeat."

Those words from 1910 chastened me. I was frustrated, and I became angry with myself. Despite the psychiatrist, despite the prescription drugs, I was still in the same state. I hopped in my SUV, got on I-70, and started driving west, towards downtown, like so many times I've done in the past. I'm not quite sure, but I likely would have continued driving until I reached the Pacific Ocean. Except, fate intervened.

As happens too often, traffic was backed up, from an accident, or construction, or something. I turned right, exiting onto Old U.S. Highway 40. The section I found myself on is a ringer for the old Route 66, parts of which still can be found across the country. I passed some old restaurants and lounges, The Bamboo Hut, The Sandbar, and a few others. They still have a clientele and are hanging on. In their heyday, before I-70 was built, they were considered fashionable and exotic, and would regularly host a parade of celebrities from Kansas City. Nearby are old motor inns, with individual cabins for travelers. I'm sure all of them are eligible for designations as historic landmarks. There was fog, and it was strange driving through it on that stretch of roadway.

A few minutes after I exited onto Highway 40, I noticed a yellow warning light. My fuel gauge showed the gas tank was close to empty. Apart from running out of gas, the low fuel light seemed to me to be a premonition of something, a yellow caution signal. That, and the fog, caused some alarm.

There was a gas station on the right, so I turned off and drove into the lot. I pulled up to the pump. After I got out, I noticed a paper note taped to the pump, stating everything had to be prepaid inside. I locked my car and walked over to the front door of this somewhat sketchy convenience store, which wasn't part of any chain.

Walking in, I straight off realized I'd made a mistake. I had just stumbled into the middle of the latest episode of our ongoing American tragedy. Three robbers, in masks, stopped and looked at me. One of them, behind the counter, and behind the plexiglass window, seemed to be in charge. A grown man, he was holding on to the bleeding teenage female store cashier's hair, blood coming out of her smashed nose. With his other hand, he attempted to point a gun at me. It collided with the plexiglass.

The other two were just large kids. Still, the nearest one looked to the man behind the plexiglass and then turned to me. He yelled, "Get on the ground, motherfucker!"

I stood there, dumbfounded. I didn't move. Something was wrong with me. I should have been frightened. I should have been getting on the ground to avoid getting my brains blown out. Instead, I looked at all of them and I smirked. I couldn't even believe I was acting like that.

The kid who yelled at me turned to his buddy standing by him and said, "Cut this fucker, man."

This kid pulled out a six-inch blade, making a couple of strides towards me. Once he was in arm's reach, I did something he certainly didn't expect, nor me. I suddenly reached out, grabbed his wrist, and jerked him closer. I wrapped my other arm over the top of his, with my hand first going down and then up, pushing against his shoulder blade, trapping him half bent over. I'm sure it was the last thing he expected me to do. It was for me.

I heard myself speak.

"It's time to get the hell out of here, while you're still alive."

The other one pulled out an even bigger knife and walked towards me. On my left, I spotted a push broom, with a long wooden shaft. I grabbed it with my free hand. I whipped it around, and the brush head slammed against the side of his head, shearing off the shaft and spiraling across the aisles. He sprawled onto the floor, out cold. The other kid wiggled free, just in time for me to whip the broom shaft against the front of his face. He ended up on the floor, next to his buddy.

The guy who had the cashier by her hair saw all this and went to the exit door from the cashier area. As he opened the door, he started to raise his gun. I had the broom shaft in my hand, with the broken off end. Instinctively, using it as a spear, I threw it at him. It was gruesome, and effective.

Looking at what the result was, I felt an overwhelming sense of deja vu.

Whenever the two kids lying on the store wake up, they'll be in handcuffs and charged with felony murder. I hope I won't be appointed to represent them in juvenile court.

I looked at the girl. "Are you okay? Do you have a phone?"

In tears, she shook her head up and down.

"You need to call your mom, dad, brother, sister, somebody to help you here. Okay?"

She barely whispered, "Okay."

I looked around for the surveillance cameras. I pointed them out to her. "Do these work?"

"Sometimes."

"Where's the recorder?"

She pointed to the door behind her. I hopped the counter, went inside, and found it. DVD, 4K. I pushed the eject button, the disk popped out. I grabbed it and stuck it down my pants.

I walked out back to the front. I reached out and grabbed her shoulders. "You can't work in a place like this. It will not end well. I've got to go. Call 911. Call your family. It will be alright. Okay?"

She looked at me with glazed eyes. She was in shock. I could hardly hear her say, "Alright."

I looked around for the store phone. Grabbing a rag, I used it to pick up the receiver and punch in 911.

I gave them the name of the store, and said there's been a robbery. They had guns. A young girl is there working as the cashier. The 911 operator asked who I was. I said I'm just a witness walking by. After that, I hung up.

I looked at the cashier, nodded my head, and left.

Driving back home, I thought about what just happened. So, life changes unexpectedly. Once again. A famous author, Cathleen Schine, once wrote, "Life is full of surprises. Why is that always surprising?" Well, it was.

It's pretty much a given that whatever mind-numbing routine I was trapped in just got obliterated. What happened wasn't one of the suggestions Google Assistant listed. My brain fog started to lift. Teddy Roosevelt would be proud. Also, Teddy Roosevelt would be pissed. I realized I could remember things that are so incredible, things that are so unbelievable, that it seemed impossible they could have been forgotten. Things that I dreamed. They were not just mere dreams. They were real. The psychiatrist was right. Carl Jung was right. My subconscious actually was attempting to communicate with me. It was trying to tell me that I had a completely different life, that I was part of a radically different reality. It was in full Samuel L. Jackson mode, and it was telling me to wake the hell up!

There was something back at my place I needed to get. If it's real, if it's actually there, maybe I'm not a raving mad lunatic.

CHAPTER 32: APOTHEOSIS

"Occasionally, we dream of a past as it occurs." Zoe Eliades

I woke suddenly. Our rooster was crowing. The sun was just rising. Thankfully, there was plenty of time to grab the hydria and fetch water from the well for breakfast. What a strange dream! I was flying in the air with dragons! It felt so real. I'll tell my mother about it at the table. Perhaps it means something.

Getting up, I rubbed my eyes. I put on my tunic. I grabbed a leather cord and tied it around my hair, making a ponytail. I walked out of my room towards the front door, picking up the old hydria along the way. I heard another rooster, our neighbor's, and some small birds were chirping. They were getting an early start at finding whatever they find. I saw my friends at the next two houses and waved at them. We all got on the path to the well. I hugged Chara while we walked. I saw Orien up ahead and run after him. We got into a foot race to the well, like we've done so many years. We were both laughing by the time we reached it. The soft fields of barley looked like golden ocean waves, even with just a light breeze. Some more houses now had thin trails of smoke rising from their chimneys.

This has been my village all through my childhood. My friends are here, and I've taken lessons here. My father travels a lot, but he is always here when we need him. Strangely, my mother travels too, but there's always one of them around. My mother tells me that on my sixteenth birthday, there's a surprise. That's today!

Walking back, with some water splashing, we are much slower. The old beggar woman is in our village. I call her that, but she's not. She never begs. It's just that all of us give her food and water. She is very kind. I'm not sure where she goes and comes from.

She was close to the path, so I walked over to her.

"Hello, Inricea. Good morning to you. Would you like some water? I have it filled up if you'd like."

She was sitting on a log, but looks over and smiles at me. "Good morning, Dionaea. Thank you so much. You are always so kind to an old woman like me!"

I always found it strange that she would know my name, but she always remembers.

"How could I not be? You are a friend to all of us."

For some unknown reason, there was a wistful look on her face, and tears in her eyes.

"Inricea, why are you crying?"

"Oh, Dionaea. It's nothing bad. It's just that you've grown up. Today is your birthday, right?"

I smiled, remembering that. But I felt bad Inricea was crying. Maybe my birthday made her feel older.

"That's nothing to cry about. I'm just a year older."

She laughed. "Well, you're right. It's just that, for you, it's special."

I said, "Thank you," not knowing what else to say.

Making it back to my house, I saw my mother looking in the distance. There was a sail, from a galley that apparently just landed on the beach, down below. It wasn't my father's ship.

I hugged her. She looked at me and said, "Happy birthday, my beautiful daughter. Let's just stay inside for a little."

That was alarming. She seemed worried. I saw her looking at Inricea.

There was yelling in the distance, from the road between our village and the sea.

Looking at Peirate while hiking up the slope, the first mate stated his thoughts. "Perhaps this is not a wise action. We need rowers, and more slaves to sell, but this is a Greek village."

Peirate was a pirate. But he was also a slaver. Athens had an insatiable need for more and more slaves, to work its silver mines. Peirate sold all his slaves to them, for a good price. But now they were short on rowers. They needed more, badly. Then, from the sea, they saw the chimney smoke from this village.

Peirate replied. "It will be of no consequence. We will not sell them to Greeks. We will use them up on our ship. After that, we'll sell them to the Persians. They will happily buy them, even if they are used up, because they are Greek."

Peirate had fifty men. They were all tired of rowing. They gladly went with him to grab as many villagers as possible to ease their burden on the ship.

They took their weapons, nets, and ropes, and followed the road to the village.

Dionaea's village was small, with perhaps fifty houses, several hundred inhabitants. They did not believe that there would be pirates, slavers, invading their peaceful settlement. It was unheard of, and a complete surprise, to most of them. By the time they realized this, the pirates, the slavers, were in the middle of the town, seizing anyone they saw. Several of the villagers attempted to defend it, with their poles and swords. Nets were thrown on them. They were knocked down, and tied with ropes. There were too many to fight off. Yet, the pirates did not kill them. They were only of value alive. Several women and children ran toward the other end of the village, but that way was blocked by a group of Peirate's men.

I was shocked, stunned, to see my friends, the children I grew up with, struck, and tied, with rope wrapped around their necks. I started crying, then I became angry, furious. I ran towards them, tackling one of the evil men. I clawed at his face. He threw me off, laughing. They pinned me to the ground and bound me with ropes.

Inricea was standing away from me, watching all this. The pirates seemed to ignore her, perhaps because she was elderly, and of no use to them as a slave.

The unthinkable began to happen. One of the pirates, grabbing Chara, knocked her to the ground, ripped her tunic, and undid his belt.

I heard my name called. Looking around, I saw Inricea gazing at me, and calling out.

"Dionaea, today is your birthday!"

I stood there, looking at her, thinking Inricea has gone crazy.

"Dionaea, today is your birthday. Today, you are sixteen."

I looked at Chara. She saw me. She was crying, hysterical, and screamed for help. Yet, my hands were tied. How could I help her?

In the midst of all this there came a sudden, strange silence, as if everyone knew something was changing. A warm wind blew in from the sea. I felt it on my face. It grew stronger. It was no ordinary wind, and it carried a whisper of music. Sometimes, music brings back memories. This music was familiar. It was from a different time. A different place. It was sacred music, and it brought back sacred memories.

I held my hands up and studied them. My hands. They seemed larger. I barely moved, and the ropes binding them burst apart, with a sharp cracking sound, startling everyone. The ropes fell to the ground. I looked around. I was taller, much taller. I looked at my hands again. They were glowing.

I am sixteen years old today. I am sixteen, and I remember who I am.

I saw my mother. There were tears in her eyes. She looked at me, in awe. And she had the widest smile, the most magnificent grin, I've ever seen.

The filth, the pirate, who touched Chara, I looked at him, and he gaped at me in sudden terror. I changed him into the snake he was. Chara did not hesitate. With glee, she stomped on him, squashing him into the dirt.

I walked towards Inricea and smiled. She smiled back, and I recalled that smile from other places, and other times. I stopped and turned around, facing the pirates. They looked up to me, with fright and horror, and averted their faces.

These pirates were not Greek. If they were, they would never have come here, to do this, at the village of Dion, the village where we live, on the foothills of Mount Olympus. The sacred village, where the Temple of Zeus is located. Zeus, king of the gods, who lives on Mount Olympus. Zeus, who is my father. Yes, I am Dionaea. I know that. Sometimes I am called Cytherea, which in Greek means Lady of Cythera. I have had many roles through the ages and I have been given many names. But, always, I have been a goddess, and though people have forgotten, a warrior goddess.

I looked up to the mountain and I saw his lightning bolts. Thunder reverberated through the village. The ground shook. My father was angry. This group of slavers and pirates followed my gaze and saw the purple, churning, storm clouds, filled with lightning, at the top of the mountain.

Looking at these evil men, I knew their fate. I would arrange it for them.

"Brash, ignorant men. You have profaned our village. Your wretched desire to enslave others can be sated elsewhere. There are men north of here, who are not Greek, who are of ill will, who you may enslave, to work the silver mines of Athens. That is, if you believe you possess the strength to capture them. Do you? You will see them on the shore. I bid you fair winds to sail there."

They stood there, petrified with fear.

"Now, flee to your ship, evil men. I am not cruel, but if you hesitate, if you look back, I will turn you into pigs."

Stumbling and crying, they fled to their ship. Pushing it off the beach, they unfurled its sail, on which was painted an eye-catching design. The wind filled it, and sped them to their fate.

I sing of Her, gold-crowned and beautiful, whose dominion is the villages and cities of all Hellas.

The moist breath of the western wind wafted her over the waves of the loud-moaning sea in soft foam.

And there the gold-adorned daughters welcomed her joyously.

They clothed her with heavenly garments, which the daughters themselves wear when they go to their Father's house to join the lovely dances of the gods.

And when they had fully decked her, they brought her to the gods, who welcomed her when they saw her, giving her their hands.

Each of them prayed her to be his wedded wife, so greatly were they amazed at the beauty of violet-crowned Cytherea.

Hail, sweetly-winning, coy-eyed goddess! Hear my song.

Eternal goddess, remember us this day.

Chapter 33: More Russians

Miloslav Volkov was a happy man. His life had turned out well. He had an American wife, two children, and a beautiful house. His business was successful. He was worried after the Russian Federation invaded Ukraine. He was, after all, its Honorary Consul in Kansas City. Technically, his law office was the local Russian Consulate. But, people in Kansas City are a friendly lot, and they understood his parents emigrated from Russia thirty years ago, when he was a young teenager. Since then, he became fluent in English, started using Michael as his first name, attended college and subsequently obtained a law degree from U.M.K.C. Taking advantage of his Russian heritage, and his fluency in Russian, he developed an expertise in immigration law. The major corporations in town came to him when they needed an individual from abroad to obtain legal status so he or she could legally work for them. They paid very well. In addition, he received legal business from the many Eastern European immigrants in the area.

Tuesday was always a good day, after all the immediate crises over the weekend were resolved on Monday. Walking into the front door of his office on Holmes Street in Midtown, he thought not too much of the two middle-aged gentlemen sitting in chairs in the reception area. They looked up at him as he smiled and waved on his way through the next door to his office.

After settling in, his secretary, Sarah Whittaker, came in.

"The two gentlemen sitting in reception would like to see you. They don't have an appointment."

"What do they want?"

"They didn't say. Except one of them did mention they knew your parents."

"Mike" Volkov caught his breath. Because, he did not know his real parents. The ones who claimed they were when he immigrated to America, he knew, were in the KGB, and deep undercover. For that matter, initially, so was he. Even though they immigrated to America when he was fourteen. When he was twelve, he was recruited from an orphan's home in St. Petersburg and considered himself fortunate to be selected. After he completed college, they were recalled back to Russia. He chose to remain in America. He was never called upon. He moved away to the Midwest, to Kansas City, and attended law school. That earlier part of his life was long forgotten.

He felt himself starting to perspire. His stomach tightened. "Okay, have them come back." Then, catching himself, he said, "No wait, I'll get them."

Walking through the door to the reception area, Mike smiled, reached out his hand and greeted them. "Privyet."

They both stood up. They were not smiling. The closer one said, "Zdravstvuyte. We speak American, if that is easier for you."

Mike looked at him with some apprehension, because he sensed that was an insult.

"Well, then, alright. Let's go back to my office."

After walking back to his office, they sat down. Mike sat down in his desk chair. One of them then promptly stood up and began inspecting the different photos and certificates in his office.

"Miloslav Volkov, you've made quite a life for yourself here in the middle of America. You've come far, since your time at the Polnaya Alekseevsky Orphanage in St. Petersburg."

Mike Volkov closed his eyes and took a deep breath. "Yes, I've been very lucky." Obviously, these men wanted something from him.

"We're here from Mother Russia. We hope you haven't forgotten who you are."

"It's been a long time. No one has ever asked anything of me."

"Listen kozyol, Mother Russia needs your services. You will assist us, will you not?"

"Of course, it's just been a long time. Tell me what I can do for you."

The two visitors looked at each other and smiled. The one sitting down stood up and reached into his sports jacket. Mike braced himself. It seemed he was going to take out a gun. Instead, a long rolled-up paper was pulled out.

Rolling out the paper on the desk, the man said "My name is Fyodor Kiselev. This is my first time in Kansas City. We have business here. This photograph is from one of our assets. Don't ask me what."

Looking at it, Mike realized it was a high resolution satellite photo of a wooded area, with several roads on the sides. The roads were labeled.

"This is what we want. We need you to research this property. Find out who bought it, when, and find out who is living there right now. It has to be done in a completely secret manner."

Mike Volkov figured he could find out online or by visiting the courthouse. The county recorder has maps of the entire county, with each parcel's legal description. With the legal description, he could easily get a title history and trace ownership. The tax records also have a public database.

Mike Volkov looked at them and smiled. "Okay, this is no problem. I have completed several real estate transactions for my clients. The property records in this county are well-organized and accessible. When do you need this?"

The two Russian agents looked at each other and then at Mike. "Tomorrow."

"Alright. I'll get right on it. How do I contact you?"

"You don't. We'll come by tomorrow at noon, Da?"

"So be it. Tomorrow at noon then."

The men seemed to be in a happier mood. They shook hands and left. Mike was not too bothered by the deadline. He'd done title searches on deadline before and could get it ready by then. He figured he could do most of this online and may not even have to visit the courthouse. It would depend on what he found.

The FSB, the successor to the KGB, was mystified by the disappearance of their agents, right when they received a report that a technological breakthrough by the Americans was successfully stolen. They already knew of Raymond Langstaff. After the event, when the plane they were on went missing, their other assets in the area noted Mr. Langstaff's reappearance. The Russian Federation operates dozens of spy satellites, of all types. One of them, with very good cameras, actually followed Langstaff's automobile to the residence and surrounding forest that was on the photograph given to Mike Volkov. As it turned out, other satellites detected a number of anomalies that either went to this location, or departed from it. This aroused their curiosity even more. The United States has a very open society. So, it was relatively easy to send several additional assets to the Kansas City area from New York and D.C. An elite Spetsnaz unit, assigned to the FSB, was smuggled in via the southern border, with assistance from one of the cartels they had relationships with. They were going to retrieve their agents, or exact revenge.

Mike Volkov did do a title search. What it came up with piqued his interest. Deeds were filed in the nineteenth century documenting ownership by the Younger family, a prominent family in Lee's Summit. Indeed, until a few years ago, the city had an annual festival, the Cole Younger Days. Yes, the Cole Younger who was close friends with Jesse James and Frank James and rode with William Quantrill and Bloody Bill Anderson as members of Quantrill's Raiders. The guerrilla group that rode into Lawrence, Kansas, burned it to the ground, slaughtered almost two hundred unarmed, defenseless men and boys, and thereafter leisurely rode down to South Texas. It was described as a mass execution. After the Civil War, Cole Younger continued his ugly career as a member of the James-Younger gang, along with Jesse and Frank James. They participated in the first daylight bank robbery in the United States, and began robbing trains, sometimes by derailing them, stagecoaches, and other banks in at least a dozen states throughout the middle of the country, callously murdering many innocent people along the way. The Younger family, including brothers Jim, John and Bob, all had interests in the land.

There have always been rumors that all the money, paper and gold and silver, that the Younger and James brothers had collected through their long criminal careers was hidden at various places in the county. Many said that the loot was hidden in caves that only members of the James and Younger families knew of. Money laundering in that time was not a sophisticated practice, as it is now, and it would have been very difficult for members of the Younger or James families, or their close friends, to spend large sums of money, or sell gold, without creating a great deal of suspicion.

Mike Volkov researched all of this. The large parcel of land that was in the satellite photograph given him was still wooded, completely undeveloped except for one large house with several structures nearby. There was title in the Younger family until it was purchased by an Aegeus and Helena Eliades in 1955. What was striking is that title has never changed since. That's seventy years ago. It must have changed hands since then. But there was absolutely nothing in the property or tax records to indicate that. Mike Volkov studied the satellite photo more closely.

The man who called himself Fyodor Kiselev, along with his partner, returned the next day. Mike Volkov gave him a full title report, and told them it was very odd that there were no real estate transactions for the property since 1955. The Russians maintained their poker faces. He left out any information about Jesse James, Cole Younger, and hidden treasure.

Mr. Kiselev, as he was getting ready to leave, faced Mike Volkov and said, "I want to remind you that this is completely secret, we never came here, this never happened, and to never tell anyone. Is that understood?"

"Yes, completely."

The other man walked over to the window. Looking out, he stated, "We want to make sure you understand this. You have a window in your office. Windows are very dangerous, da?"

Mike Volkov paled. He looked down and then said, "Da, I understand completely."

It began in the early morning. The location was thoroughly scouted by the Spetsnaz unit. They searched for a time and finally saw a small opening at the far eastern end of the wooded tract. The target, the Eliades residence, was located at the western end, with a driveway leading up to it. The plan was to enter through the opening in the bramble, and work their way through the woods until they reached the residence. There, they would cut off the electric and telephone lines. Fyodor Kiselev would go with the unit. His partner, the other FSB agent assigned to this, was in a van parked on the road going past the driveway, on the west side. In the van was an electronic device that would jam cell phone communications in the area. At some point, he was to travel up the driveway and collect whoever they'd captured.

The Spetsnaz leader, Egor Ostrovsky, thought this plan foolproof. As the sun was rising, they hopped out of a van at the eastern side. Running into the opening, they all were met by cobwebs and thorns that ripped at their clothes. Branches seemed to reach out, lashing their limbs. After twenty or thirty feet of making their way through that, they reached a more open area. Spiders were crawling over them and were in their hair. Disgusted, they spent the next several minutes brushing them off. Sergeant Ostrovsky looked around. He felt some disquiet. It seemed like a different world. This was a forest of shadows, and the shadows played tricks with one's eyesight. Hidden shapes seemed everywhere, concealed in shade. A forest creature suddenly darted past them, so quickly they were not quite sure what it was. The trees were very large, blocking out most of the light. The air was thick. They heard sounds. A piercing bugling call, perhaps from an elk. Next, a high-pitched barking. Most disturbing to them, they heard an animal roar in the distance.

Sergeant Ostrovsky looked to his men. Their faces did not display confidence. "Okay, spread out, five meters apart. Let's head west. Look for a trail."

Without being told, they took the safeties off their weapons and chambered rounds. Going forward, they weaved between the giant trees.

<hr />

Parked on the side of the road at the western side of the woods, Fyodor Kiselev's partner, who currently went by the name of Vitaliy Romanov, waited. He called on their radio but received only static. He turned on the cell phone jammer. Mr. Romanov was an assassin, a poisoner. He greatly enjoyed tossing people out of windows. He also considered himself a Russian intellectual, in the tradition of Nabokov, Pushkin and Tolstoy. He thought so mainly because he's read their novels. Therefore, he looked with contempt upon American culture.

He waited patiently. After a few minutes, he was surprised to see a van pull up behind him. Looking at the side mirror, he could see the driver was a rather heavy, middle-aged woman. Her van was filled with children.

She walked up to his door, with a big smile on her face. "Hi there. Are you stranded? Can we call someone for you?"

Vitaliy Romanov thought to himself. *Only in America would idiots do this.* "No. Everything is fine. Thank you for stopping."

"Okay, just checking."

As she drove off, it occurred to Vitaliy that people in this country were clueless. No where else would a woman stop and offer assistance to a man parked along an empty street.

A few minutes later, an elderly man in an ancient, decrepit pickup truck pulled alongside him and turned on his flashers. He rolled down his front passenger window.

"Hey buddy. You out of gas? I can give you a lift."

"No. I'm waiting for someone. I appreciate it."

"Okay then. Just checkin on ya."

As the old man drove off, Vitaliy Romanov shook his head. Looking at the back of the pickup as it passed by, he spotted a fake rubber scrotum dangling from its trailer hitch. With a contemptuous expression on his face, he thought to himself, *Look at that. Americans! Ignorant. Totally without any sense of culture. What is it with this place? Don't these Neanderthals mind their own business?*

Not more than two minutes later, he saw flashing red lights in his side mirror. *Oh, no.*

The attractive female officer approached his front side window. "Good morning sir. Can we be of any assistance? Are you out of gas? Will your vehicle not start? If you need a tow, we have a towing service we recommend that's agreed to a pre-set fee schedule."

Crazy fucking Americans. "Uh, no officer. I'm just waiting for someone to come here. I'm fine. Thank you. I'll be leaving very soon."

The police officer looked at him strangely. "Okay, sir. Mind if I ask? Just what are you doing parked out here?"

Thinking quickly, the FSB agent said, "I got lost. The person I am supposed to meet is coming here, so I can follow his car back." Vitaliy Romanov was left-handed. He wrapped it around the Glock nine millimeter squeezed in the door's side pocket.

"Okay. That's makes sense." She turned around and started walking away. Then, she turned back, and with one hand on her holster she stated, "Just as a matter of routine could I see your license and registration?"

He took a deep breath. "Sure. Let me find it." Just as he was raising his gun, he spotted two more police cars from the opposite direction rapidly cruising down the road towards him. Turning to his left, he was astonished to see the beautiful American police woman, with lightning speed, draw a .40 caliber Sig pistol and point it at his head. At that point, he then concluded that he truly, absolutely, despised American suburbs.

They found a trail. It was generally in a westward direction, so they started following it. They counted on reaching the residence in ten minutes tops. After a few minutes, they looked up to the sky. The sun was not where it was supposed to be. Instead of behind them, it was due north. One of the men pulled out his compass. The needle was going in circles.

The trail ended at a small open structure. It appeared to be a temple of some sort. It was made out of marble, with Doric columns. A worn, grooved, and discolored stone table was in the middle of the stained stone floor. Above the front, there were sculptures of horses, men with spears and chariots chiseled into the marble. They heard a sound, off to the side. Looking quickly, they all saw him. A man's face visible, between the brush, then he disappeared. There was a movement, and the sound of a horse galloping away. They all looked at each other.

Sergeant Ostrovsky used his short-range radio and attempted to contact Vitaliy Romanov. There was just static. Looking at his cell phone, it displayed a series of ones and zeroes over and over. He looked over at Fyodor Kiselev.

"Okay, what the hell is this place? What's going on?"

Fyodor Kiselev was confused and disturbed by all of this. It was supposed to be a simple operation, and yet they were now lost in what should have been a very small tract of woods.

One of the men pointed it out. A bright light a distance away, rapidly zigzagging through the trees. It was a brilliant, platinum-white ball of light. It moved almost instantaneously from one part of the forest to another. Approaching the men, it grew larger. In a heartbeat, it stopped directly in front of them. It was the size of a car, floating in the air, and glowed so brilliantly they could not look directly at it. Attempting to block the light, they raised their hands, and saw the bones silhouetted inside them, with their skin a translucent red. Sergeant Ostrovsky felt himself rising in the air. Only the tips of his boots were touching the ground. Then, instantaneously, it disappeared. Leaving only an afterimage burned into their eyes.

Afterward, they all stood still, in complete silence, in shock.

Sergeant Ostrovsky recovered his senses first. Boiling with fear and rage, he looked around and spotted the FSB agent. He pondered shooting him dead.

"Kiselev, you bastard. What the fuck was that? What in the hell is going on here? What have you gotten us into?"

"I don't know. I don't have any idea what's going on here. This is insane. Whatever it is, it doesn't make sense. Forget the fucking house. We need to get the hell out of here. Let's just go back."

"Okay asshole. Fine. But tell me, which way do we go to 'just go back'?"

They wandered in the woods for several hours. At one point, Sergeant Ostrovsky thought he smelled ocean air, which made no sense. Eventually, they noticed sunlight ahead, and an apparent end to the forest. As they approached it, they felt their grip on reality loosening. The elite Spetsnaz unit and the FSB agent found themselves on a bluff. From that unexpected promontory, they gazed out over a wine-dark sea, meeting a bronze-colored sky at the horizon. To their right, a galley rowed across the water. It slowly turned to port as its main sail was raised. An enormous eye was painted on the sail. As it turned to face them, the wind shook the sail, and it looked as if the eye, gazing at them, winked.

CHAPTER 34: TREASURE HUNT

Miloslav Volkov was excited. He went out and purchased a metal detector and on Saturday told his wife and kids he had to work at the office. Instead, he drove out to Lee's Summit to go treasure hunting in the forest. The more he researched the prior owners of the land the FSB agents wanted to know about, and the more he looked at the maps on the land, the more he convinced himself that he could find the James-Younger gang treasure. The treasure obtained by years of robbing banks, stagecoaches, and trains, and all the murders that went along with that. Collectors would pay millions for the coins alone. He could find nothing to indicate where the loot had been spent or where it might have been taken. The only plausible explanation is that it was still hidden somewhere. What better place than somewhere in the forest that their family owned for so long? Earlier in the week, he stopped at a sporting goods store and purchased a pair of hiking boots. Standing in front of a full length mirror, he very much liked the way they looked.

He drove around the tract of woods several times, stopping and starting. Finally, he saw a break in the brambles and bushes. He drove down the street and found a place to park his car behind a row of shrubs overrun with weeds. Before going any further, he sprayed himself down with bug spray. Miloslav Volkov hated bugs. Taking his cell phone, a folding shovel, and his new metal detector, he walked up the street to where he spotted the break. Yes, a trail was there, so he pushed his way in. He knew he was trespassing, but he felt it was far enough away from any houses so no one would notice. Besides, he was a lawyer. He could talk his way out of any trouble.

In the very first minute, he began to regret this whole undertaking. He walked into spiderwebs that wrapped around his face. Thorns on the vines and branches raked and gouged his forearms. Still, he kept on going, and after some distance he broke into the open. His ears picked up a different set of sounds from just a few minutes ago out on the street. An owl was hooting and the sounds of frogs or toads would start up, and stop when he was walking. But, other than that, there was strange silence. No wind blowing, no sounds from car traffic. No noise from airplanes and jets traveling far up in the sky. It smelled differently, too. It was a woody smell, maybe from all the old bark on the large trees. That, and a wet earth odor. Walking a little further, he heard something that alarmed him. It was faint, very far away. The sound of a flute. A single instrument playing a tune. There was an eerie, haunting quality to it. It had to be from some distance away, and he concluded that the only reason he heard it was because it was so quiet.

Looking around, he thought about how to approach his search. He decided it was only logical that, if treasure was buried, whoever did it would have wanted a landmark for figuring out its location later. The trees looked like they could be used as landmarks. But, there were quite a few of them, and they all looked like they were several hundred years old. Still, he might as well start. Turning on the metal detector, he adjusted the signal gain and began a sweeping motion around the nearest large tree. He proceeded to do this several times, going from tree to tree, without any solid signal. He tested the machine earlier in the week with some silver and a gold ring, so he knew what a good response would look and sound like. After a good twenty minutes, he took a break.

This is going nowhere, he thought. *I'll just hike around for a while.*

So "Mike" Volkov walked around the forest, eventually coming across a trail. Taking the trail made things a bit easier, and he followed it for around fifteen minutes. There was a small creek he stepped over. Looking ahead, there was a sharp slope into a ravine. He walked up to it and took a peek. His heart jumped. There was a cave opening.

Standing outside the cave and looking in, he considered his options. This might be his only opportunity. He had his cell phone, with a built-in flashlight. There's no harm in just going a few feet inside to check it out. So Miloslav Volkov took the first step, then the second. Switching on his cell phone flashlight, he pointed it around. The cave continued on into darkness. It was about five feet high, He was five and a half feet, so he bent over while looking around. Taking some more steps, he crept around a bend in the cave. Switching on his metal detector, he swept it back and forth, and was disappointed there was no signal. Looking back towards the entrance to verify its location, he walked forward a little to cover more ground. There was a beep! He narrowed the sweep to where he thought the loop was when it beeped. Again, a distinct signal. Kneeling down, he brushed away some of the damp soil, and used his fingers to dig a little. Using the detector once more, he narrowed it to a clod of dirt. Pulling it apart, he found a coin. Spitting on it and wiping the mud off on his pants, he could see an image of a woman with a diadem on her head. On the back were three "I"s. He assumed that meant the Roman numeral three. Looking closer at the side with the face, he saw a very small number below it, "1870!" Exuberant, throwing caution to the wind, he walked some more into the cave. Sweeping the metal detector back and forth, he forgot to keep track of his position. There was another beep, a stronger signal. Digging through the dirt, he found this one too. A smaller coin, a dime. Or, actually a "Half Dime," which was what was printed on its back. He wondered if there was silver in it.

A half hour later, Miloslav Volkov suddenly realized he had foolishly walked himself into a serious predicament. He played the light around. There were two passages. He was not sure which one he came from. To his left, he noticed there was something chiseled into the cave wall. Around a foot long, it was an image of a double edge ax, with a handle. The edges were curved, like crescent moons. Slowly walking some more down a passageway, he noticed a faint pattern scratched into the wall. Examining it more closely, it appeared to be the diagram of a maze. He hoped it would show the way to the exit, and it seemed to do just that. He was not far away, and his despair started to dissipate.

There was a sound, like something striking a stone surface. He turned around towards it, and from the same direction came a deafening, reverberating roar. Some animal, something, was bellowing. It was echoing down the passageway. He froze. There was a beast in here with him. How could that be? He heard what had to be hooves, and they were getting louder. Looking around in a panic, he spotted a passageway behind him, away from that sound. Picking up his metal detector and his shovel, he darted down the passageway. Fearing he was going to become catatonic, he concentrated on his breathing. Looking at his phone, he desperately hoped to make a call. But, of course, there is no phone reception in the labyrinth.

———◆———

There was an extensive and well-publicized search for the missing attorney. Helicopters with infrared cameras were used. Hundreds of posters were printed and plastered all over the metropolitan area. He was well-liked by the legal and business community, so a great number of people participated in searches, along with most law enforcement agencies. He did not practice criminal law or divorce law, so there were no disgruntled clients or opposing parties who were motivated to do him in. His car wasn't located. It was green, parked behind thick weeds and shrubs, not visible from the street and mostly not visible from the air. After a week, the search petered out.

People started speculating. At every court hearing in Jackson County, the judges, attorneys, and clerks exchanged with each other the latest rumors they heard. Perhaps he had a midlife crisis. Maybe he wanted to return to Mother Russia. Possibly he was murdered in a seedy part of town while soliciting sex or attempting to purchase something illegal. But all of that was mere conjecture.

———◆———

Two weeks later, a delirious, shrieking, crazy man was reported running down the middle of State Highway 350, naked, in broad daylight. The Highway Patrol was called. He kept on screaming at the cars passing by about a half-man, half-bull, which was chasing and attempting to gore him. Also, there were centaurs. He saw them! He screamed at the officers who surrounded him, wanting them to make the guy playing the flute to just stop.

Chapter 35: Rumours of War

"The Peloponnesus and Athens were both full of young men
whose inexperience made them eager to take up arms." Thucydides
"A sentence that explains much history." Will Durant

For many years, scientists, historians, intelligence services, even science fiction writers, have speculated about the possibility of an unknown, breakaway, technologically advanced group or culture surreptitiously co-existing with modern society on our planet. The existence of such a group could explain many of the mysterious UFO and underwater events which have occurred since the mid-1940s. Recently, well-researched papers have been published about this possibility. They've stated that, if there is such a secret group, their presence may become widely known should nuclear war become imminent. Their interests, and their survival, would be threatened by such an existential threat, and they would likely take action to protect themselves.

There's also been conjecture that such a group, or society, could be extremely advanced in some technologies, but if they are separate from our very large, modern technological society, they may not be so advanced in other areas. Some have speculated that such a group may well secretly exist alongside, and actively participate, in our modern society to avoid such a dilemma.

———◦○◦———

The black Tesla Model X made its way north on Interstate 49. No one was driving. The sole passenger judged it best that he allow the sedan's autopilot to operate in full self-driving mode. The front gate opened as the vehicle arrived at his residence, and the vehicle made its way up the driveway to the circle drive before shutting down. Despite the multiple high-capacity fuses guarding its power system, smoke was rising from the bottom of the vehicle. Aegeus Eliades was furious.

Earlier in the day, a courier hand-delivered a restricted report from MI6, code named *Rumours of War*. The British intelligence agency made it immediately available to U.S. intelligence. In it, MI6 made an unqualified determination that war with China was imminent. After reviewing it, and consulting with certain individuals in the U.S. military and intelligence communities, Aggie felt old passions rise. War was coming.

He rushed through the front door and entered the main room. Zoe was there and they looked at each other.

She saw the red face, the veins protruding on his neck and forehead.

"Father, what is it?" Zoe rarely addressed him in such a formal manner. She sensed his mood.

Aegeus collected himself. "At one time, we were interested in the affairs of man. That was long ago. Only the threat of nuclear annihilation has caused us to follow human events again. The idiotic demagogues of this age have gone too far now. I fear we must do something drastic."

Zoe, suddenly alarmed, asked, "What happened? Why?"

Staring out the window, he replied. "I've had lengthy conversations with several individuals today. From both military and intelligence services. All are concerned with an urgent report that was just transmitted. I've read it, and it reaches a conclusion that is difficult to argue with."

Zoe turned around, looking for a chair. Sitting down, she said, "Tell me."

Aegeus took to a couch. He concentrated on taking a deep breath. "It isn't pleasant. The British intelligence services have produced and shared a formal finding that war between China and the U.S. is at hand. China will soon invade Taiwan, setting it off. Its military is surreptitiously moving all its units into position as we speak. But, what is concerning is what will happen. They've concluded that the Russian Federation leadership, realizing the U.S. will be consumed with that struggle, and coordinating with China, will move on to the remainder of Ukraine, Estonia, parts of Finland, as well as Moldova, and as many other places as they feel are appropriate. The same logic holds with North Korea. That regime will move on South Korea, regardless of whether South Korea assists the U.S. Japan is bound too tightly to the U.S. to avoid this war. Iran will likely see its opportunity to strike its neighbors, for the same reason."

Aegeus took another breath, and continued. "The timescale for all this is disturbing. There will be rapid escalation, with no party able to accept defeat, no party possessing the political will to walk away. Subsequently, there will be tactical nuclear strikes by whichever party is losing. After that, counter-strikes. The Brits have concluded that, politically, these adversaries are simply unable to back down. U.S. military and intelligence leadership is greatly alarmed and at a loss as to how to avoid this. They're now resigned to war as a near certainty and are gearing up. Presently, any small incident could immediately set this scenario off. Yes, it's happening. Nuclear war is knocking on our front door."

Zoe processed the implications, and grew horrified. "This is madness. We're sharing the planet with suicidal lunatics. We aren't even a party to any of it, and what you've worked so hard to avoid for so long might come to pass regardless. Father, I remember what you told me so many years ago, during another crisis. 'We have to accept the world as it is – not as we want it to be. If one exists, one cannot simply withdraw from the world he finds himself in, but has to act in it. At some point, it is unavoidable.' So, again, we have no choice but to act!"

"We have limited options. We can act, but if we do, it will reveal everything. Our lives, our people. We will have to radically change how we live on our own planet. Our presence will no longer be a secret. Do we really want to spend all our energy, all our time, and delay all our own goals, so we can deal with and micromanage all these insanely malfunctioning governments? That is not the life we want. You know our tasks, our goals, lie elsewhere. This is not the agreement we made with Truman so many years ago. Nuclear war has always been our red line. If it comes to that, we will intervene. We will act, and our actions will be harsh and they will be devastating."

Zoe looked at him and smiled. "We have our own sources of intelligence, father. Far, far superior to anything that these nation-states, who hate each other so much, possess."

Aegeus, calming down, looked at his daughter and smiled. "Yes, we do. I will call on your mother tonight, She is overdue. She is the one with true foresight. Also, Eleni certainly needs to know. I suspect she already does. She may be outside. Her conclusions are of no small consequence. Especially if we need to call upon the Filoi."

"They will gladly help, no matter what. Just as we always assist them."

"I know. That gives me no small amount of comfort. The Filoi will view any such war as a breach of their promise, even though they would not have caused it. And, the Filoi never break their promises."

Zoe, looking at her father, stood up. Smiling, she noted, "Neither do we."

Aggie, more relaxed, took a deep breath. "Okay, tell me about Essie."

Tears formed in Zoe's green eyes. "He's back at his place. Thoroughly confused. Not knowing what is going on. He visited a psychiatrist recently. He convinced him he has amnesia because he was depressed."

"Zoe, we had to allow time for his subconscious to reorder his memory. I have seen this before. He is strong. All his old memories will be put back where they should be. I heard about his actions there. You know, he impressed many people who are very hard to impress."

Zoe beamed. "I am so proud of him. But what a price to pay."

Later, Zoe went back to the kitchen and exited through the back door to the side yard. A crow was sitting on a tree branch nearby. Zoe looked at it, and smiled. It flew off.

———◆○◆———

Aegeus stayed seated for a while. He stared at some of the wall hangings. Old memories came back. He smiled to himself and contemplated their role in human history.

Human behavior can be so shockingly horrendous, so indescribably immoral. Yet, we have never intervened in modern times. And neither have the Filoi. Why? To intervene even once exposes our existence. It would then take all our time and all our energy. There have been countless horrors, mass murders, world wars, genocide. To stop them would have likely required massive destruction and far too many deaths. That, or the constant manipulation and oversight of politicians, military officers, philosophers, and religious leaders. We have our own goals, our own aspirations, many far removed from this planet of ours. Still, Zoe is right. There are options. We have worked so hard and endured so much sacrifice to stay apart. Is now so different? Every age has its dictators, pure evil. In the past, we've called them tyrants. Those who exercise almost complete power, unrestrained by laws, the people, and other leaders. Now, they're called Party Secretaries, Supreme Leaders and Presidents. They all have the same pathological profile. They impose hyper-nationalism, and promote hatred towards others, to keep themselves in power. Those who live under such rule are so manipulated and enthralled that they are essentially enslaved. They have no recourse from injustice. Most aren't even aware of this. Something is fundamentally wrong with the human psyche. Even glorious Athens in its golden age existed on the back of its massive number of slaves.

This constant cycle of war, caused by those who do not remember the last, cannot continue. Why? The unprecedented danger from the demagogues in this new age is that they possess nuclear weapons. Weapons that can exterminate all life on the planet. This is my people's world as much as theirs. We will not stand by and watch it all burn down. We will defend it, no matter what the cost.

———◆○◆———

Aegeus stood up, looked around, and strolled out through the front door, walking into the main yard. Standing there, looking at the beautiful green lawn, he spoke to the open air.

"Okay, Eleni, we need your thinking. War is coming. A nuclear holocaust. How much of that ten thousand years of data and experience of yours can you go through to help on this?"

After some disturbance in the air, a football field-sized silver orb, touching the tops of surrounding trees, began to materialize.

"Aggie, quite a lot, to be honest."

"You've encountered this situation before? How did it turn out those other times?"

"Mostly good. Humans here are, of course, much more unsettled in their social structure and governance. But, that is not unprecedented. The easiest method would be overt action. We remove the tyrants, the dictators. They certainly deserve it. But, consequently, countries are thereafter bereft of any leadership, leading to lengthy periods of chaos. That, invariably, turns out badly. Regardless, I know you have little interest in serving as a dictator, tyrant, or elected leader, to take their places."

"Absolutely none. What is the current status on the various nuclear weapon arsenals?"

"The sheer numbers alone reflect an aspect of human civilization that can be characterized as a group psychopathy, a suicidal death wish. Currently, 13,080 nuclear bombs and warheads are deployed, of many different designs and various means of delivery. Several on hypersonic missiles. Some on nuclear-powered torpedoes. The vast majority are possessed by the Russian Federation and the United States. Besides that, there are numerous storage locations stockpiling various nuclear weapon parts. Some can easily be accessed to quickly build even more nuclear weapons. As you know, their existence is a major unknown factor in the question of human survival."

"I assume you are privy to the same information I received today. The intelligence report concerning what is developing in the South China Sea."

"I've had access to the various conversations between members of the Chinese Politburo, as well as discussions between the Russian Federation President, their Prime Minister, and their Federation Council. The Russian General Staff is already updating war plans in anticipation of China's pending moves. That report, unfortunately, is correct. The British have reliable sources in both the Russian intelligence services and the Chinese political leadership."

"How do you suggest we handle this?"

Eleni, slowly rotating, and growing brighter, responded.

"We've done this before. It's not our first rodeo. This is what we suggest. . . ."

CHAPTER 36: CROWS TALK

Pulling into my driveway, I am on overdrive. I have to look for something and find out, immediately. I barely get the front door open before slamming it back. I rush upstairs and go into the spare room, the room with a mountain of ancient, faded clothes, junk I don't use anymore, and other miscellaneous stuff that takes up too much space and I should just toss. A room that perhaps symbolizes what my life had come to. I'm not quite sure what I'm looking for, but I start throwing handfuls of clothes over my back, shoving dusty boxes of old paperwork to the side, half of them with their bottoms busting loose from age. Scattering more useless stuff on the pile that covers the entire floor, I catch a glimpse of something metallic, dark yellowish. Sticking out of a pair of old ripped jeans is a metal handle with leather wrapped around it. I slowly pull it out. Covered in greenish patina except for the bright edges and the bottom of the pommel is a beat-up, thick, gouged bronze sword that I know deep down has always been mine. Relief floods through me. Because, those who are delusional aren't aware they're delusional. Holding the sword in my hands, it is physical evidence I'm not delusional. I know, I am positive, that I am completely, absolutely, sane.

I don't know if what had happened was planned. I don't know if it was coincidental. It was certainly serendipitous. Because now, I know. I've run out of gas before. I've dealt with cutthroat goons before. I've used this sword. There's something else in my life besides the mind-numbing, vanilla, mediocre world I found myself trapped in. There is a separate reality from that. I was part of it, and for some unknown reason it's been hidden from me.

I look around. A wave of claustrophobia comes over me. I'm having trouble breathing. Everything is closing in. I start down the stairs and leap down to the landing. Going to the front door, I jerk it open, step outside, slam it shut, and walk into the driveway. Whereupon, a murder of crows waiting there begins a cacophony of cawing. They take flight and swirl around me. The large one lands on my right shoulder. The others land around my feet. I look to my right, eye to eye with a non-human intelligence. It caws, very quietly. It caws "koe." All of them join in, uttering the same thing, louder.

"koe, koe, koe, KOE!"

More of my lost memory returns. I smile. Then, I laugh. I feel tears on my cheeks. They are tears of joy. There is a beautiful woman who loves me. I think she's a Greek goddess. All the crows are shouting her name.

The gate to the driveway is closed. I hit the buzzer on the keypad and speaker box. I hold the button down and say, "Hi. Surprise. It's Essie Kemp. I remember. I remember you. I remember extraordinary things. We have to talk." No response. I do it again. Nothing. Looking up, I see the surveillance camera. I smile and wave. I hold down the button, and I say "Jehovah's Witnesses." Nothing. After a few seconds, I try once more. "Pizza."

I hear a buzz and the gate starts opening. I get in my SUV and travel up the driveway I've been on so many times before. Apparently, they still appreciate a sense of humor.

I pull up and park near the circle. As I'm getting out, I spot a lone figure standing at the front door. Long black hair, tall, smiling, with a face red and wet from tears. The most beautiful woman in the world. I run towards her, and we merge in a tangle of arms.

CHAPTER 37: SHE RETURNS

I n the evening, Aegeus Eliades knew it was time. He stepped outside and strolled into the woods. It was beautiful weather and the surrounding forest was alive with activity. He chose a little-used path. After a few minutes, he reached an intersection of several trails. It was watched over by an ancient statue of a woman with three faces. Turning right, he continued his walk, arriving at an open area with a small marble bench. Aegeus stopped and surveyed the surroundings. The sun was setting. The scenic view, from the hill he was on, was of the Little Blue River Valley, and the plain between the river and the surrounding hills. The perspective brought back an unbidden memory of the Asopus River, the plain it passed through, and when he called for her, long ago, while at war. It was a different age.

He was furious. Fearing the enemy cavalry outflanking them, his line had withdrawn, despite the oaths they took. Knowing what was at stake, he refused to do so, and he steeled himself to face the enemy alone. One solitary man against thousands, quickly marching towards him.

He recited a hymn of her wisdom and her courage. A hymn first sung by Homer. The Persians, sensing victory, rushed forward and were almost upon him. Then, a flash of metal to his left, where there was no one before. A warrior, taller than any other, wearing brilliant armor, brighter than the sun, holding a spear and a shield with the face of a Gorgon on it, stood with him. The Persian line hesitated.

The Spartan general, Pausanias, was growing impatient with their diviner, who again insisted that the sacrificial goat intestines gave unfavorable omens, and they thus should not attack the Persians. He heard cries behind him. Turning around, Pausanias was shocked to see his close allies, the Tegeans, madly rushing forward onto the plain. He spotted what they saw. Looking back at the diviner in disgust, he growled, "There are far better omens on the field of battle. Save the goats for our feast."

None of the Greeks could miss the sudden appearance. The Spartans, wearing their red cloaks, quickly formed up a crimson phalanx, intent on sweeping all in front of them. The other Greek allies, with their bronze helmets glinting like gold in the sun, stopped their withdrawal and rushed forward. All wanted to fight alongside the Greek god.

With a voice all on the field could hear, she said, "Those who burn our temples will face our wrath." With a beauteous smile, turning to him, she whispered, "Any who threaten the one I love will face a cruel death."

——◦○◦——

With that memory on his mind, Aegeus smiled, and chanted out loud what he recited so many years ago, when he called for her:

Of she who is Guardian of the city, I sing.
Dread is she, and with Ares she loves deeds of war,
the sack of cities, the shouting and the battle.
It is she who saves the people as they go to war and come back.
Hail, she who is!

Hear our song, grant us good fortune and victory!

———————◦———————

The tranquil sunset exploded with light. Radiant beams of the setting sun shot out, and ignited the sky with crimson flames. The gray clouds turned orange and red. The forest drew silent, in anticipation. Out of that silence came the lonely hoot of an owl.

"So, you are called to war, mighty Aegeus? Those who would oppose you are unwise."

Turning around, he faced her. She stepped out of the sudden mist, without guise, wearing an embroidered white robe, with a golden belt, black hair, woven and wrapped, and a diadem on her head.

With the greatest joy, surrounded by mist glowing from the last rays of the sun, they embraced.

Aegeus spoke. "Once again, the world weighs on us."

"Does it? How could it? Do we not have command over time and space? What mere mortals can stand against that?"

"There are many tyrants, with many new weapons."

"Has the world been too much with you? Have you perchance forgotten who you actually are? You are more than man, more than any petty tyrant. Remember who you are!"

With that, Aegeus grinned, and grew in stature, such that he would tower over any man.

"You know I have impeccable foresight. Take action now. Show them what their foolishness will result in. Mortals play with the end of all things, and they do not even realize it."

Stepping back and gazing over the valley, she said, "Just as we intervened on the plains of Plataea, to save the future, we must do so again. The Filoi have seen this before. They will stand by us, just as we stand by them. They will sorely need us in the future. We will not let them down."

"So be it. The world wants to go to war? We shall show them what they wish for. We will act."

In a softer voice, Aegeus said, "Our daughter is troubled. What of her betrothed?"

Helena Eliades smiled. "Our future son-in-law will come into his own. He will recall his past, and he will conquer it. In so doing, death will lose its power. He will remember the fearsome warrior he is. Now, I must take leave and go to her. True love causes worry, but she worries needlessly. I will be with you later this evening.

Helena Eliades full well knew that the littlest things change the course of history. If she had not appeared at Plataea, Pausanias would have continued watching his diviner slaughtering goats, with the Greeks themselves being slaughtered in the end. Athens would have no Golden Age, Western Civilization would not come to be, humanity would not travel the galaxy in the future, and change it forever. Smiling, she realized that Aegeus fathomed as much when he refused to retreat and faced the Persians alone, and she once more recalled just how much she loved him. As her father said, her vow of chastity was not for all eternity.

That night, after many had retired to their bedrooms, the regional National Weather Service Doppler radar detected a sudden storm cloud forming over a Kansas City suburb. The meteorologist on duty thought it odd. There was rotation, however, they put off issuing a warning until its direction was determined. It never moved. Multiple lightning strikes were detected. People standing outside their houses, apartments, and condominiums observing it that night all agreed. It was awesome.

Chapter 38: Aegeus Has a Visitor

It was a beautiful, bright spring day in Missouri. Everything was flowering and blooming, to the point that it was difficult to think of dark things. Many places on Earth do not have seasons. For that matter, many places throughout the galaxy do not have seasons. For those who grew up in locations where there were, and who now struggle to remember what it was like, there is a never-diminished desire to return home and experience them again, and reminisce over the passage of time.

Looking up into the sky, a careful observer might perhaps have noticed three spots of blurriness, in a triangle formation, moving across the sky, between and through the cumulus clouds, at a rapid clip. The formation took a circular route, as if on a tour of the region. It eventually came to a location above Lee's Summit, stopping abruptly, and slowly lowering to the ground. If one were to see the landing, the blurriness would dissipate as brilliant silver ovals manifested, hovering a mere foot above the ground in an open area next to a beautiful, large, isolated house in the Kansas City suburb. Openings appeared in them.

Aegeus Eliades stood up and observed his friends and colleagues at the working lunch he was hosting. The group was just finishing up the entrées, some of them grabbing desserts and staking out their chairs in the great room. They were from all continents, and many places elsewhere. Men and women, young and old. Many of the young were old, and many of the old were ancient.

"Okay, just grab what you're eating or drinking and bring it in with you. We have to address the issues that have brought us here today. Don't worry about making a mess. I never intended this place to be a damn museum. We live here, so I think it needs to look like that."

One of his friends responded. "Aggie wants us to trash his house."

That generated quite a laugh from everyone. Some were tempted to do just that, but the great room could pass for an exhibit hall at the British Museum for all its exquisite furniture and wall hangings.

When they were all there, Aegeus stood up. There was an abrupt change. A sudden heightened sense of awareness appeared on his face, a squinting of his silver-flecked eyes. He turned to his right, towards the front entrance of his house.

A massively built, Olympian-like man strolled in. Everyone saw him and immediately stood up. Tall, with long black hair, Mediterranean tan, a weathered face, a thin white vertical scar going down his left cheek, and eyes with silver in them. He looked human but unmistakably different. Wearing a textured black jumpsuit and a utility belt, he gazed at all of them, broke out a huge grin, and in a loud, deep bass voice exclaimed, "Well, you asked that they send someone."

CHAPTER 39: THINGS ARE NOT GOING WELL

"We are in a crisis. Things are coming to a head. North Korea fired an ICBM over Japan, unannounced, last week, traumatizing the entire nation. Guam was put on full alert. The month before, Kim Jong Un resumed nuclear testing, exploding what North Korean media claimed was a thermonuclear hydrogen fusion bomb. Russia, after withdrawing from the new START treaty, claims it has fully tested and is deploying its new hypersonic missiles, complete with thermonuclear warheads, in a strategic role. Russian state media also brags about a ludicrous, long-range, nuclear propulsion-powered torpedo, complete with a thermonuclear warhead, it claims can destroy coastal cities. China, meanwhile, refuses to sign any nuclear weapon reduction treaty and is rapidly building out hundreds of new ICBM sites for its newest version of the Dongfeng strategic missiles, complete with MIRVed warheads, the designs of which were allegedly stolen from the U.S. Sandia National Nuclear Laboratory."

"Chinese warships, allegedly armed with tactical nuclear hypersonic missiles, continually harass U.S., Japanese, South Korean, Filipino, Australian, British, and Indian warships in the South China Sea, sometimes in those nation's own territorial waters, and elsewhere. Their long planned invasion of Taiwan is imminent. Russia continues to threaten nuclear retaliation if Ukraine retakes the territory Russia previously seized. Russian warplanes harass U.S. and NATO airplanes flying near Ukraine, the Black Sea, and the Baltic and North Seas. Iran will soon have several nuclear devices and has continually sworn to exterminate Israel. Pakistan and India consider each other rabid dogs and have nuclear missiles aimed at each other which can reach their targets in less than a minute."

Aggie Eliades continued. "They act like they have no knowledge of apocalyptic nuclear war, and express no concern over accidental launches. It seems hard learned lessons of war have not been passed on to later generations. In an age of thermonuclear weapons of mass destruction, this is an existential flaw. In their ignorance, they possess no fear of annihilation. Their fail-safe, security, false alarm mechanisms and machinery are in many instances decrepit and, in parts of Russia, almost nonexistent. All the nuclear powers have submarines capable of firing dozens of ICBMs with MIRV warheads, yet they almost certainly will have their communications cut off in a conflict. None of the ICBMs have self-destruct mechanisms after they are launched. They're actually designed that way. And they can relatively easily be launched by mistake, or accident. The U.S. flies sixty-year-old strategic bombers around the world with thermonuclear weapons onboard, and every decade or so one of the planes crashes, or one of the weapons is dropped by accident. The Russian military is equally guilty of the same actions. Mistakes and accidents are an unavoidable aspect of human behavior, no matter what safety protocols are adopted."

"Yes, we've forestalled the development of anti-gravity propulsion, and its consequential ability to travel almost instantaneously anywhere on the planet. Clearly, that helped to preserve the continued viability of the mutually assured destruction doctrine. But, this present state of affairs seems to ignore the ratio-nality behind that doctrine. There is now no fear of nuclear catastrophe. The political leaders and the general populace of the entire planet go about their everyday business with hate and contempt for whoever they believe their enemies are, though their perceived enemies change every decade. They all think nothing of the threat of nuclear war. I'm not sure quite how to change this state of affairs."

Looking at everyone there, and turning to the new arrival, Aggie said, "To be succinct, the human population on this planet is living on borrowed time. We have no subtle remedies, no unnoticeable methodology to stop this suicidal drive."

The new arrival, who strolled to the buffet table during this presentation, was drinking a bottle of Corona beer. He looked over at them and smiled.

"The human race is a strange species that on a regular basis allows psychopathic maniacs to lead millions into wars that serve no purpose other than their own self-aggrandizement. Our hard-learned knowledge has taught us that in the end, each people must save themselves from themselves. While any immediate crisis might be resolved, more will appear unless the people, through the experience of solving it themselves, can stop any evil that appears in the future. There are many outside threats. That is what the Filoi can deal with, to keep the promises we all made at the beginning of this age. Just recently, one of your own traveled with us, encountered, and dealt with some of them. At some cost to himself. I just spoke with him again outside. Internal cultural flux is complicated, even with our A.I.s advising us, but what we can do is grant your people more time to grow in wisdom. You know who I am. We've been here before. Many times. You don't think that we can change this world's suicidal trajectory? What do they say in this country?"

He tilted his head up a bit, and said, "That's right ... hold my beer."

Chapter 40: Colonel Travinsky

Colonel Igor Travinsky took the staff car and drove over to the air base to be on hand as the Mig-29 landed. Major Shaskovich, shaken, was well-trained and made a clean three-point landing. He taxied over to his hanger, where Colonel Travinsky waited, Engines turned off and the canopy rolled back he hopped out and climbed down the ladder rolled over to the plane. He spied Colonel Travinsky and immediately saluted.

"Where are your missiles?" Colonel Travinsky asked.

They both approached and looked under the port wing. What they saw was amazing. The missile pylon was missing. Around six inches of it was all that remained attached to the wing. There was a completely perfect cut, not even any melted metal at the edges. They walked over to the other wing. It was the same.

Colonel Travinsky said. "These particular missiles are designed to be tracked on radar. Our operator detected nothing falling from your plane. The beam used for this could just as easily slice your plane in half. It is significant that was not done. Even though your plane was sent up there with the intent to attack the object, following the standing orders. This is further proof that the standing orders must be changed. These craft are not hostile. This encounter is extraordinary, yes. But, not unprecedented. Major, your conduct was exemplary, you did nothing wrong and exhibited calmness under great stress. It will be so stated in my report, along with my recommendations."

Colonel Travinsky saluted the major, turned around, and walked back to his staff car. A photographer turned on his camera and started taking photos of the bisected pylons.

Chapter 41: Reunion

"I seem to have loved you in numberless forms,
numberless times, in life after life,
in age after age forever." Rabindranath Tagore

Zoe Eliades and I, oblivious to the world, continued to embrace each other, neither of us desiring to ever let go. Finally, I realized I had to figure out just what was happening to me.

"Zoe, my mind is full of empty spaces. There is so much I can't remember. I don't even know what I did last week. I need to know."

"Maybe I can answer that for you."

We turned around and were taken aback by the sudden appearance of a massive man in a black jumpsuit. Behind him, completely silent and hovering close to the ground, were three enormous silver orbs. People were quietly disembarking from them.

"Esmond Kemp, your memory loss was intentional. We thought it unwise for Zoe to interact with you. It would have almost certainly triggered a premature recovery of your memory. As it so happens, a lot of good that did since you had your little encounter today. You've got to stop running out of gas. Memory is resilient, with many alternate pathways and duplicate storage regions. Many times, that can be a curse."

"I'm sorry. I feel like I should know you, but I don't."

The man in black looked at Zoe, smiled, and nodded, then turned to me. Grinning, he said, "My feelings are hurt. You don't remember me?"

I glanced at Zoe, who, blushed, with wet cheeks, smiled at me and shrugged. I looked sideways at this man. He seemed human, but perhaps more so, had a rather impressive scar on his face, and was one of those people whose age is impossible to figure out.

"Um, no."

"I am called Theseus here. An old family name. But, I've been called any number of names. Some I do not care for. I am Zoe's uncle."

So, Theseus and I shook hands.

"Esmond, by chance did you bring along an old beat-up sword?"

I turned around and went to my SUV where I left the sword, having brought it along for some reason. I grabbed it and walked back.

Theseus asked, "May I?"

I handed it to him pommel first. Theseus took it and weighed it with his hand.

"These old bronze swords are so thick, it seems they can more effectively be used as clubs than cutting weapons. Still, this one has some hidden qualities."

With that, he twisted the pommel at an angle. There were etchings on the blade, partially filled in by the patina. The patina started flaking, and the etchings became more distinct. Stepping back, Theseus tossed it up into the air. Oddly, it kept going.

"Essie, can I call you Essie?"

"Sure."

"Essie, raise your arm up and hold your hand out."

A brilliant flash of gold flew past us, curved around, and the sword's grip slammed against my outreached hand.

"Jesus Christ, why didn't someone tell me it could do this?"

Theseus looked at Zoe, then me. Laughing, he said, "Well, that was the problem. I assumed someone did. It would have been good for you to have known a while ago."

"I suppose this is one of those swords that has its own name?"

"Sure, it's, um, the Sword of Esmond."

Zoe rolled her eyes.

So, Theseus took his leave, having a meeting to attend inside the house. Leaving Zoe to explain what the hell was going on.

⸺⊷◉⊶⸺

As mentioned before, it was springtime. In Missouri, this means an infinity of different shades of green, everywhere. The forest surrounding the Eliades mansion is primordial, with well-kept trails weaving through it. The giant trees created enough shade that, even at noon, it seemed like evening while walking among them. We strolled across a small meadow, where a symphony of violets, hyacinths, crocuses, irises and daffodils were all in bloom. Their fragrance filled the air. We resisted the temptation to pick them.

"Essie, what happened to you occurred while you were grizzly hunting with Uncle Ted. Not here, but off-world. There's a nomadic group that regularly engages in intrigue with the Filoi. They avoid direct confrontation, but have always caused trouble when they can do so undetected. They began releasing these creatures on a planet where people we support are living. It was hoped that we wouldn't notice, by inserting seemingly natural animals there, but we did. So, Theseus, Uncle Ted, wanted to go hunting with the newest member of the family. This is crazy, isn't it? But, we fly off-world in sentient, semi-organic orbs and engage in a great number of surreptitious activities to keep various cultures alive and thriving. Anyway, more of your memory should be back by the end of the day."

"Grizzly hunting seems like fun."

"Not when it turns out they were enhanced. They weren't grizzlies anyway. From my understanding, they were genetically engineered predators. Released to kill every person in that region. You had a head injury, according to my uncle. In fact, you had a number of injuries. Still, I shouldn't be so upset. You survived. That threat had to be taken care of. I know those people. I've been to that beautiful planet. They were in danger. For you, well, we know now that you suffered a brain injury, and then went deep space for a day to get back here. That's not really advisable in that condition. Regardless, the recommended medical practice was to do nothing, since the brain recovers all its misplaced memory on its own. Essie, I care for my uncle dearly, and Theseus is a very famous man, but I let him know in no uncertain terms that I did not care for the liberties he took with the man I love. You know though, he told me, you were awesome. To impress Theseus is no small thing!"

That explanation for the memory loss seemed superficially plausible. But, I thought it through. And realized it didn't make any sense whatsoever.

"Zoe, if this injury I got caused amnesia, wouldn't it make sense for you to talk to me when I got back? I mean, talking to you could have brought back lost memories, right? Yet, you were told to stay away, so my amnesia would continue? Your uncle said the memory loss was intentional. It just doesn't make sense. You're covering something up, probably for my own good. But, still, you've got to tell me what the hell is going on."

She looked at me, her face red, perhaps realizing I was right - the story made no sense. She then smiled and muttered, "Damn lawyers."

Stopping on the trail, I took her face in my hands, kissed her, and whispered, "Tell me what's really going on here."

Zoe, eyes watering, whispered back. "If I tell you, what happened at the end of that trip may happen again."

That worried me. Still, there was no question about this. I had to know. "Tell me anyway."

Zoe, laughing, hugged me.

"Essie, do you remember getting that sword?"

I thought about that and it caused some confusion.

"This must be part of my amnesia. I remember using it but, really, I don't."

"Essie, this is where I get sick to my stomach, worrying about you. My mother gave you that sword."

This caused even more confusion. "Zoe, I don't know why, but I've never met your mother."

Tears coming from her eyes, she said. "Oh, yes you have."

"I would think I would remember meeting your mo ...."

"Monkey Mountain."

"What?"

"Monkey Mountain."

I recalled first going to Monkey Mountain. The thorns, the snow, the flying saucer. Then, to my utter astonishment, I recalled a woman in the middle of the field, who touched my forehead. And caused a carousel of strange visions and unbearable regrets:

———————◄○►———————

After my close encounter with the saucer, I wandered around basically lost and in a daze. Eventually, I came across the meadow that was my original destination. It was a beautiful view, covered in virgin snow. I spotted someone standing in the middle. Whoever it was, the person was standing where I planned to take my photos. I headed over there. I wasn't exactly threatening, plowing my way through the snow with a camera and tripod.

As I approached I called out. "Hi, there. Great weather. What brings you here?"

The person was a tall woman. There was a sudden stir in the air. It was darker, and I was stunned to realize it was late afternoon. Yet, I started out around noon, and it was only a twenty-minute hike, even in the snow. Was I blacked out or unconscious for a time? I don't know.

She turned to look at me. She smiled. For a moment I thought she was the woman I encountered at the grocery store. Looking around, I was confused to see no footprints leading up to her. I'm sure she realized I noticed this. I looked at her more closely. She could have been that woman, or any woman for that matter. My recall is strange at this point.

And then, I heard her voice. In my mind. I don't know what she said. She spoke in some language I couldn't understand. It was lyrical, melodious.

Nothing was making sense on that mountain, and I was utterly bewildered. Had I somehow ingested a hallucinogenic? Gazing at her, speechless, I saw she was wearing a cloak. No jacket or coat. Her very long, braided black hair was in a classical weave, and wasn't something seen these days. Her eyes had silver in them. She reached out her hand, and her palm touched my cheek.

I experienced an epiphany of some sort, as if a veil was torn away. There were vague flashbacks of past times in different places. Love, heartbreak, adventure, journeys, fathers, mothers, sons, daughters and wives. I wanted to forget it all. To keep from going insane.

Opening my eyes, I realized I was on my knees. I looked around. There was a woman at the far end of the meadow, walking into the trees. An animal was there waiting for her, all black. But its size seemed wrong.

<hr />

"Zoe, who is your mother?"

"My mother is Helena Eliades."

"Zoe, really, who is she?"

Zoe Eliades, beautiful, tall, strong, confident, stood in the middle of the woods with me. We were completely alone. It was strangely quiet, not a sound anywhere. She closed her eyes then, and I understood she was looking into herself to determine just what to tell me, and just what the consequences might be if she got it wrong.

"Essie, this is going to be long-winded. I'm sorry. We knew each other when we were kids. Life took us to different places. Somehow, and I'm not so sure if it was just serendipity, we met again. My people, and they are your people now too, we have to live on Earth for parts of our lives, for our families. We are human, after all. Our planet's gravity and atmosphere are required for us to make babies, and to raise them. Our children cannot grow up on our ships, the Filoi planets, or on most other worlds we visit, without many possible difficulties. Our DNA is specific to Earth, and we protect our planet, even though we travel the galaxy with the Filoi. We are long-lived, and our well-founded beliefs are that there is a nonlinear continuity, and a universality, between lives. We are a family of old souls, and we experience life in many different roles. When we die, we rejoin the Soul of the World, always knowing that we will be reborn. Through all of this, we believe our consciousness, individual, and universal, our psykhē and pneuma, survives and permeates all human life. Pythagoras, Virgil, Socrates, and Plato have all written of this."

Zoe continued. "My mother taps into this, lives this. The Filoi and our people transcend space. We can travel otherwise insurmountable distances, sometimes instantaneously. A few of my people though, including my mother, can also transcend time. They tell us time is an illusion. Even Einstein said this. When she sees people, she can choose to see what their paths have been through time. She takes this as a given. She knew you when you encountered each other that day. There's an expression we use. 'The mercy of forgetfulness.' She lifted your forgetfulness, and you had too much to bear as soon as she did that, for your timeline is long. She saw that and quickly lowered that wall. But, by doing so she made it easier for you to recall the past, and that sword also has its own effect. This is the good part, though. She knew you, and she told me that we're blessed, because she saw that we met again and that we would be together."

For a time, I was truly speechless. All I could do was look into Zoe's eyes and hold her hand. Eventually, I found my voice.

"My forgetfulness, this amnesia when I try to recall the recent past, what has caused that? What happened?"

"I want to blame the sword. But it was the trip you took, the expedition, with Theseus. It is something that is time-honored, that is expected of new members of our family. Our family tests prospective husbands by having them undertake a dangerous task. We still need to quell your inner turmoil, and that's as good an answer as I can give you now."

Zoe paused for a moment, and she had that same look, apparently contemplating if she should say more.

"When you got back, you were in a bad way, Essie. You began to experience many memories from long ago, and I'm not just talking about this lifetime. You were overwhelmed with thousands of years of memories. No one can deal with all of those at the same time. You told me you could recall your deaths, many deaths, your children's deaths. Like they just happened. That is something you really should not be recalling. Not in that way. No one should. Theseus said you had a head injury and you lost blood. I don't believe he told me everything. More must have occurred. And that sword has an ancient history. For you, well, we soon recognized that we had to block your memories for a while. Your subconscious, your subliminal mind, can still process them, and resolve them. Given some time, it will. That's a certainty, Essie. Believe me. All your past was so much closer to your awareness after you encountered my mother. Well, the sword yes, but to be honest, I don't want to say this, but also from us being together. It was even more difficult to cause forgetfulness when the person you went on that trip for was by your side. You had nightmares, and it was unbearable for me to watch you in your nightmares. That's why we had to be separated, so we could make you forget everything for a while, so your memory could heal, and it was awful."

She paused, and wiped a few tears from her cheeks. She took a deep breath, looked at me, and smiled. I understood then that, as much as I've been tortured over this, so has she.

"Essie, my people have a learned strength that most others do not. We are all masters at forgetting. We have to be. Life is unbearable otherwise. It is taught in Buddhism, the ancient Greek mysteries, even written in Virgil's *Aeneid*, that reincarnation, the transmigration of souls, is too painful should previous memories carry on to the next life. Even in our current lives, many times we must forget and move on. But, dreams are our Achilles's heel. Powerful memories can be expressed in dreams, and some are so painful it cripples us. So, we learn to selectively forget, and also to selectively remember, when it is an aid to our current affairs."

Zoe drew closer. She wrapped her arms around me and whispered into my ear.

"My mother told me that you have a virtuous soul. You have your third man, and your inner memories, the memories that your subconscious is the keeper of, give you strength. But, if they are too close to the surface, too unfiltered, or improperly suppressed, they have the potential to turn anyone into a madman."

"Zoe, I've been told that a way to deal with bad memories, to forget them, is to create new ones. It only makes sense. They obscure the old ones. So, fresh memories help, over time. Zoe, I remember that sword now. It was in the field when I was at Monkey Mountain later, facing the Russians. It likely saved my life. So that was when she gave me the sword?"

"Well, I want to say this precisely, Essie. She did not give you that sword. Like I said, my mother recognized you. She returned your sword."

I whispered, "Who is your mother?"

Zoe turned her head to me, her eyes glistening. She hugged me, and then stepped back.

"Essie, in this life, here and now, my mother is Helena Eliades. That's true. But, this is not her only aspect, her only identity. That's true for all of us, including you. We all have many roles. My mother has been given many names. She was known in other places, other times, as The One With Gleaming Eyes, The One Who Fights in Front, The Destroyer of Giants. She was known as Parthenos, Glaukopis, Pallas, Promachos, Ergane, Polias. In your past, you knew her by those names."

Chapter 42: The Night That Brought Everything Back

Zoe

I know it's raining outside. Strange, because I don't see outside the window, and
I hear no raindrops. But I know it is. Essie is here with me, asleep, thank God.
Should his pain surface again, along with everything from his past, I'm not sure
what to do. Do we make him forget again? If one endures a year, twenty years, a
hundred years of pain, is it meaningless, is it mere vapor, once it goes away? I believe
it does change a person, either in a good way or in a bad way. Perhaps it is up to that
person to figure out which.

My mother believes painful memories, all memories, have value. Most believe
music has value, yet it is ephemeral. Is it? Music stays with a person and has the
power to change. But only if we recall it. So perhaps with pain, for it to have value,
for one to give it value, and not waste it, one must recall it. I know my memories of
pain are very well hidden. Yet, I'm able to recall and make use of them when I wish.

Why do I love him? Even before this trip, he hid his trauma, his own pain. He
suffered over several years, and it made him cynical and depressed. On some level,
he must have known his trips to the Irish Wilderness were attempts to lose himself,
lose his memory, all to somehow stop his pain. He wanted to torture himself, and

contemplated his death, to hide the past from his awareness. Yet, strangely, that pain also made him more gentle, more empathetic. That's why I love him, because his pain made him kinder, and with other men, it turns them into cruel creatures.

Essie

That night I couldn't sleep. I turned over and looked at her. How can a man who's lost everything, somehow, after so many years, suddenly have everything? She heals me, she makes me whole again. It shouldn't be possible.

I left Zoe in the bed and sneaked out, passed the front door, and strolled through the yard. A storm had come through, clearing the night sky and chilling the air. Looking up to the sky that night, with no moon, the stars were brighter than ever, like a bucket of diamonds scattered across black velvet. They sparkled, and glistened, and they reached into my mind and revealed memories I didn't know existed. I saw a shadow glide silently through the air and land on a nearby tree branch. I squinted and saw that it was a little owl. It was a beautiful, magical creature, and as it examined me I kept an eye on it. I felt someone's arm wrap around mine. I turned my head and Zoe smiled. We both looked up at the stars. And, despite the pain that it would cause, my memory of that trip, and what happened to me, returned.

Chapter 43: The Trip

Theseus made a compelling case. "These are people facing an existential menace. They're our friends, we've hunted and explored with them countless times over the centuries, and they need our help. There are interstellar groups we have polite disagreements with who do not want humanoid life to dominate on certain planets. Especially planets with approximately 1G gravity and oxygen-nitrogen atmospheres. They want to claim the planets for themselves or their favored species. But mainly, they just want us not to have a presence there. They are deceitful and believe they can exterminate people without us becoming aware of their actions. They have mistaken politeness for weakness. They vastly underestimate us. They are not the first to have made this mistake. This is one of those occasions. There are bear-like creatures naturally on this planet. But what this group has done is modify them to create powerful, intelligent predators that would, over several years, kill most of the people, leaving their continued existence nonviable. It was planned to make this look like a natural occurrence, mother nature at work, survival of the fittest. These friends of ours, these people, who we call the Kitren, would hunt these bears, as they've done for thousands of years. But now, the bears would be hunting them, and killing them. And, the bears will go to the villages and kill there."

"We cannot use technology in front of the Kitren. For all the usual reasons. We have no need of worship, and we don't want them traumatized by a display of modern weaponry. Their society would simply stop its progress and become unstable if our technology became widely known. So, that's the scenario. We have several teams going there. You've got a sword. You'll need a spear too. Are you up for this?"

I glanced at Zoe. She just shrugged her shoulders and smiled.

I responded, "Sure, this seems like fun. I've never been bear hunting before."

Zoe gave Theseus an inquisitive look. He looked at her and said, "We use three-man teams. One of the members is camouflaged, virtually undetectable, and acts as a sniper when appropriate. He usually goes to the high ground and oversees the whole area."

She did not look satisfied. "These 'bears.' Just how enhanced are they?"

"Not really sure. That is part of why we're handling it this way. We want to know how smart they are, and how they react to us. Don't worry, we'll have our ship a couple of miles up above. And you know my ship. She'll vaporize anything that gets too close."

I spoke up. "How do you handle the oxygen requirement? Surely, this planet's atmosphere can't be that close a match to Earth's."

"Well, it's fairly close. That is the reason why the planet is somewhat contested. But, we have a methodology that provides us with a close in atmosphere without even being noticeable. You'll have an oxygen-nitrogen environment surrounding your head, with something similar to a magnetic field keeping it there."

Zoe pulled me to the side and whispered. "This is not a cakewalk. It is not a mere hunting trip. It will be dangerous. It is intended to be dangerous. Essie, you are expected to go, and it would be shameful if you didn't. But, listen to me. Make me proud."

She smiled. I saw a flash of something new in her eyes then – an extraordinary toughness that was very well hidden.

Theseus continued. "When our team arrives on location, I'll want to visit with the town leader. It used to be a small village when I first visited, but now a town.

They know we come around now and then. As far as they are concerned, we are distant cousins from out of town who don't know the dialect very well. The Kitren are, well, you'll like them. They have an avid curiosity and an extraordinary sense of humor, which all of us have found to be an indispensable survival trait. For a few of us, their culture brings back old memories. I suspect a couple of them know a lot more about us than they are letting on."

"Anthropologists would love to be in on this."

"Yeah, there are two I know of tagging along."

So we mustered up by Theseus's ship. Now a black ellipse, it was hovering a few inches above the ground. We all said our goodbyes. For everyone there, it was just a routine thing. For me, well, I was the new kid on the block. I looked at Zoe and waved. She nodded at me, not wanting to make a spectacle.

We embarked and took off. In just a few minutes, we approached and entered a much, much larger craft. These ships are fascinating. They go faster than light, and the perception of time passing while in them is completely untrustworthy. I experienced some nausea. For me at least, there was a lounge chair affair that I lay on and the back lowered. The interior of the ship is surprisingly uncomplicated. One individual was standing in a corner viewing a very impressive hologram and manipulating some parts of it with his hands. The hologram stayed with him as he walked around. Probably not surprising for anyone who is up on scientific advancements, but I was impressed. I felt the ship's presence, or, I should say, its consciousness. It was comforting. It seemed to be female, but that might just be to ease some initial anxiety. There was no communication with me, but then it wasn't my ship. In fact, I got the impression it wasn't anybody's ship. It was more a member of the group assigned a task, along with everyone else.

The technology is probably beyond my ability to understand, both from how it travels inconceivable distances and the actual material it is made of. I do not believe that what I saw in the interior was a false memory. Clearly, the human race has much to look forward to as the future approaches. One thing I thought odd, no, I thought was rather cool, was that on the larger craft, there was a long plank of ancient wood on display. It was embedded into a central bulkhead in one of the main spaces. Maybe ten feet by three feet by four or so inches. I was in the Navy, so naturally it appealed to me - a plank of wood displayed on a most modern ship. I examined it more closely. There was some lettering on it. It looked like Greek lettering to me.

So, there on display, almost certainly a direct connection to an earlier time. Really, this is a powerful thing - a feeling of continuity is immensely important to people, and cultures. It occurred to me, just how old is Theseus? Is he a plank owner? How old is this ship I am embarked on? If it's Greek, was it counted in the Catalogue of Ships? I smiled to myself. This embedded plank was a most ingenious resolution of that philosophical paradox, the "Ship of Theseus," or perhaps more correctly an elegant avoidance of the same. Regardless, I then understood why I was supposed to go on this little trip. They very much wanted me to become immersed in this new tribe, this culture and society.

I don't know how far we traveled, or how long it took. For me, I just laid down in one of those lounge chairs and became lost in thought. I really lost track of time. I'm sure I slept a few hours. Regardless, we arrived, and before we disembarked I met up with several more men and women, who all made a point of introducing themselves. All very human, but with certain quirks. One woman was rail thin, as was the man she was with. There were several who had the very solid build of Theseus. This, I am told, is a result of many years on certain planets or moons. They all carried swords, spears, and some bows and arrows. Several carried what looked like rifles, and I saw them carefully wrapping the same in camouflage fabric.

Theseus approached me with a short man. "Esmond, I want to introduce Kalay, who will save our asses if we get ourselves in trouble."

I realized he was our third man, and he was packing a rather impressive rifle.

"Kalay, good to make your acquaintance. I certainly want to stay on your good side."

"Good to meet you, too. Well, this will be an interesting trip. A scientific expedition, though it could be mistaken for a hunting trip."

Theseus said, "We do want to get some biological samples from these creatures. We also want to determine if they are reproducing on this planet. At some point, if we can, we'll make a short visit to the town I've visited before and determine its status."

Looking at me, he continued. "We've learned to not display our technological weapons, and certainly to not allow their use to be seen. It is truly disruptive to a society that cannot understand how they work. It just creates too much trauma, so we always put a good deal of work into avoiding ontological shock."

Several three-person teams deployed around the planet. Kalay, Theseus, and I were transported down by the same black orb that took us up to the main ship. We disembarked. The first thing I noticed was that the orb had almost no visibility as we walked out of it, and it was remarkable. I thought of the almost magical ability octopi have to change color, matching the immediate environment. The second thing was the weird trees. We trekked through a forest of them. The trunks curled quite a bit, like they were in no hurry to rise. They had a smooth surface and most had a burnt brown color. The leaves were circular and were green and silver. The green faced the sky and the silver faced the ground. It made for a weird effect when the wind blew. The tree roots started several feet above the ground, which created hidden, shadowed areas at the tree bases. I spotted a few stars in the sky, visible even though it was midday.

Anyway, we were on a new planet. I sensed the field around my head keeping the oxygen nitrogen level correct. We were issued rather interesting Kevlar-type undershirts to wear beneath the basic textile shirts that I assume were in use in the area. We reached a ridge that overlooked the village Theseus wanted to visit. The village itself overlooked a small river, with an undulating crop field of radiant yellow in the flood plain. Several thin columns of white smoke rose from chimneys sticking out of thatched roofs. Some people were moving around, women and children. They, at least from a distance, looked very human-like.

Theseus knelt and used binoculars to survey the surroundings for a long time. After a while, he turned around and talked to us in a low voice.

"Well, I was planning on visiting the village. But, now, I sense that it might be too disruptive. They are on guard because of these new intruders. What I think is best is to stay here until nightfall and see what approaches it after dark. We can make ourselves invisible easily enough with what we've got. It will get dark rather quickly. It might be wise not to move around much when it does. We've got a good position here."

Theseus, gazing through his binoculars again, noted something new. "Well, this is interesting. There are several stone structures in the town now. They look fairly substantial. That speaks well of these folks. They have enough confidence in their future to build something permanent for it. Perhaps, that is why these new predators were brought in."

Kalay spoke up. "I don't want one of these things sneaking up on us. We don't know how good their night vision is or their sense of smell. But, I suspect we'll find out."

So we waited for a while. It did get dark. This is something I won't forget. Nighttime on this planet. The stars came out. Many appeared quite differently from ours. Several were red. Some, very bright white diamonds. There seemed to be more stars, and they appeared closer. It was a beautiful sight, and I had to remind myself to pay attention to the closer surroundings. At one point we saw a luminescent blue-green cloud moving across the landscape, morphing into different shapes, against the background of stars. Apparently, insects of some sort. A one-of-a-kind vision. The cloud crossed a creek, briefly changing it into a bright ribbon. Reaching the crops in the flood plain, it created a moving splash of green.

It caused me to reminiscence why I left the Navy. All those remarkable events, extraordinary, incredible sights, and I would look around to share them with someone. For the most part, I could never really do that. The more wonderful the things I saw were, the more incomplete, and the more lonely, I felt. So, it troubled me that Zoe was not around to share that beautiful vision. I recall looking up to the stars, and wondering if, somewhere out there, she was thinking of me.

———◦———

"Something's over there." Theseus pointed to the right.

There was a large black shape to the right of the village and slowly approaching it.

Kalay pulled out his long-range weapon, looked through his scope, and spoke. "I'm heading left twenty yards or so for a better angle. There's more than one."

Theseus looked at me, and in a low voice said, "These things likely know we're here. Esmond, your sword might be very useful in a few minutes."

I felt the pommel of my sword, thinking I'd much rather be gripping an automatic weapon.

A minute later, Theseus whispered, "We should space ourselves apart a dozen yards or so. The one by the village is now moving toward us. The others surely have seen it change direction, so they know we're around here too. They just don't know what we are."

Theseus took off into the dark. At this point, if I was a rational human being, I would have been worried. Here I am, an ordinary human, on an alien planet apparently being stalked by uplifted, modified alien predators in complete darkness. Under a night sky with red stars and an amorphous blue-green sparkly cloud floating all over every which way. Accompanied by, I'm not quite sure, maybe a Greek god, or at least his second cousin. The things we do for love!

The beast that was heading toward us stopped. I spotted two more of them a distance behind it, traveling toward the village. They were headed to a spot that was lit up, and I could see that it was a playground or game field of some sort. I caught myself. Children were playing there.

I whispered. "Theseus. Kalay. Hey, Theseus!"

I picked up some pebbles and tossed them to where I thought Theseus might be. Nothing. I tossed a rock to where I thought Kalay might be. Nothing.

The first grizzly, or whatever the hell it was, had stopped, and it was between me and the other two creatures and the children. Horrified, it occurred to me that it intended to block me from what was going to happen. A slaughter of innocents.

My face flushed. I started breathing more heavily. The spear I brought along was on the ground, I felt around for it and picked it up. I felt my sword pommel. I remember my thinking. *No, no children dying tonight.*

I stood up and started down the rise, straight towards this God knows what. I saw it shuffling around, knowing I was approaching. The spear was not that comforting. I would have gladly switched it for a full-size pike, with a metal point. At about ten yards, it started to charge. So did I.

I should have died right then, but this monster decided to roar at me. When it did, I threw, or more exactly, jammed, the spear into its mouth and down its throat. I managed to dodge its massive body as it tumbled by me.

I could see I had not much time. These were kids. They may be on another planet, maybe another species, but they sure looked like kids to me.

I sprinted at these things. No spear, but I did have this clumsy, thick, bronze sword. It worked well for our ancestors all through the Bronze Age so, hopefully, it will do the job.

They saw me. Stopping, and turning around, I saw their eyes. Large, intelligent, maybe a little too intelligent. They didn't charge me. They waited. I wished I had a twelve gauge, with deer slugs.

———◆———

Up on the ridge, two dark silhouettes were barely visible. They were observing everything.

Kalay spoke. "Should we help him?"

Theseus responded. "Naah. This is his. But, you know, I'll bet he has no idea about that sword."

———◆———

I approached a point between the village and these giant creatures. They separated and approached from opposite sides. They didn't charge immediately, and I was thankful for that. Perhaps they were wary after seeing what happened to their buddy up the hill. When they got closer, I backed up, maybe ten yards. These truly were monsters. Some vague similarity to grizzlies, but their front paws had elongated digits and vicious claws. Their eyes were much larger. To me, they were abominations. There was a boulder to my right and I stood closer to it. They turned slightly away and started to move past me. Some rocks were on the ground. I picked one up. I threw it hard at the closest one, striking its nose, or whatever passed for one with these. The impact made a satisfying sound. That had to hurt. It stopped, grunted and snorted. Maybe it was in pain, maybe it was talking. The other one charged. I thought that was the end of it for me. Using both hands, I held my sword straight out towards it. Apparently, not wanting to run itself onto the blade, it stopped right before my reach. Still, its front arms were far longer than my sword. Dodging the blade, it made a dash at me. I slashed at it, managing to cut into one of its arms. It didn't stop. It swung its other arm at me, and that hit me hard. I was hurled against the boulder, and my head smashed against it. There was a sudden pain and burning in my chest. I started to black out. Shaking my head, I looked down, and I was sickened when I saw a huge gash across my ribs. So much for the Kevlar undershirt. It was shredded, and my clothes were soaked in my blood.

The creature, apparently convinced that I was no longer a threat, acting on its monstrous arrogance, stood on its hind legs, reaching an incredible height. It towered over me, and roared in triumph. This affront to nature, this obscene cross between a Grendel and a grizzly bear, was exalting in its domination over the puny creature cowering in front of it.

Looking up at it, what crossed my mind came out of nowhere. How so many thoughts can cross one's mind in an instant, when facing certain death, and where they come from, I don't know. But, what I suddenly realized was what this thing had no way of knowing about us, all of us. In our past, our ancestors, our great, great, great-grandparents, not only survived but conquered a brutal world by hunting and killing monsters of every sort imaginable, and they did it with the most primitive of weapons, made from rocks and sticks. What it did not know was that I, and every human alive, are the genetic offspring of those ancestors. That is our legacy. We are monster killers.

Realizing that, I grew ashamed, and then I grew enraged. I knew I was going to die. The certainty transformed me into a madman. Accepting my fate, I stood up to my full height. Surprised, it turned its head to look down. We made eye contact.

Without thinking, I kicked it. It was an insane thing to do. But I kicked it, right between the legs. As hard as anyone could do. I was wearing boots. It bellowed out an enormous noise, and immediately went back to all fours. Suddenly, we were face to face.

Kalay - "Did I see that right?"

Theseus - "Now we know they have balls."

There was a movement in my hand, a reminder. My sword. I saw the opening. Again, without thinking, before it could turn its head, I jammed the blade into its eye socket. Up to the hilt. I was lifted off the ground by holding onto the grip. It shook its head, making an earsplitting howl, but I knew it was finished.

I yanked it out just in time to sense the enormous shadow of the other one standing over me. Its huge mouth with spectacular fangs and its foul breath. Its front arms swiped at me. I blindly stabbed upwards into its neck. There was a grunting sound, and I was slammed against the boulder, again. I tumbled off it, and the creature crashed on top of me, making a hellish, gurgling, howl. Abruptly, there was just complete blackness and a crushing, dumbfounding weight.

It was an eternity. I slowly became aware of myself, but only to wonder if I was alive. There was no light - just nothing. Was I dead? Was this how those who are blind and deaf experience consciousness? I had no sight, no hearing. Was I really dead? This wasn't supposed to happen. I wasn't supposed to die. Not then, not when I found love with Zoe. Not when I had so much hope. A new beginning. I thought of the Greek Mystery religions. Lost in eternal nothingness. Demeter's pleading for Persephone's return to the upper world. I felt tears rolling down my cheeks. That, ironically, that gave me hope. Maybe I was alive. I realized I was breathing, but barely and with great pain, for there was an unbelievable weight on my chest. It was slowly constricting my rib cage. I didn't have much time.

I heard sounds. Muffled noises. Were there people up above? They grew louder, and the mass on top of me moved, rocked sideways, and began rising. Suddenly, there was extraordinary, brilliant light. It was beautiful, and I'll never forget it. I looked around and made out people, dozens of people. All around me. Men and women and children. A man was bent over, reaching down, grabbing me. I was stood up, and I saw people holding torches, grinning, hard men and serious women, with spears, swords, knives, clubs. Some were laughing and slapping me on the back. I saw Theseus and Kalay. Theseus put his foot on the beast's neck and pulled out my sword. My vision was bad, but that sword was glowing. He covered it, walked over, and put it in my scabbard. Laughing, he hugged me. It was painful.

Grabbing my arm, Kalay whispered, "Essie, we watched from above. The damnest thing we ever saw. Everyone here. It was extraordinary."

Theseus, standing next to the village leader, spoke. "You put yourself between those things and the children. Zoe said you were stouthearted. Now we see it for ourselves. She chose wisely."

I felt pasty wetness on my face. When I reached up, I saw muscle and bone exposed on my forearm. I was starting to hurt badly. My chest was burning. Theseus was talking to the village leader, laughing, and hugging several of the men holding spears. My vision started narrowing, and my knees gave out.

We were back on the ship and a celebration was going on. None of us had eaten for a while, and a buffet was laid out. I had no appetite, though. People were introducing themselves, shaking hands, hugging, and laughing about everything that happened. I met many intriguing individuals. Men and women. There were people from Earth and others who were human-looking and had to be from very Earth-like planets.

They'd collected tissue samples from these creatures and hunted them using various methods. A few individuals came by and asked if I actually kicked a grizzly the way they heard. Several women were especially interested in the story. An anthropologist on the trip told me she believes I likely started a new rite of passage for the young males in that region. I was mortified. The initial consensus was that the Kitren could handle these creatures. After all, they determined most of its DNA came from *Arctodus simus*, a monster our ancestors hunted and killed. The species is extinct. We're not.

I was not feeling well. I had stitches and staples in my arm, my head, across my chest. My head was hurting, a lot. I was seeing double. I think one of my ribs was fractured. So, I decided to call it an early evening. Or whatever time it was in space there.

I made a mistake, though. As a new member of this group, I was expected to drink a certain traditional tea, which consisted of barley, water, honey, goat cheese, penny royal, sometimes wine, and other unknown ingredients. So I did, and rather liked it. I was thirsty, so I drank some more. Kykeon is actually good tasting, and it's a very healthy drink. It is a drink well known to historians. The ancient Greeks consumed it at the dramatic climax of the initiation ceremonies for the Eleusinian Mystery religion, a religion that started in prehistory and was practiced for over two thousand years. It is perhaps one of the most inexplicable historical unknowns - just what are all the ingredients in that drink? No one knows. That is, no one knows, except the people I'm traveling with. It's said that one drinks kykeon to meet the Gods.

I had a brain injury of some kind, maybe a skull fracture. About an hour after I drank the kykeon, the ship went into hyper-drive, and I felt time twisting. One should never drink kykeon and then travel on a ship that warps time and space. I grew drowsy, and then I dreamed. I dreamed of the Irish Wilderness, when I journeyed there a year ago.

CHAPTER 44: THE IRISH WILDERNESS

There's an ancient forest in flyover country. Four hundred-year-old trees. Unpolluted streams, fresh, pure air, few hiking trails. No human noise. No humans at all. Except for me. Not labeled on any map. Maybe the locals know. But, the locals are not very local around there.

Last summer, I knew it was time to go back. Once again, I hated myself and I hated my life. It seemed pointless, ugly, and meaningless. Chasing money, everyone else chasing money. In the Navy, that was not done. Nor, I assume, in the priesthood. In those professions, people have different goals and different motivations. So, with everything becoming overbearing, I knew it was time to escape for a while into a different world where avaricious greed is not the predominant purpose in life.

I needed to head to a place that no one knew of. I canceled everything - court hearings, appointments, and meetings. When asked, I simply said I was heading south. I didn't want to share my plans. That would somehow sully them. It was important to tell no one where I was going. Perhaps that's unwise should something go wrong but, to me and I think to many people, that makes the journey more serious, more consequential.

The Irish Wilderness is a specific area in the Mark Twain National Forest, which covers a good part of southern Missouri. An immense area, with very few roads through it. It is an area that draws many hikers from around the country. Hiking trails crisscross it in most sections. Any number of maps show them. But the maps also show areas where there are no roads, no trails of any sort. That's what I have always looked for. Then, I pull up a terrain map and look for the valleys, ridges, canyons, creeks, and tributaries.

There are many areas there that are isolated, but I found one in particular that I knew I wanted to get to. No towns nearby, no roads. No trails. I took off in the first week of April. I stripped my car of anything valuable and drove down to Doniphan, Missouri. Some people there advertise that they'll watch your car and drive you to whatever trailhead, or river access point, you want. That's what I did.

I was dropped off about twenty miles north of town and started my way west to the area I wanted. Hiking up creek beds and deer traces. It was neither easy nor fun. I was wearing a stuffed backpack with lights, compass, sleeping bag, tarp, water bottle, water filter, various foods, knife, medical kit, and, as people who hike know, the list goes on and on. I sprayed my clothing and everything else with permethrin, hoping that would take care of ticks and chiggers. When I filled up my water from a creek, I made sure there was no dead animal around the bend upstream. While hiking, I saw many animals, and more than a few deer. They were certainly not afraid. They just weren't hunted much there.

I was dropped off in the morning and by five or so I figured I made it about ten miles in. So the first night I camped on a gravel bar by a large stream. It wasn't too bad. There were bugs, but certainly not enough to cause problems.

Early the next morning, I took off again. I followed the stream. Around noon time I came upon an awe-inspiring bluff. Water seeped from its many crevices and holes. The drainage stained the face with innumerable shades of brown, black, white and silver, creating an ancient appearance. Where the bluff's bottom met the creek, the pristine water, rushing up from the Earth's fathomless depths, the Soul of the World, was a translucent, ethereal, shade of blue. A blue that seemed possessed of additional dimensions. The blue that Maxfield Parrish endeavored to reveal in his paintings. I would put my hands together, scooping up the water, and in the sunlight it all but disappeared, as if I held luminous aether.

It was spring water - frigid, numbing even. A good many of the waterways in this part of the state are supplied by springs, some enormous. I've canoed on many of them. They are so stunningly beautiful Congress created the Ozark National Scenic Riverways, allowing the National Park Service to protect the region. Even though it's southern Missouri, the streams are inhabited by pickerel and trout. Herds of wild horses call the area home.

The southern Ozarks is known for karst geology, with the rock formations mostly limestone and dolomite. Up a little from the bluff was a smaller creek flowing into the one I was hiking along. Checking the map and the compass and looking up at this towering cliff, I determined that this was my destination. Now, I had to somehow get to the top.

It took a good hour to make it there. I backtracked a hundred yards or so, made my way to a low area, and proceeded upwards. Lugging a backpack did not make it easier. Still, it was definitely worth it. There was a spectacular view to the horizon of green-leafed trees on rolling hills. I went about setting up camp.

The Irish Wilderness, and the Mark Twain National Forest, were logged extensively in the past century. But, there are a surprising number of areas that were not logged because they were too inaccessible. In small canyons in between hills with cliffs, there was no way to cut down the trees and get them to a road. These areas are of course the hardest to get to. I made it to this one. A canyon down below, surrounded on both sides by cliffs, with a long stretch of immense trees, trees with trunks maybe five feet in diameter. Hundreds of them. Oak, hickory, and coming out of the bluffs, pine trees with twisted trunks. A place where the trees were never forested, never cut down.

Looking down into this hidden world, I caught glimpses of the creek weaving its way to the one I followed. There was an updraft of surprisingly cool air. A spring or a cave had to be down there in the small canyon. Something to explore later, perhaps.

I stayed up late that night. No moon, the Milky Way was painted across the sky. No city lights, no human lights. I say human lights because I did see lights of a sort. Definitely not lightning bugs. Never bright, fading at times, they weaved through the woods below, darting and stopping. I brought a small Nikon along, and I took a few shots of the horizon and the night sky, which was why I hiked uphill to camp at this high point. F/2.8 aperture, 6400 ISO, and ten to fifteen-second exposures seemed to work best. No tripod, so I laid it on some rocks with it pointed up. Not exactly a professional method. While doing that I caught sight of a satellite quickly traversing the sky, from west to east, then sharply changing course, around ninety degrees, and heading south. Without the right instruments, all one can do is speculate about those things. Who knows what it was?

It was a beautiful night. I was so happy to be there. It was cool, the breeze coming from below. An owl was hooting, not too far away. Coyotes howled in the distance, a reminder that the modern world is not all there is. The sounds, the atmosphere, the night sky, the smell of the wet earth, and the lights in the woods, created a certain sense of awareness for me. Hamlet comes to mind. "And therefore as a stranger give it welcome. There are more things in heaven and earth, Horatio, than are dreamt of in your philosophy." Of course, that would depend upon one's particular dreams.

It is, I believe, one of the reasons I did those trips. No sounds or sights of the modern world. Time's anchors then seem to be loosened, and I drift along into the past and the future. My mind comes to a point where the concept of time is meaningless, there is only the present, and the present includes the past and the future together with it.

I fell asleep then and there. I had a strange dream. In the dream, I wake up and look over the forest and the stars. I stand up and turn around. In the darkness, there is a darker shape. It separates in two and the smaller one approaches me. It's a person wearing a cloak, with a hood covering the face.

"Who are you?"

A woman's voice said, "We're the reason you've come here."

"I can't see you very well."

"You don't want to. But we had to see you, and talk to you. One more time."

We were close enough, so I reached out and pulled back her hood. She was elderly. Very, very old. She possessed a compassionate face, with thin, gray hair, and she regarded me with a penetrating gaze. She looked familiar. I saw that she was hunched over. And, she was crying.

"I am your daughter."

———————◆O◆———————

I hurl off the couch. Looking around, I frantically struggle to remember where I am. On a superluminal craft I desperately hope is headed back to Earth. Back to Zoe. Sweating so much that there are puddles of water on the couch, I breathe as fast as I can. I remember things. All sorts of things. I remember past lives, that may, or may not, be mine. I remember my wife and daughter dying, and what could have been. I remember other children. I remember myself dying, again, and again. My memory is broken, because it is not blocking out thousands of years of living. There are no guardrails, and I am struggling to contain myself and keep my sanity.

The ship senses the distress and a woman comes in. She grips my hands, and touches her forehead to mine.

Chapter 45: The Mission

It was nighttime and pitch dark. There are dozens of rooms in the Eliades house. The long hallway on the second floor is lined with solid teakwood doors, different intricate designs carved into each. The figure, jet black, was invisible as he strolled down the hallway. At the end, where the stairs were, he turned around. Then he spoke. His voice was not loud, but it was impeccable, deep, and precise. Everyone in the rooms behind those doors, despite their thickness, heard it and knew who he was.

"All right, it's time to save this sorry-ass planet. Get up, get your gear, and muster outside."

The men and women who heard him smiled. Some laughed. Wasn't Theseus born on this "sorry-ass" planet? Of course, they were already standing by, anxious to start. Doors opened, and a varied crew stepped into the hallway almost immediately. The huge orbs outside were waiting for them. Even those most amazing objects appeared eager to begin. Aegeus Eliades, ready for war, stood beside them.

At the same time, if someone happened to be sailing on the Indian Ocean, approximately two thousand miles southwest of Australia, which really is almost never the case, he or she would be witness to a truly wondrous sight of several hundred luminous orbs rising from below the ocean surface like champagne bubbles. The emerald waters lit up so to such a degree that the ocean became translucent, almost seeming to disappear. The orbs rose in altitude to several thousand feet and began to shoot off in all directions at extraordinary speed. North, South, East, West, and all points in between. If one were to witness this sight and repeat it to others, he or she would be thought to be conjuring up a fairy tale. Such disbelief has happened many times in history.

Chapter 46: The End of the World

A cross the United States, there is a vast, disjointed system of Civil Defense sirens. In the Midwest, these are usually tested every Wednesday at noon, unless there is a potentially dangerous storm system in the area. They are utilized to warn the populace of imminent tornadoes and damaging storms. Many people don't know that the sirens are also intended to be utilized for a different purpose – to warn people of an incoming nuclear missile attack.

When the sirens are tested, people under sixty just pay no heed. Those older, even though they know it's a test that sounds off every Wednesday at noon, well, they just wince. They grew up under the cloud of nuclear annihilation. Being taught to and ordered to hide underneath their school desks during regular drills. Watching their anxious parents look at each other in fear during the Cuban Missile Crisis. People at work regularly practiced proceeding, in an orderly fashion, to a bomb shelter stocked with Geiger counters, iodine pills, and water, trying hard not to contemplate what it would actually mean if it were not a drill. Many families built bomb shelters in their backyards and took firearm lessons from the National Rifle Association, so they could accurately shoot dead any neighbors who might decide to grab the shelters for themselves should the Soviets decide to destroy capitalism with balls of atomic fire.

It was much the same story in the Soviet Union, with the Politburo drumming into the proletariat that the Americans wanted to exterminate them. Red China was consumed by Mao Zedong's Cultural Revolution. In the past, the Chinese leadership insanely believed they could absorb a full nuclear strike and still have hundreds of millions of people survive to carry on the work of the Party. They now have their own arsenal of doomsday missiles.

A bright, sunny day, Thursday, July 11, 7:00 a.m., Central Time. Downtown Kansas City, Missouri. Thousands of cars, SUVs, and pickup trucks are exiting off the highways onto the city streets. The parking garages are filling up. Hundreds of people are strolling up and down the sidewalks, looking to get a quick breakfast or some coffee drink at the different Starbucks, before starting the day at work. A siren goes off. At first, people think it's a police car siren, or perhaps an ambulance or fire truck. They hear more. A number of them, from completely different directions. Some people think to themselves it must be a test, it must be Wednesday. Others think that's odd, a tornado or storm is coming on such a bright, cloudless day. Cell phones are looked at. Horror slowly spreads. People begin to realize they are listening to a quadraphonic cacophony of Gabriel's horns announcing the end of the world.

Moscow, 3:00 p.m., their time. Terror strikes. Thousands of riders are confused when the Moscow Metro stops, nowhere near any stations. There is utter quiet. The young men and women, who still have excellent auditory perception, hear it. Sirens. Sirens they didn't quite recognize. A different pattern from the distinct police and ambulance sirens heard in European cities. The sirens get louder, and it has become apparent to young and old that the end of the world has arrived.

The citizens of Beijing, most at home during the evening, also hear their imminent doom. A city of twenty-two million souls, none of them could think of a safe place to hide, for the Americans are attacking.

NORAD Command Center, Peterson Space Force Base, Colorado. Royal Canadian Air Force General Harold Maxwell, stunned, took in the hundreds of missiles being tracked on their seventy-five-foot-wide status board. He picked up the red phone.

"White House Situation Room."

"This is NORAD, General Maxwell. Missile attack. This is not a drill. We are tracking 322 ballistic missiles, tracking from both Russian and Chinese ICBM ranges. Confidence Level High. This is not a drill"

"How long until impact?"

"Nineteen minutes."

"Has StratCom been contacted?"

"General Ian Reynolds here, Duty Officer, United States Strategic Command. All stand-by strategic bombers have been ordered airborne. Standing by on order to launch missiles."

"God help us. Let me contact the President."

<hr/>

Late afternoon - the Kremlin was busy. The Russian President was hurriedly corralled down to a secret bomb shelter seven floors beneath his office. It was a satellite command center and on the wall was a display showing hundreds of missiles coming across the Northern Pacific, along with heavy bomber tracks originating from the American Midwest. Sickened, he recognized the end of everything. A young bright-eyed Naval lieutenant stood by him, holding the briefcase. Generals and colonels were standing at the opposite end of the room, staring at him, several with tears in their eyes.

"Can this, all of this, be spoofed?"

"Nyet, we have voice confirmation from our ballistic missile radars in Yeniseysk and Mishelevka. Multiple air targets. Our space command reports multiple missile launch detections from our infrared and optical satellites."

"How much time do we have?"

Someone answered, "Nineteen minutes."

The General Secretary and President of China was by happenstance at his Zhongnanhai office near the Forbidden Palace. The alerted staff escorted him into a secret shelter that also had a satellite command center. In it, he saw the approaching onslaught of missiles.

The U.S. President, who happened to be in the Oval Office when the missiles were detected, was first taken to the White House Situation Room.

"I was told there are 322 missiles inbound, nineteen minutes until the first impacts. That's what I was briefed on earlier. Is that still current?"

"Yes sir."

"Mr. President, at this time it is best to take the train to the emergency bunker."

"We both know that will do no good. It will be obliterated along with the rest of the city, and the country. Is this a false alarm? Is it a ruse?"

"No sir. Ballistic missile radars all confirm contacts. A half dozen of our detection satellites all detected launches from the Russian and Chinese launch areas."

"No time for an answer, but we had the Kremlin thoroughly infiltrated, there was absolutely no hint of coordination with the Chinese on this."

The National Security Advisor ran into the room. "Mr. President, we have verified that the Russians believe, and their radars and satellites also detected, a massive attack originating from North America, from all of our strategic assets, approximately ten minutes ago."

"What the hell. I gave no such order!"

The Chairman of the Joint Chiefs, who was present by audio-video transmission, yelled out. "That is false. Absolutely no launches have taken place. No ICBMs have launched. Most of our planes are in the air, but they have launched no missiles."

"Mr. President. You have a decision to make. Do we retaliate?"

Chapter 47: What Transpires

The Kremlin bomb shelter was a madhouse. "Mr. President. As the Commander-in-Chief, you must give the order to launch. We will lose that capacity in minutes."

There was yelling behind the President. "Let me in. This has to be known."

GRU General Anton Detiatov, accompanied by Colonel Igor Travinsky, was screaming.

"Let him in, let him in."

"Mr. President. The Americans detected hundreds of missiles heading towards them around twenty minutes ago. I couldn't believe it. Both our assets broke cover and called the embassy. It's true."

"So that's the reason they have launched this attack. Who did this? Beijing? To get rid of both us and America at the same time?"

"We may never know. It's too late now."

"Colonel Travinsky has just been giving me his report today. He may have an answer to that."

"Mr. President, the anomalies that regularly appear on our radars, they appear and disappear at will. They can appear as multiple targets and travel as fast as our ballistic missiles. They are real. They are not the Americans. They may be responsible for this."

"Mr. President. It doesn't matter. We need you to order the launch. Mr. President ....."

———◄○►———

The secret shelter underneath the General Secretary's Zhongnanhai office was overheated. Too many people in too small a space. All of them panicking. Some people lit cigarettes and the harsh smoke created a white haze over everyone's heads.

"Mr. General Secretary. We have reason to believe that the Americans were tricked. Perhaps by our Kremlin friends, though it makes no sense for them to do that. Their radars, and the two DSP satellites of theirs we have feeds from, showed launches from all of our western bases. I confirmed that no one ordered that and there in fact are no such launches. They will launch only on your order and are standing by."

"We are waiting for your order, Mr. Secretary."

———◄○►———

In the bomb shelter below the Kremlin, significant events transpired.

Turning to the Naval lieutenant, the President said, "Issue the order. Launch our missiles."

The young officer, Alexi Popov, looked at GRU General Detiatov, and then Colonel Travinsky. He knelt, opened the suitcase, flipped open the keypad cover, and he stopped.

Lieutenant Popov stood up, looked at the President of the Russian Federation, and said in a clear voice, "Nyet."

The Russian Security Council Secretary, standing nearby, screamed at him. "That was an order!"

Lieutenant Popov looked at him and said, "It is an illegal, it is a mistaken order."

The Security Council Secretary pulled out a pistol, and aimed it at the lieutenant.

There was the sound of a gunshot.

The Secretary, with a hole in his temple, fell to the floor with a loud thud, quite dead.

GRU General Detiatov stood there with the gun still smoking, pointing at the dead body.

The President of the Russian Federation looked at him, and at the dead body. He said, "The young lieutenant has a valid point. After reconsideration, I withdraw my order. Now, we wait and see what transpires."

In the White House Situation Room, a fateful decision was made. The President, his face pale, perspiration on his forehead, said forcefully "No!"

The Chairman of the Joint Chiefs spoke up, starting at a whisper, and ending in a scream. "We will lose everything if we don't launch NOW!"

The President looked around, found a chair, and sat down. With his head in his hands he said, "If we launch, yes, we would utterly incinerate half of China, western Russia, and most of Siberia. But in doing so, we also condemn Europe to death. And eventually, the entire world. No. Hell no. I won't be a party to the end of the world. Even if it means we are not avenged."

Everyone in the room, and the Chairman of the Joint Chiefs, heard this. They knew he was right. Then, there was nothing more to do, and they resigned themselves to their fate.

The General Secretary of the People's Republic looked at his advisors and smiled.

"The Russians think the Americans have launched. The Americans think the Russians have launched, as well as us. There is trickery afoot here. We may suffer a horrific nuclear attack. But China will survive and grow stronger. We will sit back and hope that we are here tomorrow to see the sun rise. It will certainly be a new world, no matter what transpires today."

CHAPTER 48: LIEUTENANT COLONEL LAMMERS

All the militaries that deploy nuclear weaponry are existentially challenged by how to prevent a rogue actor from detonating one without authority. The consequences of such a person successfully doing so include many nightmarish possibilities, including the worst-case scenario, the start of World War Three. Could a nation's political leadership not conduct a retaliatory nuclear strike if a rogue actor destroys one of their major cities? It could well be impossible.

Almost all nuclear weapon assets were alerted and deployed, one of them being a B-52H bomber out of Minot Air Force Base in North Dakota. Lieutenant Colonel Henry Lammers was the aircraft commander when they were given the order to take off and fly to their Go/No Go point. The B-52 bombers no longer carry nuclear bombs. To carry out their strategic role, they now utilize long-range-stand-off missiles (LRSO) with nuclear warheads. They don't have to penetrate Russian or Chinese airspace. The missiles do. A number of the missiles are hypersonic.

Lt. Colonel Lammers was in a conflicted emotional state. He'd been in the Air Force for thirty years. All that time he practiced dropping nuclear bombs on Russia or now, more recently, practiced going to a location over the Pacific Ocean and firing nuclear-tipped long-range-stand-off (LRSO) missiles that will do the same. It was not unnatural for him to think that, at the end of his career, he was a failure since he'd never performed his life's work.

This mission started like any other. They get the bird up into the air and proceed to a point over the Pacific, about halfway to Russia. There, they wait for the Go/No Go signal from the Air Force Global Strike Command. Colonel Lammers got the word the day before that since his retirement date is within thirty days, he will be taken off flight status. Today was his last day.

The entire crew knew this was not an ordinary mission. A number of alerts were received. They knew something was up. Regardless, they were trained to treat this flight as all the others until they received a command signal at the Go/No Go point.

The co-pilot and flight engineer, Major Billings, was competent enough, but fully recognized that Lammers was in command. Lammers wrote his evaluation report, and Billings has a wife and several children to take care of. He had no way of knowing the existential dread Lammers was experiencing, and the epiphany he had when the voices in his head kept on telling him that his entire life had come to this, his one final flight.

So, one hour later, at 25,000 feet, around 1500 miles northwest of Hawaii, they received a transmission. For the very first time, they did not receive a GO or a NO GO. They received a "HOLD." This was especially suspicious because they had always received a NO GO well before they reached their Go/No Go point. Since they did not receive a No GO they were steeling themselves to receive a GO order. Major Billings switched frequencies and requested confirmation. The signal was not strong. It was an encrypted voice transmission, the syncing delays and distorts the audio. Major Billings heard NO GO. Colonel Lammers heard GO, but he did not know if it was from his headphones or from his voices.

Lieutenant Colonel Lammers made a fateful decision. In his mind, Russia was a treacherous, perfidious, extraordinarily evil state. His entire life was devoted to training to destroy it. He had no plans for his upcoming retirement. He knew his life would soon be without meaning, without purpose. Also, he had his secret. He heard voices in his head. They only were present when he was stressed. He knew what that meant. He never told anyone about them since his flying days started, because his entire career would immediately end. Besides, he was sure he could keep them under control.

Lieutenant Colonel Lammers was told that a strike on Moscow would be a decapitation strike, and the Russian military command structure would collapse on its destruction. So he decided to act.

With the intent to reduce crew size at some point in the future, the Air Force recently upgraded the B-52H, digitally linking all crew stations, giving the cockpit the ability to release weapons, like the B-2 and B-21 strategic bombers.

"Air Crew, stand by to launch missile. Activate consent unlock. Weapons System Officer, transfer weapon release to cockpit."

Shocked, Major Billings turned his head and looked at Colonel Lammers. "What, what are you doing?"

Colonel Lammers said emphatically, "I am the Aircraft Commander. It was a GO. I heard it clearly."

Major Billings then had some self-doubt. His headphones were old and emitted feedback. Also, for the first time, they did not receive an order before reaching the Go/No Go point. It was also the first time they'd heard a "HOLD" command.

"Shouldn't we get confirmation? I did not hear it clearly."

Lieutenant Colonel Lammers turned his head to him, looked him in the eye, and said, "I heard it clearly, Major. Are you capable of fulfilling your duty here?"

Unconsciously, Major Billings looked down to see if Lammers had his hand on his sidearm. He felt embarrassed when he saw that it wasn't.

"Russia is an evil nation. We are God's lightning. God will strike it down. Just like David decapitated Goliath, we will decapitate Russia."

Whereupon, Major Billings followed Colonel Lammers's lead and both inserted their launch keys into the weapons control panel slots. They both turned their keys to the right. Colonel Lammers reached over to the red missile release handle. Twisting it to the right, he pulled it. The missile was released from its pylon, ignited, and took off. With a warhead ten times as powerful as the one that exploded over Hiroshima.

Sixty seconds later, an interrogatory was received from Strike Command.

"Confirm receipt of NO GO. Over."

Major Billings looked at Colonel Lammers in horror.

Colonel Lammers smiled. His life's purpose had been fulfilled. After thirty years of training, his subconscious had, at some point, distorted his personality. While his conscious mind always avoided thinking about it, his subconscious, not bound by conscious control, was all too aware of the nightmarish consequences, the horror, of what a nuclear weapon, a weapon he would release, would do. For him to continue to function, to survive, his capacity for remorse, for empathy, had to be buried.

So, rogue actors are a significant, known risk to the military use of nuclear weapons. Yet, militaries have never figured out how to always stop them. This missile was headed to Moscow, a city of thirteen million souls. And if it made it, it would start World War Three.

Three minutes later, with Major Billings desperately trying to contact Strike Command, and Colonel Lammers just listlessly looking through the window into the distance, they both noticed a small golden dot on the horizon. The same direction their missile went. The dot grew in size. In the blink of an eye, they were confronted with an enormous golden plasma ball directly in front of them. The effect is caused by the time/space warp field produced by the orb inside it. Inside the field, time becomes jumbled, with future sometimes mixing with past, and space contracting and expanding.

All of this happened in perhaps a second. The field moved and encompassed the B-52's cockpit. Colonel Lammers blinked and spotted a strange, lopsided, soccer ball-like object slowly tumbling toward him, surrounded by a cloud of diamonds. As it approached, he saw what appeared to be a patch of hair. Then he saw eyes, nose, mouth. He had enough time to realize that he was looking at his own head. Because, within the field, sometimes the future happens before the present. The LRSO missile's direction had been reversed, and it shot straight for the B-52. Its canard shattered the port cockpit window, creating a cloud of glass shards, and it decapitated Colonel Lammers.

Chapter 49: Major Collins Visits

S everal weeks later, a plain, American-built four-door sedan made its way down a suburban street. Unmarked. Air Force Intelligence foregoes using the ubiquitous blue sedans with Air Force markings found in plentiful supply at the many Air Force bases in the U.S. and around the world. Major Randall Collins was thankful for that. He did not want to draw any attention to his destination. Driving down a hill into the valley on the way there, he noted the many trees and the wonderful shade they produced in the August sun. He also pondered how soon it would be before all the cars driven in the U.S. would be electric. People are beginning to believe it may be quite a bit sooner than originally thought. Following his GPS he arrived at the location he was looking for, where the road intersects with a driveway blocked by a closed metal gate. There was an intercom on a post next to it. He put the car into park, walked over, pushed a button, and said "Good Morning, Major Collins here."

The speaker box replied, "You found it! Just follow the driveway up the hill."

With that, he got back into his car, as the gate opened. He started driving up the hill. He came to a large, beautiful house, with a circular drive. There were some additional parking spaces off to the side, and he drove over there and parked.

Getting out and walking towards the front of the house, he heard the unmistakable, omnipresent din of the cicadas that come out every summer and in so doing mark the passing of time. He eyed a large man walking toward him. They met halfway.

The man reached his hand out. Major Collins took it, and they shook hands.

"Good morning, Major, I am Aegeus Eliades. I am very happy to make your acquaintance."

"Mr. Eliades, I am grateful to you for allowing me to come visit you at your home."

"No problem. Let's go inside, where it's air-conditioned."

Major Collins was appreciative. He noticed he was sweating already in the heat, and his hair was wet under the Air Force service cap he put on when exiting his car.

Walking into the main room, he was offered and gladly accepted some iced tea. He found a chair and sat down, taking the opportunity to look around. From the Major's perspective, it was sensational - fine European furniture, classic works of art, teak wood ceiling beams, and several intriguing artifacts.

"Mr. Eliades, in light of the remarkable events over the past few months, I was asked to visit you and introduce myself."

"Major, it is an extraordinary time. World War Three apparently commenced, then abruptly ended, and the world is shocked and horrified."

"I wake up every morning now and have to remind myself this has happened. Mr. Eliades, what has been reported in the news is true. Every nation on the planet has agreed to give up nuclear weapons. They've agreed to submit to a remarkably intrusive inspection regime. The reason for my visit is to inquire of you as to certain aspects of how this has occurred."

Aggie smiled, stood up, and walked over to an ancient, weathered, marble frieze on the wall, about three by five feet, in which was carved a woman sitting and several men, wrapped in tunics and holding spears, standing in front of her.

Major Collins noticed it then, having previously overlooked it. Stunned, he thought to himself, *'No fucking way.'*

Aggie, grinning, turned around and faced him. "Major. It was gifted to my family long before Lord Elgin was even born."

Aggie Eliades strolled over to a burnished, mahogany writing box resting on an antique table. He opened up the top half, exposing the leather writing surface. He pressed down on a small piece of wood and a hidden drawer popped open. Picking out an old photograph from inside it, he handed it over to Major Collins.

It was an aged color photo, maybe from the early 1960s. In it, Aggie Eliades, looking exactly like he does today, was smiling, standing next to a grinning Air Force First Lieutenant wearing a garrison cap. Unmistakably, it was a very young General Odinberg. Directly behind them, hovering just above the ground, was a large silver flying saucer.

"Major, Henry Odinberg and I go back a long way, a very, very long way."

Major Collins was dumbfounded. General Henry Odinberg, U. S. Air Force Vice Chief of Staff, called him yesterday, directly from Washington, D.C. An extremely unusual thing to happen to a major. The general specifically requested that he visit Mr. Eliades. He requested, ordered, that Major Collins ask Mr. Eliades just what he knew of the recent events, and to keep everything he learned secret, only to be reported to him.

"Major, I'm sure you've been given some briefings, really just speculation, about us. General Odinberg has decided to bring you in, so to speak. There's a small group of Air Force officers who, since 1952, have kept our secret, passed it on, and coordinated with us. This was specifically authorized by President Harry Truman and the Air Force has full authority to act in this manner. We act in pursuit of one goal - to keep this planet safe from self-immolation. It is our home too. Just so there's no doubt, it's true. We raise our families here, but we travel the galaxy with our friends who come here from many light years away. We do not raise our children on star ships, space stations, or other planets. This is our home, it always has been."

Major Collins, and it might be thought of as an odd reaction, became exuberant. Tears formed in his eyes. "So, there really is extraterrestrial life? They visit the Earth? There's faster than light craft?"

"Major, yes. You can be certain of it. That, and much, much more. We created this immediate crisis. Because, the world had forgotten the horror of a global nuclear war. These recent events, as we surmised, have successfully negated that possibility for a while. Maybe, just maybe, permanently. I suspect what Henry is curious about now is what we have hidden from modern science for a number of years - anti-gravity."

"Anti-gravity? Mr. Eliades, I didn't know that was possible. I know there's been a number of programs to figure that out, including a significant one here in this area. I spent a month on temporary duty at the Naval War College several years ago. There was discussion then about just what widespread use of anti-gravity propulsion would mean to our survival. Even then, the military applications were obvious. But, every attempt to figure it out was a dead end."

"Anti-gravity and nuclear weaponry is a nightmarish combination. I think it occurred to Henry that if nuclear weapons are going away, anti-gravity propulsion will not be the existential threat it would be otherwise. And, he's right."

"So, your people have the technology? We'll get anti-gravity propulsion?"

"Major, you Americans are smart. You've already discovered it, worked it out, and experimented with anti-gravity a dozen times or so. Anti-gravity propulsion allows for extraordinary, unimaginable acceleration and velocity. But, we screwed the pooch, so to speak, We spiked the research, and we altered the testing, at Sandia, Lawrence Livermore, Los Alamos, Wright-Patterson, Huntsville. We did a number of things, including right here in Lee's Summit and Kansas City. We also did the same in the old Soviet Union. The People's Republic of China gave up. They figured if the Americans can't do it, then they can't. We tricked them into thinking that. But the reality is, we have made sure the technology is hidden. And we will continue to do so until it is certain that there is not a single nuclear warhead in existence on the planet. And, we have the ability to do all of that."

"Mr. Eliades, how? The events of the last weeks, how could all of that have been done? Concrete missile silo covers blasted open, on their own. A number of missiles launched, on their own. Some stayed in their silos, and exploded. We believe some ended up diving straight into the ocean after launching. Both ours and the Russians. Firing controls went crazy on our ballistic missile submarines. Our SSPARS phased array ballistic missile radars detected hundreds of incoming missiles, but they never hit any targets. They just disappeared. The infrared detectors on our DSP and SBIRS satellites detected hundreds of launches. Our intelligence reports, hell, both the Russian and Chinese leadership have outright said so, that the same scenarios happened to them. We had one incident with a B-52 pilot who went insane and launched a hypersonic, long-range missile with a nuclear warhead. We would never have believed what the co-pilot said, but the interior and exterior cockpit cameras recorded it all, documenting that it somehow reversed course and one of its canards decapitated him."

"Yes, about that, he attempted to commit genocide, a war crime, and in so doing would have started World War Three."

"But, how would you know about that?"

Smiling, Aggie responded. "Let's just say Eleni and I were in the neighborhood. The consensus is that it was fully justified. That, and everything that you recited, was intended to demonstrate how easily all the nuclear safeguards, all the fail-safe mechanisms, all the human reliability programs, are so much wishful thinking. One person, I'll say it again, one person, can start World War Three. Someone, mentally ill, pulls the trigger. One nuclear missile hits one city. Our best analysis concluded that no nation's political leadership could resist the demand to retaliate. And then, Major Collins, the world ends. This is reality. In the blink of an eye. Anyone in the world, who controls even one warhead, can end life on this planet. It's insanity, madness. This is what we so badly wanted to demonstrate to every human being. I believe we have."

Major Collins contemplated what Aegeus Eliades said, and realized it was undeniably true. He then asked, "Who is Eleni?"

There was an awkward silence.

Aggie said, in a quiet voice, "Okay, Major. You wanted to know how we are capable of doing all of this. I know Henry can't be here today. It's going to take him a little time to figure out how to get rid of five thousand nuclear warheads. But, he wanted you to meet her. Let's step outside and I'll introduce you."

They both got up and walked outside into the front yard.

"Major, General Odinberg trusts you, and so I also extend my trust to you. This is not for the general public. She's here."

He extended his arm.

"What?"

"Eleni, Major Collins would like to make your acquaintance."

"Hello, Major."

Major Collins looked around to where the voice came from, the large, well-kept lawn. The air shimmered in the middle. Slowly, the transparent outline of a mammoth oval appeared, more than a hundred yards long, hovering fifty feet or so above the ground. Eleni solidified to a silver metal and rose. Rotating, she grew brighter. Rising into the blue sky, she blasted upwards. Punching a hole in a cumulus cloud, she traveled at an impossible speed, with no sonic boom, beyond any person's ability to make her out anymore.

"Major, our people and our off-world friends travel our galaxy in thousands of sentient, semi-organic, trans-medium, faster-than-light craft, of all sizes, like Eleni, who I believe likes you. This little demonstration doesn't actually answer your question as to how we were able to do everything you asked about. But, then again, it does, doesn't it?"

Chapter 50: How to Explain It

I t is difficult to describe what happened after the event. Humanity as a whole had the same reaction as individuals have to near-death experiences. There was no doubt in anyone's mind that they had one. Each and every person on the planet had been immersed and obsessed with their own individual goals and pursuits, oblivious to the ever-present, extraordinary risk of nuclear apocalypse. When the event occurred, it froze them in their tracks, shocking them into realizing what was happening - the end of everything. Time stood still, and they understood they, all those they loved, all that they knew, would abruptly end in a thermo-nuclear firestorm. When it didn't happen, each and every soul properly considered it to be a miracle.

Those nations without atomic weapons demanded, screamed, that those that did get rid of them. The leaders of the countries with nuclear weapons were on the same page, and felt the very same as the populace. These things are suicidal. They've got to go.

Political leaders on all levels reached out and communicated with their counterparts in other countries. Quite suddenly, every town in the country wanted a sister city in their former enemy's nation. Overnight, participation in foreign exchange programs grew hugely popular, and became thought of as a sacred duty to humanity.

Hegel was right, there is a worldwide zeitgeist. In a heartbeat, in a twinkling of the eye, it changed.

Change, when it came, came all at once. In a way, it was just a mere quirk in people's conscious thoughts. They suddenly became conscious of their own fragility, their nation's fragility, and humanity's possible extinction in the blink of an eye. The global consciousness arose. It was realized, out of the blue, that nonproliferation and yes, disarmament, are essential for survival. It became plainly self-evident and no one could understand how anyone could have thought differently in the past.

When Charles Darwin published *On the Origin of Species*, people around the globe, after reading of the basic concept, smacked their foreheads and said to themselves 'Duh, of course! It's so obvious! Why didn't we think of that already?' People and cultures do change. Slavery, practiced throughout the world all through history, was abolished within a matter of decades in the nineteenth century. Tobacco, an extremely addictive substance, was consumed by almost every adult in the United States, privately and in every public place and conveyance, until the federal government adopted policies to educate the public about its harms in the 1960s. Almost no one smokes in public now, and far, far fewer people smoke at all.

When the dots are in plain sight, right in front of them, everyone, in an act of global consciousness, in an act of universal self-awareness, connects the dots. Afterward, no one can even understand why they did not do so before.

Chapter 51: Swimming Pools, Everywhere

"Meaning makes a great many things endurable - perhaps everything." Carl Jung

August is a hot month in the Kansas City area. For those families not on vacation, the local municipal swimming pool is a choice refuge.

Most major cities and their surrounding suburban municipalities each have one or more swimming pool complexes. The Kansas City region is no exception. Prairie Village, yes, there is a town called Prairie Village, has a fabulous one. An Olympic-sized pool for swimming laps, a large recreation pool with a shallow entrance at one end for families, an adult pool, where grownups just float around on inflatables, a baby pool, and a water slide pool. Each season has its own color and summertime's color, it would seem, is blue. With the sun-filled sky and with all these pools, there is a riot of different shades of blue.

I looked around and saw her. A stunning, tall, raven-haired woman, trying her best to hide behind sunglasses while lounging by the lap pool. Several men made their way from the adult pool to slowly walk by her, checking her out and trying to flex their muscles without seeming too obvious.

I laughed. I picked up an empty lounge chair, walked over, and asked, loudly, "Hey lady, can I use this open spot on the concrete next to you?"

She looked up, lowering her sunglasses. "Well, I'm fine with that, but my really hot husband will likely have words with you when he shows up."

"Oh. What does he look like?"

"Strangely, he looks a lot like you."

With that, the males in the vicinity knew what was up and slinked back to their pool, knowing that this astoundingly beautiful woman was taken.

I had picked up the Sunday newspapers from the local convenience store. The headlines were remarkable. The New York Times had "MILLION PERSON MARCH AT TIANANMEN SQUARE - Chinese Leadership Joins with Students." The Wall Street Journal, from yesterday, read "RUSSIAN LEADERS JOIN MASSIVE CROWD IN RED SQUARE - All Demand Total Nuclear Disarmament." The Washington Post, not to be outdone, read "NEW AGE - WORLD DEMANDS NO NUKES." Showing them to Zoe, she told me the same sort of unbelievable news headlines were all over the internet.

I laid down on the lounge chair and looked up. Music was piped into speakers around the complex. People of all shades, sizes, and shapes walked around - pale, tanned, tall, short, black, brown, obese, and rail thin. The next pool over, children screamed with joy splashing in the clear, aquamarine family pool. Looking up to the azure sky, white billowy clouds sailed across.

Zoe spotted her, between the clouds, but seemingly much higher, a single silver glint that twinkled once, as if to acknowledge, 'Yes, I'm here.'

Joe Rogan, the well-known celebrity and podcaster, once speculated that, while intelligent extraterrestrial species might find us interesting to study, they certainly would not want anything else to do with crazy primates who have nukes. That's true. But this truism leads to another question, presently an unspoken one. What happens when the apes are no longer crazy, and they get rid of their nukes?

Zoe looked over to me and asked, "You are so exuberant, so happy again. I wanted to ask. How? Tell me how did you resolve all that you saw."

I looked at my remarkable wife. Unexpectedly, there were tears in my eyes.

"Zoe, it took a while for my mind to process, to put everything back in place. Yes, I saw very sad, horrible things from the past. But, then, as I sorted through everything, I saw the future. A wondrous and astounding future. A future that gives purpose to everything that has happened to all of us. And Zoe, it is bright, so very, very bright."

-To Telos-

Author's Comments

P eople are fascinated by Greek mythology, the possibility of extraterrestrial life, and evidence of a shared consciousness manifested, sometimes, in our dreams. I certainly am, so I began writing about them, and this story is the result. I started having random, strange dreams, which actually began during the pandemic. But, so did half the country. Newspapers and magazines published articles about this widely occurring phenomena. One weekend while this was going on, I was at an estate sale and found an old book authored by nineteenth century American psychologist and researcher William James. In it, Dr. James described the remarkable research of a Frederic H. W. Myers. I tracked down and did my best to absorb that man's two volume treatise, *Human Personality and Its Survival of Bodily Death*. I also came across a novel by Thomas Mann, *The Magic Mountain*, in which he described, in powerful language, a character's very curious dream. All three of these gentlemen described how we all, on occasion, have peculiar and detailed dreams that simply cannot be accounted for by what we've experienced during waking hours. It is surely one of life's mysteries. I suppose Carl Jung would call all of this a synchronicity. Anyway, that's how the chapters that touched upon dreams ended up in this tale.

We live in dangerous times. Just like in the 1960s, we've suddenly become more aware that we live under the cloud of a possible nuclear holocaust. It really is an insanity. There is the *Treaty on the Prohibition of Nuclear Weapons*, sponsored by the United Nations. It currently has ninety-three signatories, https://treatie s.unoda.org/t/tpnw/participants. I don't believe any nation that possesses these weapons is a signatory. I don't have any answers except that, like in the novel, there has to be a change in the global consciousness. I just hope that it won't take some horrific event to change the current state of affairs.

The U.S. Air Force has gone to extraordinary lengths to suppress the public's curiosity concerning all those anomalous objects that fly through our skies and confound our pilots. I want to believe they do so in good faith. A reason put forth over the years for their actions is that they've got craft with anti-gravity propulsion, and they'd rather not admit to them, or put them on public display. Considering how tense the world situation has become, they may well be justified in doing so. Still, if they are suppressing knowledge concerning the existence of extraterrestrial, or ultraterrestrial, intelligence, simply because the generals believe the public can't handle the truth, that would be an opprobrious violation of our basic right to know, which many legal scholars argue flows directly from our First Amendment rights.

In Brian Muraresku's fascinating book, *The Immortality Key*, he suggests that the kykeon provided to the participants at the Eleusinian Mystery ceremony may have contained a hallucinogenic. He could well be right. The ceremony must have changed somewhat from century to century. However, if I were the chief hierophant (priest) conducting the ceremony, I would think twice about surreptitiously giving a hallucinogenic to a Roman emperor, or Greek and Roman generals, or various other kings and queens, all of whom went through the ceremonies over the many years it was in existence. Many participants were very sophisticated. Many in high positions had constant concerns about being poisoned. It is a mystery. If it were a Christian ceremony, the Catholic Church would state that a real metaphysical event would explain the numerous extraordinary experiences the participants reported. That's how Fatima was explained. Every saint recognized by the Catholic Church had to be credited with at least two documented miracles. So, what's fair is fair. Perhaps Persephone, or Demeter, or

Pluto, really did make an appearance. Maybe they're still around, and live next door.

There is a Kansas City National Security Campus. The people there create top secret material for Sandia and Los Alamos National Laboratories. A great deal of what is fabricated has to do with nuclear weaponry, but the extremely hard-working and brilliant people who apply their talents there work on many other things as well. Currently, Honeywell actually does, under contract to the U.S. government, operate both Sandia National Laboratories and the Kansas City National Security Campus.

When the Russia Federation invaded Ukraine, one of the first units intended to reach Kyiv was a military police unit tasked with locating and imprisoning Ukrainian politicians, military and police officers, lawyers, professors, teachers, and the list goes on. They were either going to make them disappear into a gulag, or outright murder them. Imagine the consequences if the United States and Europe had no nuclear weaponry, while the Russians had their six thousand nuclear bombs, missiles and torpedoes. No one wants these weapons around, but, what can we do when adversarial countries possess them in such numbers?

Several sources document UFO/UAP and anti-gravity research at Sandia and Los Alamos. *Loose Threads*, by Daniel Elizondo and others, accessed through Medium, and, of course, *The Hunt for Zero Point*, by Nick Cook, are two of them.

In the past, Western Electric provided the government with sophisticated and unique instruments and parts. Its enormous building in Lee's Summit is still being used. It has tunnels. The company was at the forefront of America's high-tech economy in the forties, fifties and sixties. Harry Truman made an extraordinary request to executives at Western Electric to take over management at Sandia. The General Manager at the Lee's Summit Western Electric operation went straight to Albuquerque to become Sandia's Executive Vice-President.

Southern Missouri, and northern Arkansas, have a long, documented history of black triangle UFO sightings. Some were extraordinary. In recent years, House Bill 1261 was introduced in the Missouri state legislature to officially name Piedmont, a small town in Wayne County, Missouri, as the official, state recognized, "UFO Capital of Missouri."

Is there a secret breakaway society hiding somewhere in the world? Many believe that's a possibility. Secret societies are human nature. Secrets bind people together. The greater the secret, the stronger the bond. To avoid stagnation, such a human society would also likely look for new members. This is, of course, assuming the members are human, or humanoid. If they possess remarkable technology, overt use of the same would certainly be avoided when possible.

Navy ships home-ported on the West Coast regularly deploy to the Indian Ocean. When doing so, they cruise at around fourteen knots, twenty-four hours a day. There are multi-week periods during which no land is visible, and the crew enjoy unobstructed, 360 degree views of the entirety of the horizon. They sail across approximately eleven thousand miles of ocean, averaging several miles in depth, the stalking grounds of sperm whales and giant squid, eventually arriving on station somewhere between Diego Garcia and the Persian Gulf. For members of the crew, the deployments create an unforgettable sense of how enormous the world is. When traveling on modern passenger jets, people just aren't able to experience this. Our planet is unintuitively large.

At certain times of the year, the waters of the Indian Ocean appear almost invisible during the evening and night. Enormous amounts of bio-luminescent plankton are brought to the surface by uplifting ocean currents. It is quite astonishing to observe destroyers and other Navy warships, even aircraft carriers, appear to be floating in air. Researchers have uncovered nineteenth century whaling ship logs documenting the same phenomena.

Closer to home, the Olympic National Park has been described as a lost world where people regularly disappear and so rugged sometimes it takes half a day to just hike around a fallen tree. Even in southern Missouri and northern Arkansas, there are indeed lost canyons and enormous, unexplored, cave systems. The vast majority of the Amazon rain forest remains intact, uncultivated, and, for the most part, unknown. The scale of Canada's Auyuittuq National Park, located at the ends of the Earth, is incomprehensible. Massive stretches of unexplored forests, ocean depths, mountains, and jungles can be found around the world. Immense expanses of Antarctica remain mysterious, almost inaccessible.

I suppose the point I'm trying to make is that the world is extraordinarily, incomprehensibly, large, and it is still full of mysteries. There are lost, unexplored regions everywhere. So, a group, a society, unknown to most of the world, perhaps hiding in some remote location, or in plain sight, or both, is a possibility. As Donald Rumsfeld would say, the world is full of "unknown unknowns."

Speaking of "unknown unknowns," there are longstanding, unanswered questions about the 1952 Washington, D.C., UFO event. Something certainly happened. One question people have is, "Why?" What was the motivation, the purpose, behind the UFOs making such a public demonstration? It stopped after two weeks. What caused it to stop? Also, why was there a decrease in UFO reports across the country after 1952? There are perhaps more mundane answers to that question - the government wanted the public to ignore them, and several experts publicly ridiculed the reports of sightings around then. There was hope that the "All-Domain Anomaly Resolution Office," newly created pursuant to federal law, would produce previously undisclosed records answering this question, while researching the "Historical Record Report" it was statutorily obligated to complete. Of course, it didn't.

Superluminal travel is a facet of many science fiction stories. Yet, many physicists say it is, practically speaking, impossible. All I can say is that, in 1890, almost no one could have conceived of a Boeing 787 flying around the globe, or a Space X rocket traveling to Mars. Physics is overwhelmed with inexplicable mysteries - quantum entanglement and non-locality, dark matter and dark energy, quantum tunneling, wave-particle duality, non-quantum action at a distance, quantum superposition, the unexplained, primordial galaxies at the edge of the visible universe that the James Webb Space Telescope has detected and, of course, those very real, unexplained, anomalous objects that travel our skies. In the words of a recent U.S. President, "There's footage and records of objects in the skies that we don't know exactly what they are. We can't explain how they move, their trajectory ...." There are equally incredible statements about these objects from

Directors of the C.I.A., Directors of National Intelligence, and all those Navy aviators. So, superluminal travel is still included in my list of possibilities.

The world we live in really is full of mysteries.

BIBLIOGRAPHY

Books

Cook, Nick. *The Hunt for Zero Point*. New York: Broadway Books, 2001.

Coulthart, Ross. *In Plain Sight*. New York: HarperCollins Publishers, 2021.

Elizondo, Luis. *Imminent: Inside the Pentagon's Hunt for UFOs*. New York: HarperCollins Publishers Inc., 2024.

Green, Brendan. *The Revolution that Failed: Nuclear Competition, Arms Control, and the Cold War*. New York: Cambridge University Press, 2020.

Grotstein, James. *Who Is the Dreamer Who Dreams the Dream? A Study of Psychic Presences*. Hillsdale: The Analytic Press, 2000.

Evelyn-White, Hugh Gerald, trans. *Hesiod, the Homeric Hymns, and Homerica*. London: William Heinemann, 1914.

James, William. *Memories and Studies*. New York: Longmans, Green, and Co., 1917.

Jung, Carl. *Flying Saucers: A Modern Myth of Things Seen in the Sky*. Princeton University Press, 1979.

Kahn, Herman. *On Thermonuclear War*: Princeton University Press, 1960.

Kean, Leslie. *UFOs: Generals, Pilots, and Government Officials Go on the Record*. New York: Penguin Random House, 2010.

Kelly, Edward F., et al. *Irreducible Mind: Toward a Psychology for the 21st Century.* Rowman & Littlefield Publishers, Inc., 2007.

Loeb, Avi. *Interstellar, The Search for Extraterrestrial Life and Our Future in the Stars.* New York: HarperCollins Publishers, 2023.

Mann, Thomas. *The Magic Mountain.* New York: Alfred A. Knopf, Inc., 1927.

Marler, David and Alexander, John. *Triangular UFOs: An Estimate of the Situation.* David Marler, 2013.

Muraresku, Brian. *The Immortality Key: The Secret History of the Religion with No Name.* New York: St. Martin's Press, 2020.

Myers, Frederic H. W. *Human Personality and Its Survival Of Bodily Death.* London: Longmans, Green, and Co., 1906.

Powell, Robert. *UFOs, A Scientist Explains What We Know (And Don't Know).* London: Rowman & Littlefield Publishing Group, Inc., 2024.

Shepherd, William. *Plataea 479 B.C.: The Most Glorious Victory Ever Seen.* Osprey Publishing, 2012.

Periodicals

Ekmektsioglou, Eleni. *Hypersonic Weapons and Escalation Control in East Asia,* Strategic Studies Quarterly Vol. 9, No. 2 (Summer 2015).

Hennings, Thomas. *Constitutional Law: The People's Right To Know,* American Bar Association Journal Vol. 45, No. 7 (July 1959).

Ivester, David. *The Constitutional Right To Know,* 4 Hastings Constitutional Law Quarterly 109 (1977).

Parrington, Col. Alan. *Mutually Assured Destruction Revisited,* Airpower Journal Winter 1997.

Renner, Rebecca. *The Pandemic is Giving People Vivid, Unusual Dreams. Here's Why,* National Geographic 15 April 2020.

Weaver, Cathy. *Why Am I Having Weird Dreams Lately?,* New York Times 13 April 2020.

Online

Division of Perceptual Studies, Department of Psychiatric Medicine, University of Virginia. *Frederic W. H. Myers.* https://med.virginia.edu/perceptual studies/wp content/uploads/sites/360/2016/12/KEL10.pdf (accessed November 21, 2024).

Elizondo, D., et al. *Loose Threads.* Daniel Elizondo, accessed via Medium .com, https://omega-point.medium.com/loose threads af8f652ee8cb (accessed November 21, 2024).

Emerson, Ralph Waldo. *The Over-Soul.* https://emersoncentral.com/texts/essays/first series/the over soul/(accessed November 21, 2024).

Feynman, Richard. *Richard Feynman. Why.* YouTube, uploaded by Firewalker, 2 April 2012, https://youtu.be/36GT2zI8lVA?si=YA8LZ0D_hAR78ZpQ (accessed November 21, 2024).

Tingley, Brett. *The Truth Is The Military Has Been Researching "Anti-Gravity" For Nearly 70 Years.* The War Zone, 29 October 2019. https://www.twz.com/3 0499/the truth is the military has been researching anti gravity for nearly 70 years (accessed November 21, 2024).

U-S-History.com. *Western Electric Company.* www.u-s-history.com/pages/h 1802.html:#~:text=It%20developed %20breakthrough %20technologies%20in-made%20the%2020th%20century%20work (accessed November 21, 2024).